The Ussir pilot was swinging too far to the right. If he kept swinging, and if what the Jassans had told Harry was true, that Ussir fighting craft was going to run into—

Screee-boom!

—the Shield right about now.

A direct dead-center hit.

Harry got up out of the hole he'd dug in the sand, watching the fragments of the Ussir fighting craft, blown apart by a purple ray fired from somewhere inland, flutter to the ground. Well, that answered a couple of questions for him.

There *was* a Shield.

And it *did* work.

Also by Ward Hawkins
Published by Ballantine Books:

RED FLAME BURNING

SWORD OF FIRE

a novel by
Ward Hawkins

BLAZE
OF WRATH

A Del Rey Books

BALLANTINE BOOKS • NEW YORK

A Del Rey Book
Published by Ballantine Books
Copyright © 1986 by Ward Hawkins

Library of Congress Catalog Card Number: 86-90854

ISBN 0-345-32735-7

Manufactured in the United States of America

First Edition: July 1986

Cover Art by Ralph McQuarrie

CHAPTER 1

The end of it all was not far off now. In seven turnings of the planet Essa, the island of Tassar would sink beneath the sea. Let the end come. Welcome it.

These were the grumbling thoughts of Old Mind.

The shaking was becoming much more severe with each passing day. Delicate balances, grown fragile with the centuries, were being disturbed, thin lines were becoming even thinner, mirrors were becoming transparent. The end, in a matter of days, would find very little left of Old Mind to wipe away.

Even now thoughts were difficult to hold.

Only memories, the treasures of the aged, were clear.

Old Mind easily recalled those distant times. Those long-ago centuries when the Beings of Essa had had the vision to see, the courage to dare, the will to attain the unattainable. Distant galaxies had come within their reach. Other Beings had become known to them; other knowledge had been shared.

And then—the war with the Xrix!

The Beings of Essa had stolen the Lassa Crystal from the Xrix!

They had brought the Lassa Crystal home to this galaxy, to this solar system, to this planet, Essa; and here, on the island of Tassar, they had used the Lassa Crystal

1

to build the Source, from which their light and energy had come in all the centuries that followed.

Then, to protect the Lassa Crystal from any effort by the Xrix to retrieve it, they had built the Shield. An inverted half globe that covered the island, the shield was a force-field containing computer-controlled weaponry—automatic, invincible, eternal—which now protected the Lassa Crystal and the Source from all who would approach for any reason.

Old Mind grumbled on...

The powers of Old Mind still brought information Old Mind could monitor.

Was there hope?

A new race of Beings had been found by the Essans. Two of these Beings had been brought from the planet Earth to the planet Essa. In these two Beings there was the will, the fire, the courage, the daring of the Ancients. Could *they* succeed where the Essans were failing? Could *they* terminate the Shield? Could *they* rescue the Lassa Crystal before it sank beneath the sea with the island of Tassar?

The Beings from Earth had the will to try.

And soon they would try.

Their striving—against each other as well as against the Shield—would be of interest. But Old Mind held no real hope for the Earth Beings. However strong, they were not the equal of the Ancients. None like the Ancients would ever come again.

The Beings from Earth were too late.

The sea would win.

All would be swallowed, gulped into oblivion.

In oblivion, there would be release...

And comfort at last.

Old Mind grumbled on...

CHAPTER 2

Harry Borg was not sure about the leg. He thought it might be broken. It hurt like bloody hell, that was sure, just there below the knee where the lower body panel of the rented car had pinned the leg so neatly between two deeply embedded rocks. Harry was sure he could not have designed a more secure trap if he had tried all day.

After the crashing, bouncing descent down the long slope from the roadblock—down several hundred yards of great, blast-broken rock, Harry falling free like a Ping-Pong ball down a staircase and the car pursuing him like a demented demon—the car had given a final lunge and had crunched down, catching his leg with the uncompromising authority of a grizzly bear trap.

Damn it all!

He looked up the slope.

Two of the assassins were lying where they had fallen on the slope below the road. One was dead beyond any doubt. The other was dying. He had cried and called for others on the road to help him, and when they hadn't come, he had just cried, his crying slowly getting weaker. Harry had thought it would be merciful to shoot the dying man again and end his fear and pain, but he had not been able to bring himself to do it.

The poor bastard . . .

3

The others wanted no part of the wounded man. Or that open slope, since all of it was within range of Harry's weapon. They had opened fire when Harry had rounded the turn, blowing out his windshield and tires, causing him to lose control, blast through the guardrail and take the long fall down the slope. They had started down to make sure he was dead, and when Harry had killed one of them and mortally wounded the second, they had scrambled back to the safety of the road. Then they had tried to kill him with quick shots taken while lying on the road under the guardrail, but Harry was caught on the downside of a huge, broken-faced rock that deflected their shots, sending the bullets screaming off into the canyon to join the echoing of earlier shots as they *ka-whack*ed about in the empty hills.

They had stopped shooting five minutes ago.

In that last, violent, shattering instant on the road, Harry had seen five men. That meant there were three still intent on killing him. And it needed no second guess to know how they were going to do it.

They would go a half mile up the road, climb down the slope out of his view and range, cross the shallow stream and climb up the slope beyond the stream, then come down the ridge to a position above him on that side. There was plenty of cover over there. The pine trees grew among the rocks, thick in places, scattered in others. From any one of a dozen spots that Harry could see, they would be able to see him, fully exposed, at a range of about two hundred and fifty yards.

"A turkey shoot," Harry said.

And he cursed softly.

It shouldn't take them more than thirty minutes.

Harry turned to lie flat on his back. He placed his left heel carefully on the battered metal of the car, hunted for the best possible purchase for his hands in the rocks beside him, and strained to push or lift the metal enough to free his leg. It was an enormous effort by a very powerful man. His neck corded, his eyes bulged, his mouth tore in a violent grimace.

"Leggo, you sucker!"

No use.

With a hard fist, he dented the metal in angry exasperation, then collapsed, his breath exploding out of him. Except for that trapped leg, a deep abrasion on the side of his head that had left his ear and neck and beard-covered jaw bloody, and a lot of bumps and bangs, he was unhurt. He looked up the slope he had tumbled down.

"Lucky to be alive," he admitted.

Then he argued that.

He had his damned leg caught, hadn't he? They were going to shoot him in another thirty minutes, weren't they?

What was lucky?

Lucky was the fact he hadn't lost his .38 Police Special in the fall; that had saved his life at the cost of two of theirs. Unlucky was the fact his weapon was not a Jassan esso. With an esso, the sidearm of the Jassans, he could have used the purple ray to cut a neat hole through the metal of the car and let himself loose in a moment or two. But the Jassan essos had the problem shared by all weapons: They ran out of ammunition. His esso had been out of ammunition since the fight in Washington, D.C., and the nearest reload was quite literally out of this world—in the world called Essa, in the country called Jassa.

"Damn blast it!" he swore.

But it didn't help.

Harry Borg looked to be about forty, though he was actually in his late sixties. At six feet four inches and two hundred forty pounds, in perfect physical condition, he was a fair giant of a man. He had dark blue eyes beneath strong, dark brows, and an uncompromising jaw beneath a short-cut reddish-brown beard. The single gold band, clamped, blood-caked, in the lobe of his left ear gave him the look of a pirate. But he was, he had to admit, anything but a pirate now. A Christmas goose was more like it.

Ready for the ax.

He was lying two-thirds of the way down a slope below the private road to Ahmed Hassad's vast underground complex known as Globe One on the eastern side of the Rocky Mountains in the western United States. The elevation here was above five thousand feet, and in late April there was still snow among the trees and on the higher ridges. The air had a clean bite. A crow cawed from a tall pine, and the call echoed across the gorge, a hollow sound. Gravel rolled, rattling, perhaps dislodged by a passing deer on the upslope above the road. But for the most part it was as silent as a cathedral on a Monday afternoon. A pair of buzzard hawks wheeled and sailed in a sky that was clear and dark blue.

They had no interest in Harry . . . yet.

He could look down at the stream below and follow its course as it tumbled, melt-fed, through a rocky gorge toward a valley several miles distant. He measured the day that was left and knew darkness would not save him. He tightened his down jacket around his shoulders and neck and sprawled against the upslope rock—if he looked dead enough in their binoculars, they might come close enough to give him a shot or two. He wanted to kill at least one more of them before they finally killed him.

Earlier—only a day ago—Harry Borg had been at the Red Rock Motel, a motel owned by Terrance Daly, and Harry knew now that a wiser, more cautious man would have known what was going to happen.

The motel was six cabins, all clean, all with comfortable beds, on an all but abandoned stretch of highway that crossed a desert in Arizona. There was a gasoline pump and a few groceries to help the odd traveler in need, a water tank, and little else. It was not unusual for hours to go by without a single car passing on the road, which was exactly the way Terrance Daly wanted it. When asked why he would operate a motel on a road so poorly traveled, he had a stock answer.

"A man's got to make a living somehow."

That was his kind of gentle irony. The truth was, he liked to be alone.

Certainly, there were few places on this busy Earth where a man could be more alone than on a distant part of an Arizona desert. At night the sky was a great roof of stars, billions beyond counting. The air was soft and clean though sometimes hot. The dark hills kept a respectful distance. The small mammals, the reptiles, and the night birds were too busy with their lives to bother. And the silence was enormous.

Terrance Daly was sixty-four, a slight man with pale blue eyes and thinning, reddish hair. He had flown wingman for Harry Borg in Lockheed P-38s in World War II, and if there had ever been a better time or a better place to cement a friendship than a dogfight over Nazi Germany, neither man had ever heard of it.

When Harry Borg had been an aging alcoholic—and that had been before all the business with Jassa had begun—the Red Rock Motel had been the only place he'd ever gone, when the need of going anywhere had come upon him. It had never been said, but it had been always understood between them that if Harry were going to kill himself with booze—and he had been within countable bottles of doing just that—Terrance Daly had a right to be the man with whom he shared his last drink. They would sit out back, chairs tipped against the wall, hearing the distant yap of coyotes, watching a sliver of a moon, hearing the soft whooping of an owl, saying nothing for hours, sipping whiskey . . .

Dying, if it was to come to that.

Then the world of Jassa had changed it all.

When Harry Borg had returned from Jassa and had come again to the Red Rock Motel, he had come as a man of forty-odd, a big and powerful man full of ginger, his dark blue eyes glowing with lusty life.

"Harry," Terrance Daly had said, head tipped, his pale blue eyes wryly amused. "I don't know what you're on to get you in the shape you're in, but you put it in a bottle with a nice label on it, and you've got your fortune made."

Harry had roared his laughter.

"It's going to take me all night to tell you about it," he'd said. "Right now I need shelter for some friends."

"Always welcome," Terrance Daly had said.

Even those friends who had come in the flying saucer were welcome. Even though they were reptilian, even though their eyes were large and golden, even though their pupils were vertical slits, their tongues forked, their hands eight-fingered . . .

Any friend of Harry Borg was a friend of his.

"You're a purty little thing," he had said to Sissi.

And when Sissi, a female of the species, learned from Harry what Terrance Daly had said, he had won her heart. Guss and Los Ross were no more difficult to put at ease. After the merciless attention they had suffered at the hands of the United States government—they were aliens from another world, for mercy sakes! What more exploitable subjects could there be?—they were deeply grateful for simple hospitality.

"Y' see, they need a day or two," Harry told Terrance Daly. "Ross, here—" he'd put his arm around the shoulders of the Jassan, who wore spectacles crookedly on his short muzzle and a soiled smock always wrongly buttoned "—has to find a new, what he calls a Point of Proximity, to get back to a sanctuary in Jassa."

"Sanctuary? Their folks want to hurt them?"

"Their folks said no. Said they would have a safe welcome. But the way things are these days, who can you trust entirely?"

"Better safe than sorry," Terrance Daly had agreed.

"And these lads, too," Harry had said. "Like me, they're wanted."

"These lads" were his cadre. They were wanted, as Harry was, because Ahmed Hassad had used his tremendous wealth and influence to shift suspicion of having set the nuclear bomb that was to have destroyed Washington, D.C., and begun the final holocaust from himself to Harry and the lads.

The lads were Chad Harrison, white-haired, deeply tanned; Homer Benson, wide-shouldered, big-handed; Arnie, knuckle-faced, a hard charger; and Eddie, a lithe, slick-moving black. Not one of these was yet twenty-one, but all had been battle tested in Jassa, on the planet Essa. All were combat soldiers.

"Got plenty of room," Terrance said. "For as long as you need it."

They had needed it for two days.

Since the Jassans—Guss, Sissi, and Los Ross—had suddenly taken their ship and disappeared from Washington, D.C., all the government agencies thought they had gone back to that mysterious other-dimensional planet from which they had come—one still not understood, or described, or even quite believed by American scientists—taking Harry Borg and his cadre with them. There had been no hue and cry, no search to speak of. Here, in the middle of nowhere, in a distant Arizona desert, in the Red Rock Motel, under a billion stars, where the silence was so vast the sound of a quiet human voice would carry a mile, all the fugitives had found a place where they could have a few moments to be alone.

A few moments in which to say good-bye.

Out of courtesy to Terrance Daly, the humans spoke vocally as well as telepathically, and for Terrance Daly it was the same as if the three Jassans were sitting quietly reading minds. What did it matter if they could talk or not? After all they had done to save the planet Earth from a final holocaust, they were entitled.

And while Los Ross, wearing a helmet studded with antennae and knobs, worked with his ship's instruments searching for the Point of Proximity, there were the few moments at Terrance Daly's table with good friends, with good food and wine, with memories shared of other times and places.

Los Ross had found a Point of Proximity on the second day.

"This is *our* POP," Harry told the Jassans in the last moment. "We can use it to stay in touch. I'll see to it Terry knows where I am at all times. You need me, you come back through here and talk to him. He'll find me, any hour, day or night. Okay?"

"Okay," Guss agreed. "Los will set up a monitor here. If you need us, you come out here in the sands, lift your head, and call. We'll hear you. We'll come."

"My good friends," Harry whispered.

He had a special good-bye hug for Sissi. The little Jassan female, the loveliest of her kind and surely the bravest, had a special place in Harry's heart. As he had in hers. She caressed his bearded jaw with her delicate forked tongue and whispered in his mind. "You be careful. Please?"

"If you'll take care of Guss for me."

"What's this?" Guss asked. "I'm not a klutz anymore!"

It was an old joke—but were there tears in those golden eyes? In a few more moments, the Jassans took ship and they were gone.

Then Harry had to part with his young men.

"How do you say you're proud?" he asked them. "How do you wrap it in silver paper and red ribbons? How do you say thanks?"

"We should come with you," Chad Harrison said soberly. "I don't trust Hassad. God knows, you shouldn't."

"All I'm goin' to do is go to Globe One and pick up Lori and Sam. I'm not even going to *see* Hassad. I'll stay outside Globe One and call them out."

"You taking his private road?"

"Hell, yes! I'm goin' to drive right in there."

Harry shook hands with each of them, then wrapped each in a bear hug. "I'll send Sam back to you in Reseda. Get on with proving you're not terrorists. Get on with your lives. Get on with your education. Take the NFL apart when you get there."

"See you," they said, faces strained.

He strode quickly to his rented car and got out of there, tires smoking. A man can't shed tears in front of his troops, now, can he?

But roaring down a highway, he sure as hell could.

And then, driving down the private road that would take him to Globe One, where his wife, Lori, and her bodyguard, Sam Barnstable, were being held, he had run into the roadblock.

The roadblock and the killers of Ahmed Hassad.

The fusillade of fire...

The first indication that Hassad's killers had gotten to the far side of the stream was the rattling sound of a small rock falling, kicked loose by a clumsy boot, and a muffled curse.

"C'mon, you suckers," Harry whispered.

He watched the far slope through slitted eyes, waiting for that first shot from his would-be killers. When it came, it was wide, hitting the slope ten yards below him and to the left. Two hundred and fifty yards is an extreme range for a good shot, an impossible range for a bad one. The weapons, as Harry remembered from those brief seconds on the road before they had destroyed his windshield, were shotguns and handguns. But there must have been a rifle; he thought the first shot had been from an AR-16 or something like it. The high *crack* had sounded like a military cartridge.

Very effective in the hands of a sharpshooter.

He waited, unmoving.

"Hey! Borg!" a voice yelled. "You're a sittin' duck!"

Tell me about it, Harry thought.

They wanted some response, wanted to know if he was dead or very seriously wounded, going on the assumption that no man who was not dead or wounded would be able to remain motionless knowing he was in an exposed position and about to become a target. And they were right. While Harry was not moving in any way they could see, his right hand, holding the revolver, was not motionless. It was quivering with an uncontrollable eagerness.

"You want us to kill you?" the voice yelled. "We can, y' know!"

Harry still gave no reply.

Then, as if to demonstrate their ability, they began firing a steady volley. The muzzle blasts and the delayed echoing off the canyon walls made it sound as if a small war was going on. All the shots were wide, some striking rocks and whining viciously away, others thudding as they burrowed into bare earth.

"How about it, Borg? Had enough?"

Silence.

"He's dead." Though the voice was over two hundred yards away, it carried perfectly, echoing hollowly in the vast silence that followed the fusillade. "Gotta be dead."

"Ain't so sure. He's a tough bastard."

"All right, let me shoot. You watch. I can reach him from here with this piece."

There was another moment of silence, then a bullet whanged into rock just above Harry. The flat *crack* of the rifle muzzle blast came an instant later.

"You're too high!" a voice said. "I seen the dust it kicked off the boulder right above 'im!"

In the silence that followed, Harry knew the rifleman was taking aim again, lowering his sights, and he waited, motionless, cursing. This was how a deer felt caught out in the open, he suddenly realized, in that instant before the bullet killed it. This was how a bear felt, standing erect before a hunter—a bullet was going to hammer into him in another moment, and there wasn't a bloody thing he could do about it.

Ka-whack!

The bullet ripped through Harry Borg's jacket at his shoulders, tearing fabric but sparing flesh.

"Y' did it! Y' did it!" a voice yelled triumphantly. It was a young voice.

The owner of the young voice had seen the fabric rip and had called it a hit. Close, sure as hell, but no cigar. Harry gave a convulsive heave and flopped limply.

"There, y' see? Right there, he died!"

Harry, scanning the far slope, placed the young voice among the rocks below and to the right of the rifleman. Now, through slitted eyes, he saw the young man rise up from the cover, holding a revolver carelessly.

"Easy!" an older voice cautioned.

"Heck! He's dead!" The young man's voice had a hysterical note that spoke of great relief as well as triumph. "I can see where y' hit 'im!"

The young man left the shelter of the rocks and pines and came down toward the creek. At the bank he must have had a moment's doubt, because he paused there to stare up the slope toward Harry's motionless form.

"Y' think he ain't dead?" he said finally. "Okay! I'll prove it!"

The young man lifted the revolver and fired, one-handed, three deliberate shots. From a .357, by the sound of it. The shots came near, but only near. All three missed.

"Y' see that?" His voice held a note of braggadocio. "Ain't no man going to lay there and get shot at like that if he ain't dead."

Confident now, the young man crossed the stream and began climbing the slope. Two men farther up the far slope—one with the AR-16, one with a shotgun—moved out of their cover to watch. They had apparently believed the young man's reasoning: Their weapons were held in crooked arms, muzzles pointing down. But there was still enough adult good sense in them to persuade them to wait and see.

As the young man moved up under the crown of the slope, Harry lost sight of him, but he could follow his progress by the rattle of dislodged rocks. Then there was heavy breathing—the slope had become very steep and required a lot of effort—and finally the young man came into view ten feet away. He had to scramble a little to cross and find a place where he could stand and look down at Harry.

Harry's face was tipped up, eyes mostly closed, as he tried to look as dead as he could. He saw a narrow-faced man in the uniform of Ahmed Hassad's private security force, a young man in his early twenties with buckteeth and large ears and the bright round eyes of a small animal. Now the bright eyes moved off as the young man turned away to call to the others.

"He's dead, all right! He's—"

Harry shot him.

The young man's face came back, mouth gaping, eyes wide, unbelieving. He tried to bring his revolver to bear. Lacking the strength, he lurched forward. He must have died midstride, because he was dead when he fell on Harry. Catching the body, Harry turned it so it lay on the rocks between himself and the far slope, a barricade of sorts.

"You bastard!" a man screamed angrily.

Both the remaining would-be killers scrambled back into cover, and in a moment another volley of shots came. Only two bullets struck the corpse protecting Harry, causing it to jerk twice under the thudding impact. The body could not stop the AR-16. The bullets penetrated, passing through. But mushroomed and out of velocity, they merely buried themselves in the shoulder of Harry's thick jacket.

The shotgun was worthless at that range; it was only an expression of senseless rage.

"You're gonna die!" one of the killers yelled.

"Tell me about it!" Harry answered.

"We got you nailed down, you turkey!"

"What's the score?"

Their answer was more shots, fired in a frenzy.

"You got three dead! And I'm still alive," Harry yelled.

No answer.

"Three-zip! That's the score!" Harry took a cold pleasure grinding their faces in the truth.

Still no answer.

And Harry knew why. They had realized that with the corpse protecting him from their angle of fire, they had to move again to a better angle. Probably upstream. Looking that way, Harry could see several places from which they would be able to see him, from which they could shoot with the high-powered rifle and still be safely out of range of return fire from his handgun.

"Turkey is right," he said grimly.

It was only a matter of time.

CHAPTER 3

Lori Borg, the wife of Harry Borg, five months pregnant with Harry Borg's child, was holding a handgun in each hand. She fired one and then the other at the center of a locked door. Tears were streaming down her cheeks and her vision was blurred, but there was no way she was going to miss that door. Or miss the first one of Ahmed Hassad's killers who might come through it.

But they wouldn't come.

"Come on!" she screamed. "Come *on!*"

"Mom!" Tippi cried. "You're goin' nuts!"

Tippi was Lori's daughter, thirteen and gamine-wise; and both mother and daughter had reason to be insanely distraught. The security guards had shot Sam Barnstable.

They had shot him twice!

They had shot that enormous, lovable giant of a kid whom Harry Borg had left to protect Lori. Sam had said no to the security guards when they had come for her. He had said it quietly, a young bull of a man, six-four, two hundred and sixty pounds, and not yet twenty-one; and he had moved between Lori and the two security guards Hassad had sent to get her.

He had said no again.

And they had shot him.

It had been clear, then, that they had planned on shoot-

15

ing him from the beginning, because the shooter had had
one hand behind his back, pistol cocked, and had simply
brought it around and fired point-blank without warning
of any kind.

The shooter had died an instant later. One shot had
not been enough to stop the young, quick-smiling, button-
nosed behemoth; a dozen shots could not frighten him.
Even with a bullet in his side he had knocked the gun
from the shooter's hand, reached out with both his huge
hands, and broken the neck of the man who had shot him.
Lori would always remember the *crack* of it, like a stick
breaking. The second guard, whose pistol had been holstered because he had thought one shot would be enough
to kill Sam, had stumbled hastily back out the door, drawing and firing. One of his shots had grazed Sam's head,
clubbing the big youth down, though the guard, in his
frantic haste to escape, had not seen that happen. Lori
had reached the door then, closed it, and locked it.

Now, with the security guard's pistol in one hand and
Sam's revolver in the other, she was standing between
her fallen protector and the killers out in the hall and,
weeping, she was blowing bullet holes in the door, screaming her fury.

"Mom, please!" Tippie pleaded. "You're pregnant!"

Lori didn't hear. Or it didn't matter. Or perhaps the
child she was carrying was fully with her, furious, too.
Together they were beautiful. The distended belly made
no difference. Her beauty lay in her wide-spaced gray
eyes, her good solid cheekbones, her generous mouth.
She was wearing her ash-colored hair in a single thick
braid that reached her waist. Her red, loose-fitting blouse
revealed already swollen breasts, her black pants hugged
long legs, her fit and shapely body glowed with strength.

Sam was not dead ... but was he dying?

His telepathic communications were distorted, inco-
herent. Lori could hear names of friends, football signs,
a whispered call for his mother, for Harry Borg. The shame
of it, the pain of it, had her raging, not at the shooter
alone but at Ahmed Hassad. He had to be the one who
had ordered the attack. She knew that now. She knew
Hassad had never, never intended that Harry come and

get her. He had lied! He had lied to the United States government. He had lied to Harry. He had lied to her.

He had lied, lied, lied!

Damn him! Damn him! Damn him!

She sent another bullet through the door, seeing it only vaguely through her tears, her ears numbed and deafened by the muzzle blast. Tippi's ears were numbed, too, but most of all she was frightened. She was not frightened for herself. She was frightened for Sam, whose blood she was mopping; for her mother, who was raging; and for the child her mother was carrying. All this would damage both mother and child beyond fixing.

"Mom! Please! Stop it!"

Tippi, at thirteen, was still growing; the beautiful girl she would presently be was as yet only described—budding breasts, hips beginning to swell. Maturity was only just now thinning a child's round cheeks, but the bright brown eyes held knowledge beyond her years. She was untouched, to be sure—her good sense made that certain. She knew it all and delighted in knowing, but she was satisfied for now with only that—she was a bright child, a good child.

After she had been returned from Jassa, Hassad's people had found her at George Bushby's and had brought her here for what was supposed to have been a joyful reunion with her mother.

"Mom! Please!"

And her mother heard the clear, pleading young voice coming through her screaming rage. She lowered the guns. Tippi ran to her then, pulled her back until her legs caught on a chair and she half collapsed, the guns still in her hands.

Now Lori saw a hole appear in the door as a fire ax, swung from the side, knifed through an upper panel. She somehow knew what was coming next. She put her one arm around Tippi.

"Sorry, love."

"The baby, Mom?"

"He's all right."

And then the canister of tear gas came through the hole

they'd chopped in the door. It hit the floor and began twisting and squirming as it spewed a cloud of gas.

Lori fired two more shots through the door—just to empty the guns.

When the horrible, throat-grabbing, eye-blinding, coughing hour of semiconsciousness had passed—she was vaguely aware during that time of rough hands, of being strapped on a gurney, of herself, Tippi, and the badly wounded Sam being rushed along corridors—Lori found herself, still strapped down, staring up at the ceiling of a surgery.

It had to be a surgery.

There were the big lights . . . there were the gray, featureless, sterile robes, caps, and masks . . . there were the tiled walls . . . there was the smell of fresh blood . . .

"My baby!" she screamed suddenly, writhing against her straps.

A mask-covered face came then to hover over her. "Your baby's all right. You're all right."

"The blood! I can smell it!"

"Your bodyguard was injured. They're saving him now."

"I'm all right, too, Mom!" Tippi's telepathic voice cut through Lori's panic. "They've got me tied down, but I'm okay. Mom! Mom! Can you read me?"

Lori began to stop trembling. "Yes, love. I read you."

"Take it easy," Tippi pleaded.

"Yes . . . yes, dear." Lori had control now. "They didn't hurt you?"

"Not much. That gas, a little bit. You sure you're okay? They gave you a shot, I saw 'em do it."

"Whatever it was . . . I'm coming out of it."

They were both silent—telepathically.

But they called to each other vocally, reassuring each other. Vocally, because they would be expected to want to know about each other and did not want the others to know they had been communicating with the telepathic powers given to them by the Jassans. And they listened, tensely, worriedly, to the surgeons, the anesthetist, the surgical nurses, as they worked on the sheet-covered figure that, by the bulk of him, could only be Sam Barnstable.

Terse orders, terse responses . . .

Then, finally, "You close."

Straining her neck, trying to see from her tied-down position, Lori saw a tall, elderly man turn from the table, dropping his mask, tiredly stripping off his gloves. He had a kind face, deep-scarred with lines that might have been caused by a lifetime of worrying about the lives of others; he had concerned brown eyes behind smudged glasses.

"Is he . . ." Lori asked.

The surgeon came close to the gurney where Lori lay strapped. He seemed not to want to see her, not to want to admit her presence. But he could not totally ignore her.

"He'll live," he said in passing. "If that's all there is."

"All there is?" Lori questioned, alarmed.

But the surgeon was gone, with no further response, through the large metal swinging doors. In a few moments they were all to go—nurses, anesthetist, everyone, snapping off the huge surgical light to leave the room in sudden dimness, pulling down masks, dropping instruments on trays, snapping off surgical gloves—going quickly, as if not wanting to be caught there, leaving only Sam, breathing quietly on the operating table, and Lori and Tippi, strapped to gurneys, alone.

Alone with the smell of blood, of ether, of antiseptics.

"What's goin' on?" Tippi whispered in the stillness.

"I don't know, hon," Lori answered.

"Why'd they leave Sam? Shouldn't he be in intensive care?"

"He should."

"Well, geeze! Why'd they leave *us*?"

Lori was afraid to think. "Forgot us, maybe?"

"My ass!" Tippi said.

"Tippi! Shame on you!"

"I just said it for you, Mom."

"That you did, hon. That you did."

They were silent a moment.

Then Lori called to Sam telepathically. "Sam! Sam! Can you hear me, Sam? It's Lori, Sam. Tippi's here, too. You're going to be all right, Sam. The doctor told me you're going to be all right."

She lifted her head, twisting, and found she could see

him. He was lying as they had left him, and there were
straps to hold him now, straps that cut into his huge, sheet-
covered body and bound his big arms at the wrists. His
head was a swath of bandages; his eyes were covered,
heavily blindfolded. There was a bulge at his lower chest
that told of more bandages. As she watched, she saw him
roll his head slightly and saw a change in his breathing.

"Sam." Her telepathic voice was as comforting as she
could make it. "Can you hear me now? Sam, talk to me.
It's Lori."

The first groping thought-voice transmissions began to
come through. "Ma'am . . . ma'am . . . you there?" His head
moved again, but, blinded, he could see nothing but darkness. "Where—where are you?"

"Close by, Sam. Only a few feet away."

Sam drifted back into unconsciousness, then slowly
returned.

"They—they shot me. I'm—I'm sorry . . ."

"It wasn't your fault!" Tippi exclaimed. "The sneaky
bastards!"

"Tippi!" her mother said.

"Well, they are!"

"Tippi . . . Mrs. Borg . . . sorry."

"No need to be sorry, Sam. Tippi was right. They were
sneaky. But they paid for it! You made them pay."

"Some kind of a bodyguard I am."

"Only the greatest, Sam." Lori was crying now. "You
did fine! It's going to be all right. Harry will be here soon.
With Chad and Homer and Arnie and Eddie. I promise
you! We're all going to get out of here in just a little while.
You rest now."

"Where are we?" Sam asked.

Lori looked helplessly at Tippi, tied on another gurney.
Tippi was shaking her head violently. Lori knew she was
saying, "Don't tell him! Don't tell him!" She didn't tell
him . . . exactly.

"In Globe One," she told Sam. "In a room together."

"I smell blood. Iodine. Ether?"

"They fixed you up—the doctors. They said you're
going to be fine, Sam. Now, please rest. Harry will be

here soon, and we'll all go home, just like Hassad promised."

"Don't trust Hassad," Sam said. He was tiring; his telepathic voice was growing weak. "Don't trust him. Ever..." He slipped off, whether into sleep or unconsciousness, Lori and Tippi could not tell.

"He's so great, Mom," Tippi whispered.

"The very best."

They lay quietly then, wondering.

Why had they been left here? Here, in a tile-walled surgery that was like a bank vault. Like a grave vault, so silent, so distant from everywhere, windowless, growing cold. It didn't help to know that in Globe One they were a mile under the Rocky Mountains to begin with and that the surgery must be deep in a remote part of it. Knowing that gave them a buried-alive feeling that set nerves shaking and jaws clamping against panic.

"Why, Mom? Why?"

"We'll find out soon enough."

Longer moments passed. Perhaps as much as half an hour, though it seemed halfway to forever. And then there were voices as the huge metal swinging doors were opened. The lights became bright again, eye-blinding in their suddenness. Four men and a woman, who were not in surgical gowns, who were totally insensitive to the antiseptic, almost religious respect owed a surgery, who came in rudely pushing aside life-saving instruments, making way for their own greasy-looking appliance of wires and clips.

"The guy on the table," one of them said. "Big sucker, ain't he?"

"What're you doing?" Lori demanded. "He's hurt! Leave him alone!" They were tearing the sheet off Sam's unconscious body.

"Sorry, lady. We've got our orders."

Now Lori saw them stringing wires, attaching clips to Sam's body.

"You filthy bastards!" she screamed. "Stop that."

They ignored her, exchanging knowing grins between themselves. Then they became most serious and diligent as the swinging doors opened to admit the man Lori considered to be the most evil man on Earth.

Ahmed Hassad.

He did not look evil.

He looked anything *but* evil.

A big man, a most handsome man, Ahmed Hassad could have won millions of female hearts had he chosen motion pictures as a career instead of the career that had made him probably the richest individual in the world. He stood six feet four, beautifully muscled, trim. His face seemed deeply tanned, but it was the blood of the Middle East that made it so. Large, expressive eyes, almost black, smiled from beneath long lashes. He had short, curly black hair, a short, straight nose, and a wide mouth that could move into the most engagingly charming smile, revealing very masculine dimples on either cheek and perfect teeth. He was wearing, as usual, carefully fitted and tailored slacks and a red silk shirt open at the throat.

"Mrs. Borg," he said. "You misbehaved again."

He smelled richly of cologne.

"You stink!" she said. "You stink of garbage!"

"Brut," he corrected. "I rather like it."

"I'm going to kill you one day," she said through clenched teeth.

"I know you'd like to," he answered, unperturbed. "And I can't say I blame you. You have been badly treated." He shook his head slowly. "But you're going to be treated even worse now."

"How could that be?"

"We're going to start with that young man over there," Hassad went on. "I think you can see the wires are in place . . . yes. He's unconscious now, but he'll awaken, you can be sure." He turned his eyes back to her. There seemed to be a liquid shine to them. Was it anticipation?

"It depends on you, of course," he said. "You can spare him all that discomfort."

"You're trying to scare me. You won't hurt him. No one could!"

"I can if you don't answer my questions."

"You're lying," she said. "I don't scare. I won't tell you anything."

Hassad shook his head. "I don't think you understand how serious I am. Or why I'm serious. The aliens have gone, Mrs. Borg. Back to their world. They left without notice. And without permission. And they took your husband and his young men."

"I don't believe you."

"It's true," he said. "And now we're back to square one, you and I. You, your daughter, and the young man there are my only—*only,* mind you—source of information about that other civilization. Do you have any idea how important that information has become?"

"Worth billions, I'm sure."

"Many, many billions. An entire world, an entire civilization, even more advanced than ours, close by, accessible, untapped in any way—the meaning of it, the importance of it, is almost beyond comprehension."

"Good!"

"And why do you say that?"

"Because I know about it, and you don't. And you can't scare me into telling you word one."

Her gray eyes were wide, blazing, defiant, hating. Her voice held all the contempt, all the venom she could manage. And it reached him, imperturbable as he pretended to be. She saw the oil shine in his beautiful dark eyes brighten.

"We'll see about that," he said.

He looked over at the man who was standing beside a dirty metal boxlike appliance he'd set on the clean white counter top. Lori could see a dial—a rheostat, she knew—a meter with a swinging needle, and wires that extended to the clips on Sam's body. A cord from the box had been plugged into a wall outlet.

The man who was to operate the device was about forty, almost bald, with bright blue eyes and moist, pouty lips. The woman standing at the head of the table holding Sam—a middle-aged, female executive type, not a nurse—held a hypodermic needle upright, carefully discharging air from the vial. A slimmer, younger man moved in to stand near Tippi; he looked like an innocent devil. The other man, older, sandy-haired, fatherly, came to stand near Lori. He laid a gentle hand on her shoulder.

She still couldn't believe they would do it.

But at Hassad's nod, the man at the appliance flipped

a toggle switch. A red light glowed. At another nod, the man turned the rheostat carefully. The needle swung—and Sam's huge body leaped against the bonds, straining. His yell was a sudden, wild cry.

"What was that?"

His telepathic voice was soaked with pain. His head, swathed in bandages, rolled from side to side.

"God—Mrs. Borg—are you there?"

"Yes, Sam." She was horrified.

"What the hell happened? Jesus, the pain!"

"Oh, Sam..."

Then Lori screamed at Hassad, "Stop it! Stop it!"

"Will you tell me what I want to know?"

"Damn you, stop it!"

"Will you answer my questions—"

"No!" Sam's voice, hoarse with pain but totally defiant, cut in. "Tell that son of a bitch nothing, Mrs. Borg. I can take it." He was panting heavily. "I can take anything he's got!"

"If he dies," Hassad said, "and he may, as stubborn as he is, the wires will be moved to your daughter. Then to you. But I promise you, I will persuade you to tell me everything you know."

He gestured at the man with the device. The man began to turn the rheostat, increasing the electrical current that passed through the most tender parts of Sam's body.

Sam arched against the straps and groaned loudly.

"Stop it! Stop it!" Lori cried. She knew she was beaten. She could not let Sam endure another moment of that awful pain. "I'll tell you! I'll tell you!"

Hassad stopped the current with an upraised hand. "I rather thought you would," he said.

And it was at that moment an alarm began sounding.

The alarm was a bell, loud and insistent, that rang throughout Globe One every Friday at twelve noon to test the system and to remind the several hundred occupants of the emergency stations to which they were to go in a time of need—a fire in the depths of Globe One could be disastrous, for example. But this was not Friday. Neither was it noon.

The alarm startled Hassad and Sam's tormentors.

Hassad strode to a telephone on the wall. "Hassad here!" he said sharply. "What is it?"

He listened, his expression shocked. "Did you stop them?"

Listening...

"Why the hell not?"

Listening...

"How long ago?"

Listening...

Then, incredulous, furious: "And you just sounded the alarm?"

Lori heard voices.

"This way. Hurry!"

Telepathic voices!

The big metal doors of the surgery were smashed inward to admit four charging figures. Yellow beams swept before them, striking Hassad and the tormentors. The yellow beams missed Lori, Sam, and Tippi, because they were strapped down—missed them long enough for Lori to yell telepathically at the top of her powers.

"Not me! Not us!"

A telepathic voice, here, on Earth, so astonished the intruders that they held the yellow beam away. Then the leader saw that Lori, Tippi, and Sam were tied down, therefore prisoners, which put them more or less on the side of the intruders. The leader lifted an eight-fingered hand to hold the others, then he came to stand over Lori, his long, forked tongue flicking, his golden vertically slitted eyes wary and curious.

"Why are you tied?"

"We're prisoners!" Lori answered.

"They were torturing Sam!" Tippi cried. "Look at the wires on him!"

A second telepathic voice, in a land where there were supposedly none, was even more amazing to the leader. Then Sam added his painful transmissions. "Who is it, ma'am? Is it Guss? Sissi?"

"No, Sam. But they are from Essa."

The leader had drawn a hand weapon Lori recognized as an esso, and now he aimed the esso at the man who had worked the device with the rheostat. That one, the fat man with the moist, pouty lips, was standing—as were all the others—with unseeing eyes, with a nonfunctioning mind, rendered so by the yellow beam of what Lori knew to be a mind-blanker. The purple beam of the esso was not so kind. It drilled a neat hole through the man's chest, and through the wall behind him, and through countless other walls as well. Then the leader turned and treated the remaining three of the torturers in a like fashion. He spared Ahmed Hassad, who was standing still, mindless, staring at nothing.

"We came for this one," the alien said, indicating Hassad. "We are going to take him with us."

"But the others. You didn't—"

"Even your world can do without that kind of bassoe."

"Bassoe" was the essan name for the human species of their world, a species considered by the reptilians, who had evolved more rapidly, to be far inferior. It was a contempt Lori would usually resent mightily, but after the torturing of Sam, Lori could not find it in her heart to disagree with him.

These humans had certainly earned contempt.

"Who *are* you?" Tippi asked.

The leader faced Tippi. He may even have clicked his heels. "My name is Oss Tiss," he said formally. "Oss Tiss, of the Niss Elite Guard."

"Pleased to meet you," Tippi said. "I'm Tippi Calder. That's my mother. She's pregnant. And that's Sam Barnstable. He's our friend, and they were torturing him. They were going to kill all of us. Please get us out of here."

Oss Tiss thought a moment, head tipped. "Are you sure you want to go with me?" he asked then.

"Tippi!" Lori said quickly. "Don't you see?"

"See what?" Tippi asked.

"They—they're not Jassans, honey."

"What d' you mean?"

"They're the wrong color!"

"Oh," Tippi said.

These intruders were from the same planet as Guss and Sissi. And they looked the same, except for the one significant difference: they were not gray-skinned, as Jassans were. They were Ussirs, and their faintly scaled skins were green.

Oss Tiss waited, watching, while all that soaked in.

Then, with only a slight chilling in his telepathic voice, he said to Tippi, "We have been fighting the Jassans for over a thousand years. We are the enemy. Do you still want to go with us?"

"They'll *torture* us here!" Tippi said.

Lori knew Tippi was right.

The people here had tortured Sam, and they had been going to torture Tippi if need be, then herself, which would have meant torturing an unborn child. And since they would be the only ones left who would know where Ahmed Hassad had been taken and who had taken him, they would certainly suffer the most fiendish torment until it was certain they had given all the information they had to give.

"Good Lord," she whispered.

Oss Tiss's yellow eyes were watching her, the vertical slits narrow; his long red tongue was flicking impatiently.

What could be worse than torture?

"Tippi!" she wailed. "These creatures *eat* humans!"

"But they passed a law against it, Mother!"

"That law was passed in Jassa! These are *Ussirs*!"

Lori saw sudden decision in Oss Tiss's yellow eyes, saw him lift the yellow tube that fired the mind-blanking ray, saw him level it directly at her . . .

Tippi saw the yellow ray strike her mother, saw her mother become mindless, staring.

And then she saw the mind-blanker point at her.

CHAPTER 4

Guss had tried, on leaving Harry at the Red Rock Motel and on breaking through the Point of Proximity into their own world of Essa, to fly directly to the sanctuary of Siss State Hospital, where they could wait in safety until the government of Jassa had assured them they truly had been forgiven all previous transgressions and were now free to resume their normal lives. But, like so many of Guss's well-intentioned efforts, things had gone substantially awry.

They had run out of fuel.

And running out of fuel had not been the worst of it.

They had run out of fuel in a densely wooded area three hundred kilometers north of Larissa, and that had put them down in a densely wooded, thinly populated area known to be used for illegal activities of various kinds. Guss had known, when he had set out with the fuel container in search of fuel, that the area was dangerous, but when faced with the rock—go after fuel—and the hard place—wait for the police to find them out-of-sanctuary—he had chosen the rock, leaving Sissi and Los Ross to cope as best they could.

Now Sissi was trying her best to cope.

Alone.

She kept telling herself repeatedly that she was not afraid.

She kept saying to herself that after all she had been through during the past month—going to Earth, just she and Guss, in an effort to save the human race from destroying itself—she could not possibly ever be afraid of anything again. But that was simply not true; she could be afraid.

She was frightened halfway to insanity right now.

They kept coming!

She had used her esso twice and had killed two of them. But they wouldn't stop. They couldn't stop. They were bassoe-butchers, and this was an illegal bassoe-meat farm where Guss had set them down out of fuel, marvelous klutz that he was, and they had to kill any who could report them, because the punishment for dealing in bassoe-meat was a death of the most slow and grisly kind.

And so they kept coming—to kill her.

The second of the bassoe-butchers she had killed lay where he had fallen, not more than five meters from the flight-craft. He had hidden himself behind a fallen tree, jumping out from time to time to fire his primitive hand weapon, then he had charged the craft, intent on breaking it open and killing her—which he probably could have done, given enough time. But she had pushed a button that opened a port and, holding her esso in both shaking hands, had put a purple beam through his chest. The beam had killed him instantly. And the killing had all but destroyed her.

She was *not* a murderer!

"Please, Osis!" she had begged of her god. "I am not. I am not!"

And, more than this, she was alone now.

She was alone because Los Ross, who had been with her until the second bassoe-butcher had been killed, had done a very stupid thing. The little scientist, on seeing how shattered she had become, and perhaps because he knew she had only two beams left in the esso, had decided he would reason with the bassoe-butchers, of whom he was certain there were more. "We won't tell on you if you'll leave us alone"—that sort of thing. He had gone out, wearing his funny helmet with its antennae and knobs, his smock wrongly buttoned, his glasses crooked on his muzzle, waving a white flag.

Reason with them? Butchers? Murderers?

What a silly notion!

Sissi thought he might be dead by now.

And so, for that matter, might Guss. Guss had been gone a long, long while.

Now Guss was in her mind. Achingly. Yes. Yes, he should have known the fuel was going to run out. They had flown all over the skies on Earth, hadn't they? How many hours at high speeds? The Triss-nass was a splendid flying machine. It had saved their lives several times, and in the end it had helped save the human race. But it *was* a notorious energy eater. It carried you with great speed and luxury, but you had better not pass up too many energy stations! Yes, Guss should have been concerned about the fuel, and had he been, they wouldn't be in this fix.

"Don't be a silly little whisser!" she scolded herself.

How many energy stations were there in the world of humans? Exactly none. Then what would have been the use of Guss keeping one eye on the energy gauge? Oh, when they had reached Essa—then he should have sought an energy station first of all. But that was Guss—he somehow didn't think of practical needs. He was a creative artist, after all, who dealt in more esoteric things.

Could she really blame him?

No matter . . .

Guss had taken the container and had set off down the road at a steady lope to find an energy station. Ten kilometers, twenty—it would make no difference. Not only was he a maestro at the sissal, Guss was an Essa-class runner as well. He had often challenged Harry at what Harry had called a marathon distance and had won as often as not. But he was more than a fine athlete, more than a maestro of fragrances. In Sissi's eyes he was an earnest, caring person.

She loved him with all her might.

She was sniffling now, getting ready to cry. The mental

picture of Guss loping along, the container banging against his bony knees, doing his best for her, was overpowering.

So much had happened since she had known him.

They'd been so happy . . .

Guss had been a very famous person, loved for his work with symphonic fragrances, and she'd chased after him like a little assle, giving herself to him—and that could have gotten them both arrested: him for molesting a lissi and her for being a wayward lissi—until she had finally gotten old enough to be his mistress, which was also illegal. But he'd promised, now she was old enough, to make her his legal mate, and he was maybe even going to *keep* that promise when they got to the sanctuary.

If they ever did.

"Oh, twiss. Oh, twiss," she wailed softly.

Sissi was small even for a Jassan female, but she was what Harry Borg had laughingly but sincerely described as the Marilyn Monroe of their kind. She supposed that meant she was shapely. But she thought her eyes were her best feature. Her eyes were very large, beautifully golden, and the vertically slitted pupils could be very expressive. And her tongue, so delicate, so red—the forked, gently caressing tips of her tongue had stolen Harry Borg's heart, that was certain. And she hoped Guss's heart as well.

They had both said she was pretty.

A look in a vanity mirror told her that indeed she was. Well, maybe not right at the moment. She *had* been frassled pretty hard the past week. Her face needed a bit of touching up under the eyes, and her lips a bit of color. But all things considered . . .

She was wearing the uniform of the Red Flame Brigade Harry had had made for her: overseas cap, blouse with the Red Flame emblem on the shoulder, and weapons belt, complete with short sword and esso holster. It was a wardrobe that gave her a certain style, a perky air. Guss had called it sexy.

"But it's not *all* sex!" she told herself plaintively. "He likes *me*! Maybe not for my mind, but—"

She was distracted again.

"Oh, liss. What next?" she asked.

A herd of bassoes had drifted out of the woods. They were wandering aimlessly, baaing mindlessly.

Even as bassoes went, these were a scrawny lot, poorly fed, obviously, and badly cared for. The soft gray fur that covered their bodies lacked the shining luster of well-kept animals. Some were even patchy. All were dirty. It hurt Sissi to see them so Bassoes were nice creatures, really.

"Poor things."

Except for the soft gray fur that covered almost all their bodies, the bassoes were identical to the humans of Earth. The sad thing was that here on Essa the race had become small and fragile. Possibly it had been because of inbreeding, and possibly it had been because, since their minds had been blanked for uncounted centuries, they had lost the life-force needed to thrive. But even small and spindly, or perhaps because of it, their flesh had always been considered a great delicacy by those who could afford it.

As Sissi watched, one of the large trained beetles used to herd the bassoes raced out of the woods in an effort to round up the little humans and drive them back. Herd-beetles stood a meter high and were very swift and very capable. Easily trained, they seemed to enjoy the task of herding bassoes, rustling their golden wing shells, waving antennae, clicking mandibles.

Now Sissi heard the telepathic whistle of a herder.

In another moment she saw the herder come through the trees in pursuit of the wandering bassoes and the herd-beetle. He was a scruffy, evil-looking Jassan, half naked, mud-caked, raggedly clothed. When he saw the round silver shape of the Triss-nass, he darted behind a tree, only to appear again to fire his weapon at Sissi. The projectile pinged off the side of the craft, leaving a dent but doing no real harm. The beetle, seeing the Triss-nass, turned to face it, lifting itself high on its legs, antennae waving, mandibles clacking. It was so frightening to Sissi, who abhorred insects large and small, that she could not help but use one of her remaining shots to exterminate it. The purple ray caught the giant insect squarely, and the nasty thing seemed to explode, legs, gold wing shells, head, pieces, and guck flying all directions.

"Yissss!" the herder screamed.

His herd-beetle must have meant a lot to him, for he came out of the woods, charging insanely, firing his weapon. Sissi opened the port again and, holding her esso with both hands, as Harry Borg had taught her, she managed to stop shaking long enough to hit the charging bassoe-butcher with a purple ray.

He died instantly.

Then Sissi collapsed, quivering, sobbing. "No more!" she pleaded. "Please, Osis, no more!"

She couldn't have fired another shot even if there had been another shot left in the esso to fire. She could only sit shivering, totally devastated. The bassoes came on to wander about the Triss-nass, baaing mindlessly. She hardly noticed them, so deep was her shock and despondency, and she sat there almost an hour, fearful and alone, before Guss finally returned.

He came down the old road, the heavy container banging against his knees, panting hoarsely, his tongue hanging out like a long, limp ribbon. When he reached the Triss-nass, he sagged against the craft, totally exhausted.

"Oh, Guss..." Sissi jumped out of the Triss-nass, hurrying to help him. His mind was too exhausted to form words; he could only gasp and wave a limp hand at the container.

"Did you find fuel?" Sissi asked.

He nodded dumbly.

"Let's put it in."

Sissi had to brush the bassoes aside—they had come running on seeing Guss and Sissi, baaing, hoping for food— but working together, Guss and Sissi got the container in place, connected, and the valves turned. Then Sissi helped Guss into the comfortable seat of the Triss-nass. He sat with the gray inner lid drawn across his golden eyes. It was long moments before he could function well enough to speak again. Then what he said made little sense.

"New record."

"New record?" Sissi asked.

"Twenty Ks, carrying a tross," he said. "Empty one way, full coming back. Cross-country. Got to be a record."

"Wonderful!" Sissi said, as if she really thought so.

Males were proud of the oddest things.

He was silent, panting a few moments more, enjoying the fact that his record was one that would probably never be broken. Then he sat up with a start, looking around.

"Where's Los?"

"I'm—I'm afraid to tell you!" Sissi said.

"Come on!" Guss was suddenly alert, anxious.

Sissi put her arms around him, hid her face. None of it had been her fault, but she felt somehow that it was. And she knew he was going to be very, very angry that she had let it happen.

"Sissi! Where's Los?"

So she told him that the POP had turned out to be on an illegal bassoe ranch— "A *what*?" he asked, incredulous—that she'd had to kill three of the bassoe-butchers, and that Los Ross had gone into the woods waving the white flag to reason with them.

"*Reason?*" Guss squeaked. "With *butchers*?"

"Guss, please—"

"The stupid idiot!" Guss exploded.

"I tried to stop him!"

Sissi was pleading now. But Guss was so angered, he wouldn't listen to her. He turned to the controls and began the routines needed to restart a craft that had run totally out of fuel.

"What're you doing, Guss?"

"Getting this cursed thing ready to go!"

"And then?"

"And then we're getting out of here!"

"Guss," Sissi wailed. "What about Los?"

"What about him?"

"Are you going to *leave* him?"

"He's dead!" Guss flipped two switches, paused. "Isn't he?"

"Isn't he what?"

"Dead."

"I—I don't know."

"You haven't heard from him in an hour, have you?"

"No."

"Then he's dead!"

He flipped another switch, and the craft began to hum, to vibrate gently. Then it stopped suddenly.

"Zatty fuel!" he swore.

Another try got the craft humming again.

"We don't *know*!" Sissi said.

"Know what?"

"If he's dead or not—for sure."

"If he's been gone an hour, what else could he be?"

"I don't *know*!"

"I *do*!"

He tried the controls. The craft lifted, then sagged. The energy driver had gone dead again. Guss swore furiously. He worked the controls again, and this time, when the engine started, he raced the drive until the craft seemed about to shake itself apart.

"You don't, either!" Sissi wailed.

"Don't what?"

"Know if he's dead or not!"

"Will you, in the name of Osis, quit your flissin—"

He turned to rage at her, as furious as a Jassan could be. Then he saw she was in shambles. She had the back of her hand to her face, biting her knuckles. Her golden eyes were huge and pleading as she looked at him. She was afraid, terribly afraid—afraid of losing him if she kept on—but she wasn't going to quit. And the seeing, the knowing, hit him so suddenly, so powerfully, it almost tore his heart in two.

He reached out, caught her in his arms. "Sorry... sorry... sorry..."

After crying and snuffling, Sissi said, "You wouldn't have left him, I know you wouldn't have!"

"I hope not."

"I know you wouldn't! You were just so angry!"

"Yes." He let go of her and straightened up. "I was angry." He shook his head. "But that wasn't all. I—I guess I was really trying to to hide from—what I'd have to do— if I didn't run."

He was looking at the forest. "I can't fly this craft in those trees," he said. "I couldn't see him on the ground if I flew over them..."

Most of the trees were a hundred meters tall; many

were three meters thick. They were the great columns of
some frightening kind of a cathedral; the ranks of undergrowth were the pews of unknown devils; the narrow
pathways were aisles to an altar where evil rites must be
performed. To find Los Ross, alive or dead, he would
have to go in there, past the dead bodies of the bassoe-
butchers, into those dark and shadowed places.

"Sissi, I don't know..."

Sissi knew what troubled him.

He had never claimed to be a hero.

She wanted to say that she would go for him, that she
would take his esso, the only one with shots left, and
leave him to guard their craft with her sword—but how
can you say that to a proud male, how can you disgrace
him in his own eyes?

"You can do it," she said. "I know you can."

"But how?"

Then, suddenly, he kicked the door on his side open
and leaped to the ground. He took the esso from his holster and thrust it at Sissi. "Give me your sword!"

"No! Take the esso!"

But he jerked her sword free.

"Fifteen minutes!" he told her. "If it takes longer, I
won't be coming back. Fly yourself straight to the sanctuary!"

He turned and charged—into those tall trees, into the
undergrowth, into those dark and shadowed places.

"Los! Los! I'm coming!"

The words echoed in Sissi's mind, fading.

CHAPTER 5

Harry Borg lay watching the far slope.

The killers of Ahmed Hassad's security force were being very careful now. And the score gave them reason. From the moment their gunfire had sent him crashing through the guardrail to where he was now, halfway down the rocky slope, his leg trapped beneath the car, he had killed three of them, and he was still alive.

The score?

Three to zip!

But they were going to change that soon.

They had a high-power rifle; he had a .38 Police Special. The .38 was a fine handgun, no doubt about it, but it had nothing like the range of their rifle. They could stay safely out of his reach, and when they started shooting at him with the AR-16, armed with the NATO cartridge, he was going to be like a tin duck in a shooting gallery.

So long, Harry.

They were moving upstream for a better angle now. Looking that way, Harry could see at least three places that would give them a clear field of fire. He had been listening for some sound—a rattle of gravel, a voice—that would tell him where they were, but he had heard nothing yet. They had to be careful. Sound carried long distances in these quiet mountains.

37

And the mountains were beautiful.

Here in the canyon, among rocks and pines, where the rushing stream bounced through boulders, he could see a valley distantly below with towering snow-covered ridges and cliffs rising steeply beyond. The air was sharp here, cold and pure, and towering clouds were like whipped cream in a blue, blue sky. A crow came to roost in the top of a nearby pine. His caw was like a profane voice in a cathedral on a Monday morning, echoing. There were five buzzard hawks now, wheeling on fixed wings, riding the thermals. And why not five? There were three dead men in view. Soon there would be another.

How did they know?

"Y'all come," Harry whispered. "Supper's on the table."

Then he heard the scattering sound as a boot dislodged gravel on the upward slope beyond the stream, and he saw the quick movement of a trousered leg in the brush. With great effort, twisting his own torso almost in two, he heaved the corpse of the security guard he had killed around to place it between himself and the most likely point of fire. He managed to scratch loose a few fist-sized rock fragments to place on top of the body for added protection. When he had finished, he found that the head of the dead guard had rolled and that the glazed, cold eyes were staring at him.

"Sorry, son," Harry told him. "But it was you or me."

He turned the head so the eyes looked away.

Zing! Ka-whack!

The ricochet and the muzzle blast had come almost together, the bullet going wide.

"Damn!" Harry swore.

It was a startled curse, for the shot had come from the slope downstream, not upstream! They had fooled him, one going upstream to distract him into building his barricade on the wrong side. Fortune had favored him, though, because the rifleman, in his hurry to use his advantage, had rushed his shot and missed. Harry was working with frantic haste to move the corpse barricade when he heard the voices.

"Y' think that's him?"

"Who else could it be?"

"Any time there's shootin', it's gotta be old Iron Balls."

"Betcher ass on it."

"At ease, damn it!"

The voices were telepathic!

They came into Harry's mind weakened by distance, but they were real and not imaginings. They were the telepathic voices of the young men of his cadre. That last voice had belonged to Chad Harrison.

"Bloody hell!" Harry swore.

He turned and pounded the ground with a balled-up fist. He was furious: furious at himself for having been a damned fool, for having come out here alone to pick up Lori and Sam; furious at them for being wiser than he had been about Ahmed Hassad; furious at the fates for having dropped him into this bloody bucket of bad luck, slated to die in a few more minutes. And he pounded the ground, because he was so damned proud of the young lads, he could hardly stand it. He hit the ground with each word:

"Best—damn—soldiers—alive!"

They would follow the orders of their commander, follow them with the necessary "cheerful and willing obedience"—up to a point. And that point was when their commander suffered an attack of the stupids that endangered not only his life but the lives of two very important members of their group—Lori and Sam.

Make that three. Lori was pregnant.

"Chad calling!"

Godawmighty—sweet music!

"Chad calling Harry Borg. Do you read? Come in, sir."

"Borg here," Harry answered. "Read you loud and clear."

"God damn! That *is* him!" Arnie cried joyfully.

"Didn't I tell yuh!"

"At ease! At ease!" Chad said. "Need help, sir?"

"Does a bear need honey?"

"Clue us in."

"Where are you?" Harry asked.

"On the road to Globe One," Chad answered. "Got to be near you to hear those shots."

"Keep comin', son. You'll see a barricade. I'm on the slope below the barricade, my leg caught under my car. There's a couple of Hassad's security guards shootin' at me. They're gonna blow me away in a minute or so, the way it's going."

"Can't let that happen. Hang in, sir!"

Then Harry heard: "Eddie! Get us there in one piece!"

And a moment later: "Barricade!"

Harry winced as another shot *zing*ed! and *ka-whack*ed! A very close miss.

Then he heard the screech of sliding tires. Looking up, he saw the top of a sedan, saw gravel fly as a car skidded sideways on the road. Chad's telepathic voice came a moment later. "What've y' got, sir?"

"Two security guards shooting at me. An AR-16 and a shotgun. They're across the creek on the far slope, maybe two hundred yards. I'm on the slope below the road, pinned by the car."

"Stay quiet," Chad said.

"Have you in sight," Homer Benson said.

And then Harry saw the big farm lad, head and wide shoulders above the guardrail, calmly hooking an elbow through the sling of a scope-sighted rifle. A .30-06 by the look of it. A single shot from that big-bore rifle, the heavier, more authoritative sound, put the men on the far slope on notice.

Trouble had come to River City!

And if the sound of that big rifle had not been enough, they had Eddie and Arnie to think about. Those two vaulted the guardrail, one up the road and one down the road like two wide receivers going deep, to disappear into the woods above and below the two security guards on the far side.

Chad came straight down to Harry. By no chance, he placed himself between Harry and the killers.

"Down, you idiot!"

"Sir," Chad said. But he didn't move. His cold gray eyes had seen it all; he knew the odds, he stayed firm, he waited.

Homer's quiet voice: "Just...one...second..."

And the big-bore rifle spoke again.

The man with the AR-16 yelled in pain, fell out of the

cover, and lay still. His rifle clattered in the rocks a distance away from him. To the right, where Harry had thought the rifle was going to be, the shotgun boomed once and then was still.

"Only two, sir?" Arnie's telepathic voice asked.

"That's all," Harry answered.

"The party's over." That was Eddie, the graceful-moving black, who then said crankily to Arnie: "How many times I got to tell you, you honky hothead—a dead hero's no good to anybody!"

"I should let 'im blow you apart?"

"I was gonna take 'im!"

"How'd I know that?"

"Try thinkin' once."

And while the two close friends went on bitching, Chad grinned at Harry. "Still can't get along."

"Thank God for them," Harry said.

Homer had come down the slope, and, working together, he and Chad were able to free Harry's leg—to find it was not broken.

"Couldn't break it with a hammer," Chad said.

"Man of steel," Homer agreed.

"Wise-asses," Harry groaned. "But it hurts—hurts like hell."

They had to help him up the slope.

Once on top, Harry had to take a few moments to walk a bit, to stop his stomach from churning, to quiet badly shaking hands. When he was able to call himself repaired enough to go on, he went back to face the four young men who were waiting quietly, uneasily, beside the car. He came to a brace-legged stance, thumbs hooked in his belt, scowling. He was a rough-looking, tough-looking bruiser any time, but now he looked bad-assed enough to scare a bear. His jacket was bullet-ripped. His bearded jaw was dark with caked blood, the gold band clamped in his left ear was dulled with it. And his dark blue eyes were cold, even menacing, as he stared at them.

They returned his gaze without wavering.

Chad: deeply tanned, white-haired, six-two and still growing, the quarterback of the group, gray-eyed, capable. Homer Benson: the quiet lad from the cattle country, wide-shouldered, big-handed, with untroubled brown eyes. Eddie: the tall, lean black from south central L.A., almond-eyed, handsome, quietly proficient. And Arnie: midsize, the quick-smiling, knuckle-faced hard charger. Harry Borg was looking at them as if he wanted to give them each a year in jail. But he was thinking something else.

He was thinking that here were four of the very best.

"I told you to go home," he said. "You don't obey orders?"

"Usually," Chad answered.

"Almost every time," Homer said.

"When we can," Eddie said.

"When we oughta," Arnie said.

They wouldn't say he had been stupid, driving here alone, but they wouldn't say he had not been stupid, either. And Harry, tough-minded, but fair, was not about to call them wrong. Not this time.

"You only saved my ass," he said.

"Nothin'," they said. "Any time. A pleasure."

"I don't know what to tell you."

"Try somethin' mean and nasty," Arnie said.

Harry brought his menacing dark blue eyes to bear on Arnie, the smallest of the lads, and the grin that had begun to glow hopefully on Arnie's face faded quickly. The lad braced to attention, eyes fixed distantly, avoiding Harry's steady glare. Harry let him stand a moment. Then, suddenly, he reached out and caught the young man's head between his big, rough hands, forcing the young man's eyes to meet his own dark scowl; then he jerked the lad close and bit him on the forehead—or seemed to.

And he turned quickly away.

"Let's get out of here," he growled.

He moved toward the task of clearing the barricade.

"Geez! That was close!" Arnie breathed.

"Coulda got your butt busted," Eddie said.

But they were voices Harry pretended not to hear.

There were five miles still to go to reach Globe One. "All we want is to get Lori and Sam," Harry told the lads. "Get them and get out fast. No sweat, no hassle. We'll start at the airport, Eddie. Remember the way?"

"Perfectly, sir." Eddie was at the wheel.

They went to the private airport that had been cut into the valley a half mile from the portal of Globe One. The security guards there, after quiet persuasion, allowed Harry and the lads to take two of the company transport vehicles—small, battery-operated buslike conveyances emblazoned with the Globe One logo—and were willing to remain bound and gagged for as long as might be necessary.

"Easy dudes to get along with," Arnie commented.

"You got a pistol up your nose, who isn't?" Eddie said.

"Chad, you're going with me," Harry Borg said.

"Sir."

"Homer, Eddie, Arnie, you're reserves. Come a-runnin' if we holler."

"Sir," they said together.

The huge concrete and steel gate that stood at the foot of a towering granite cliff, a gate that could hold a nuclear blast at bay, stood wide open as they approached. The usual pair of security guards were in place on either side, just before the entrance, but they gave no special notice as Harry drove the small bus straight at them. It was a company bus, authorized for use by company personnel only, wasn't it? When they had learned otherwise, it was too late.

Harry left one side of the bus, and Chad the other.

"No trouble, now," Harry said, leveling a pistol.

"Hang loose," Chad said to the other.

They all went to the guardroom that was carved into the granite wall inside the portal gates. A glass wall faced the tunnel; a door through the glass wall permitted entry. Inside the guardroom, two uniformed security guards sat at desks. One, a sergeant, whose name tag above his shirt pocket said his name was Sergeant Olivera, looked up and reached for a telephone as Harry, Chad, and the guards entered.

"Talk to me first," Harry said, aiming the pistol again. Sergeant Olivera took his hand carefully away from the telephone. "Harry Borg," he said. "What do you want?"

"I want my wife and her bodyguard," Harry told him. "We can do it the easy way. And I'd like that best. Or we can do it the hard way. And you won't like that at all."

"Let's try the easy way," Sergeant Olivera said.

He was a lean, dark man with the look of the military about him, the gray at his temples suggesting Korea service. He had dark eyes, a thin, sharp nose, and a narrow mustache. Not, Harry thought, a man who would frighten easily.

"Have them brought here," Harry told him. "We'll take them and leave. No sweat, no bother."

"Sounds good," the sergeant said. "Shall I call in?"

"Go."

The sergeant picked up the phone. "Olivera here. Give me the lieutenant." After a moment's wait, he told the man on the other end what he had and what was needed. And he listened. Then he hung up the phone and looked at Harry with steady, dark eyes.

"There's a problem," he said.

"So?"

"You want your wife, you have to go in."

"That's not the easy way."

"It's the only way now," the sergeant said. "Orders from the top."

"Hassad?"

"Is there another top?" the sergeant asked. When he found Harry's dark blue eyes burning into his, he said, "You can take me, a gun at my back—that's the best I can do."

"I'll take you."

"It's a one-way road, sir," Chad said telepathically.

Harry answered telepathically. "They *think*. Keep my gate open . . . and give me an interval of . . . five minutes."

"Five minutes, sir!"

Harry and Sergeant Olivera rode in the sergeant's security car down the wide tunnel that led deep into the mountain. After a ten-minute drive, the tunnel widened to reveal a sight that was mind-boggling to Harry, even though he had been here before.

"What money can do," he said.

"Beats hell, doesn't it?" the sergeant agreed.

Ahmed Hassad had told the world he was building a shale-oil conversion plant of enormous size here, a mile deep within the granite of the Rocky Mountains, but what he had built in fact was a small underground city, a self-sustaining city capable of supporting life indefinitely. It was well lighted, the temperature was permanently fixed; the air was clean and purified. Harry looked down the streets as they passed and saw the vehicles and pedestrians—except for the fact that the cars were electric and the sky was stone, they could have been citizens of any Small Town, USA.

"Outa sight," Harry said.

The sergeant brought them finally to the black marble facade of a beautifully lighted and carpeted building Harry knew very well. He had fought his way out of it not too long ago.

"You can live through this," he told Sergeant Olivera as they went into the cool, softly lighted interior. "Just stay close and stay gentle."

"You got it," the sergeant said.

"My people," Harry said. "That's all I want."

"I'm with you. Easy in, easy out."

The sergeant led them into the big, beautifully furnished room Harry knew to be Hassad's personal quarters. This time, however, instead of finding Ahmed Hassad waiting at the bar, he found the big, blond sergeant of security he had known as Cecil. Cecil was wearing a lieutenant's bar now. The scion of a wealthy eastern family, a Harvard graduate with a faint lisp, Cecil was a hardened athlete who had a sadistic turn of mind. He had clubbed Harry from behind for no good reason when Harry had been here before, and he had the same police baton he'd used then, long and black, in his hands now. He tapped it into the palm of a hand as he talked.

"Harry Borg," he said. "Welcome back."

"I thought we'd killed you," Harry said.

Cecil gave Harry a cold grin. "You may wish you had."

Harry looked at Sergeant Olivera.

"All new to me," the sergeant said.

"Where's Hassad?" Harry asked Cecil.

"We don't know."

"Where's my wife and her bodyguard?"

"And the little girl? Your wife's daughter?"

"She here, too?" It was the first Harry had heard of it.

"Was here—all three are gone now."

"Where'd they go?"

"We don't know that, either."

Harry lifted the gun he'd been holding at Sergeant Olivera's back and placed the barrel on the sergeant's shoulder, aiming dead center on Cecil's chest.

"One minute," he said quietly. "That's all you've got."

The big, blond lieutenant was not visibly frightened. He indicated three framed pictures on the walls of the room. Harry knew from his previous visit that the pictures usually concealed gunports and security guards meant for Hassad's protection.

"You'd be dead a second after you killed me," Cecil said. "But killing won't solve our problem." He turned away. "Come look at a television show."

He led the way deeper into the room to a big-screen television set. "What you're going to see now is a replay of a security camera tape." He pressed the button that turned the set on. "As you know, we've got security cameras in every room, including the surgery."

The screen came to life. The sound of gunfire filled the room.

"My God!" Harry swore.

What he saw and heard almost shocked the life out of him. Lori, his beloved Lori, belly round with child, her face tear-streaked, was standing straddle-legged, looking absolutely magnificent in her fury, a handgun in either hand, shooting at the door of the room in which she was standing, screaming defiance.

"Christ!" Harry said.

Behind Lori, the huge Sam Barnstable was lying on the floor unconscious, either dead or dying, certainly bleeding. And beside the youth he had assigned bodyguard duty was Tippi, Lori's daughter, mopping Sam's blood and shouting at her mother.

"What in hell is this?" Harry demanded.

"There's more!" Cecil said quickly. "Hang on!"

Harry put off killing him then, but only just barely.

He saw his people gassed, saw them rushed on gurneys to the surgery. What Harry saw next—the tape had been edited—was Sam, wired and being tortured on Hassad's orders; Sam's first lunge from the excruciating pain again brought Cecil as close to death as he could ever get without dying. This time he was saved only because the camera had swung to focus on Hassad.

"You bastard!" Harry breathed.

"What's goin' on?" Chad's telepathic voice asked.

"Bloody hell," Harry answered. "You?"

"Two and counting," Chad said.

"Stand by," Harry told him.

He heard Lori moan, "I'll tell . . . I'll tell you!" to save Sam from further torture. And then he saw the aliens arrive.

"My God!" he said, unbelieving.

He watched the aliens mind-blank all but Lori, Tippi, and Sam. He saw the alien bending over Lori, saw the alien turn then, draw his esso, and kill those who had tortured Sam. And he saw the aliens finally mind-blank Lori, Tippi, and Sam—then, unbelievably, take Lori, Tippi, Sam, and Ahmed Hassad away.

Cecil pushed the switch, and the screen went blank. "Where'd they go?" he asked Harry.

Harry was still unbelieving. "They got away?" he asked. "Out of *here*?"

"Clear away," Cecil said. "My people don't remember any of it—that yellow light did something to them."

"Blanked their minds."

"But the security cameras recorded the trip out. They walked through the portal, into an open area—and vanished." He waited, watching Harry with cold eyes.

"Well?" Cecil asked finally. "Where did they go? How do I get Hassad back—if he's still alive? Or find out if he's dead?"

"Why?" Harry asked. "Why?"

"What do you mean why?"

But the question had not been for Cecil. Harry was puzzled.

Why would the Jassans want Hassad? Hassad of all people! A one-man slice of hell, a greater blight than cancer, AIDS, herpes, and the black plague combined. They might have taken Lori, Tippi, and Sam to save them from torture. But Hassad? No! The Jassans knew him for what he was.

"It's impossible!" he said.

"You saw it happen."

Harry was staring, thinking.

"I want to know all about those creatures," Cecil said. "I want to know why they took Hassad. And where they took him. I want to know what I've got to do to get him back." He slapped the police baton into a cupped palm. "You're not leaving here until I get the answers—all the answers."

He waited as Harry continued staring.

"Do you hear me, Borg?"

Now Harry brought his dark blue eyes, gone almost black, to bear on Cecil. He stared into Cecil's pale blues a moment. Then he answered with a voice that was low, almost a whisper. "I hear you, son."

Something in that voice got to Cecil. His own voice thinned to a tenor, faintly girlish, as he firmed his grip on his police baton. "You're not leaving here until you tell me what I want to know! Those green bastards can't get away with—"

"Green!" Harry yelled suddenly. "Did you say green?"

"Yes, green. What difference—"

"Ussirs!" Harry said.

The security tape pictures had been in black and white, but if the aliens were green, they had to be Ussirs.

"What d' you mean, Ussirs?"

"Back now—we're leaving," Harry said to Sergeant Olivera.

"You're *not* leaving!" Cecil yelled.

The yell brought Harry's eyes back to Cecil. "You're going to stop me?"

"You damned well better believe it!"

Harry stared at Cecil a moment longer. "All right," he said then. "I owe you one."

Harry holstered his revolver, then spat on the palms of his hands.

The gesture, the quietly spoken words, backed by the level gaze of Harry Borg's dark blue eyes, must have frightened the security officer. Big and hardened he might be, a blond giant in his own right, he must have suddenly recognized the danger in the man he had thought to be his prisoner—only a frightened man could have moved with such speed, stabbing with his police baton.

The blow caught Harry Borg in the midriff, driving the breath out of him with sudden violent pain, folding him. A second, whipping blow, aimed at Harry's head, missed only because Harry had rolled backward across the carpeted floor. He collided with Sergeant Olivera and knocked that man down. The sergeant stayed down. Was it to allow Cecil his pleasure with the baton? Or was it because Harry's revolver had spilled from its holster close to the sergeant's hand?

The telepathic voice of Chad Harrison reached Harry, quietly urgent. "Now, sir?"

"Not yet."

Harry regained his feet across the room from Cecil and found the lieutenant lunging forward, sure Harry was suffering great pain and all but helpless. Great pain, yes. Helpless, no. Harry drove in under the lunging Cecil, caught the big young man thigh-high, heaved him up and over, and sent him crashing into the wall behind him. The young man came out of the bone-jarring crash only to find that Harry had followed him in. Harry tore the baton from Cecil's hand and drove a cementlike fist into Cecil's belly. Cecil folded, gray-faced, gasping. Harry caught him by the back of the shirt collar and the back of his belt and threw him into a staggering run across the room to crash into the big-screen television set in an explosion of glass and splinters.

Harry's eyes met the eyes of Sergeant Olivera, who was still on the floor, the gun hidden now. When Harry's unspoken question—"You in this?"—was answered by a head shake, Harry went on stalking the lieutenant. Cecil

backed away and threw up his hands, coughing and gagging. He called for help from the guards behind the picture
gunports.

"Kill him! Kill him!"

One of the gunports dropped at once. An automatic
weapon appeared, as lethal as a cobra head, and a quiet
voice answered.

"Kill him? No. I work for him." The voice belonged
to Chad Harrison; the eyes behind the sights were his
eyes, ice-gray; his hands were steady.

"I'll be damned!" Sergeant Olivera whispered.

"Going right out, son," Harry said to Chad. "The way
open?"

"All clear, sir."

Harry closed on Cecil, took a fistful of the lieutenant's
shirt, and drove him against the wall. The younger man
was very frightened now, pleading.

"No! Please, no!"

Harry swung a hard fist against the side of Cecil's jaw.
The lieutenant's head banged into the wall, his eyes glazed,
and his body went suddenly limp. Harry let go of the
shirt, stepped back, and watched the younger man drop
to the floor.

"Move out," he said to Chad.

When Chad was gone, Harry turned to find Sergeant
Olivera bringing a revolver to bear on him. A quick slap
at his holster confirmed the gun was his own. He had a
gut-sucking moment of tension. The sergeant could end
it all for him—right now.

"That boy took all three positions," the sergeant said.

"We were here before." Harry's voice was drawn tight.
"He could have managed one or two more."

"And now you want to go after your wife?"

"That's right."

The sergeant looked at the fallen lieutenant, still unconscious against the wall. A muscle flexed in the sergeant's
jaw; his eyes, dark and cold, came back to Harry, to hold
a long moment. Then he reversed the revolver he was
holding and handed it to Harry, butt first.

"Godspeed," he said.

The sergeant's security car was still in the street outside the building, and now Chad waited beside it. The young man's face was dark with concern—for Lori, Tippi, and Sam, Harry knew—but he would hold his questions until Harry chose to speak of them.

"They were kidnapped," Harry said when they were rolling toward the portal to the outside. "By the Ussirs."

"Ussirs?" Chad asked, unbelieving.

"The green guys," Harry confirmed.

He told Chad the rest of the story. "They can have Hassad," he said when he had finished. "My wife—no. Tippi and Sam—no. These they're going to give back. That I promise!"

"Or it'll be their butts," Chad whispered to himself after a glance at Harry's rock-hard face and dark burning eyes.

"Say again?" Harry asked.

"I said, where do we start, sir?" Chad lied.

"The Red Rock Motel," Harry said. "Guss and I had a deal—if I needed him, all I had to do was go into the desert at that Point of Proximity and holler."

"Will he hear you?"

"If Los Ross set up a monitor like he said he would," Harry answered, his hands gripped knuckle-white. "And if the monitor works."

"It will be there," Chad said. "It will work."

Harry swung his dark blue eyes to meet Chad's gray ones. "You going with me?"

"Or else!" Chad said. "Sir."

CHAPTER 6

The first awareness to penetrate the mind of Lori Borg on her awakening from the effects of the mind-blanker beam was the pressure of a cool, dry palm—unmistakably not human—pressed against her mouth. Sudden fear caused her to convulse. Another hand held her firmly. To her clearing vision then came the sight of two yellow eyes with vertically slitted pupils just above her, watching her intently out of a green, reptilian face, and of a forked tongue flickering at her. It was the Ussir commando, Oss Tiss, who was holding her down. Now his telepathic voice spoke to her softly but urgently.

"Make no disturbance."

Lori was too shaken to have disobeyed even if the urgency had not been enough to hold her still. There was extreme danger—that was what the urgency had told her. Not to her alone—she lifted her head and saw the others—but to all of them.

"We've been discovered," Oss Tiss told her softly. "They may attack at any moment."

"Where are we?" she asked telepathically.

"In Jassa." He removed his hand, confident she understood the danger. "A Jassan patrol is between us and our craft."

She was incredulous.

"You? An Ussir? You're in *Jassa* country?"

"The cave was in Jassa country," he said. "The bassoe we wanted was in the cave. This was as near the cave as we could find a portal to the planet Earth."

The "cave" had to be Globe One, the "bassoe" Hassad.

"Hassad?" she asked incredulously. "You wanted *Hassad*?"

"Those were my orders."

"But—why?"

"Silence! We are near death!"

His attention had been caught by a distant movement. He stared, tensely alert; his hand ordered Lori to be still. She obeyed, afraid to move or to speak, almost afraid to think.

And he was glad that she was.

Criss! He was thinking. Is this where it ends?

Caught by an unlucky twist—a wandering Jassan patrol blundering onto his craft at the last moment, blocking his escape. After all he had been through, after the impossible mission had been all but accomplished, was he to fail in the final moment before success?

"Go," his superiors had said, handing him a picture. "Bring us this bássoe."

As if the bassoe pictured were in an open field, undefended, only a short walk away. Fools! Idiots! But weren't all superiors? When faced with an impossible task, what did all superiors do? Delegate the task to an underling so that the blame for failure, when it came—as it surely must—would fall on the shoulders of someone else.

Oss Tiss, in this case.

The scion of a family with a history of military service that went back thousands of years, a family that had saved their country, Ussir, from defeat a hundred times, that had given their country, Ussir, victories almost beyond counting. A young military genius, he had been called the pride of the Academy of Arts and War. He was a trassor now, commander of the Niss Elite Guard, the finest fighting group in all the armed forces.

The logical choice for an impossible mission.

An intelligence network, VIS, built up during a thousand years of war with the Jassans, had supplied all the needed information. The Jassans, like so many nations, would surrender even their most precious secrets if given the right persuasion. VIS knew all that the Jassans knew and perhaps a good deal more.

They knew that the most desirable of bassoes, Harry Borg, who had led the Jassans to victory over the Ussirs in the past war, was still loyal to the Jassans and therefore was unavailable to the Ussirs.

But VIS, with complete access to the extremely detailed files of the Jassans, knew of another bassoe of equal and perhaps greater strength and ability. A bassoe named Ahmed Hassad.

VIS had known where to find Hassad since Hassad's every movement after his attempt to start a nuclear holocaust had been noted by the Jassans, and was therefore known to the VIS and the Ussirs; and they had known how to create a Point of Proximity near the cave the earthlings called Globe One. They had known all this because a Jassan civil servant had committed an indiscretion that would have cost the lives of his family had it been revealed—the methods of espionage are the same everywhere.

The courage needed to go through to the planet Earth, to enter the cave, to force the bassoes to lead them to Hassad, to capture Hassad, to take him and these other bassoes away—that had been the ingredient supplied by Oss Tiss and the Elite Guard.

And they had succeeded—up to a point.

This point.

Where a cursed stroke of misfortune—a blundering Jassan patrol—had all but brought them to a miserable failure. A failure that was almost certainly going to cost all of them their lives unless he worked some kind of a miracle.

And soon.

Lori, waiting in frozen silence, becoming more and more aware, felt a sudden concern for Tippi and Sam. She found then that she was not bound, that she could lift her head enough to see Tippi and Sam. They were lying on a grassy plot, wrapped in blankets, sheltered by rocks and stunted pine trees. And she saw Ahmed Hassad lying just beyond them. They were all still under the influence of the mind-blanker beam, senseless, unknowing.

"Sam!" she whispered suddenly. "He's wounded!"

A quick, fierce pressure of Oss Tiss's eight-fingered hand made her still again, and the commando answered even more softly.

"He had been treated. He will live."

"But—what are we *doing*?"

"We're waiting."

Lori could see they were on a hillside. Across a shallow valley, perhaps a thousand meters away, a towering granite cliff thrust out of a range of rugged mountains—on Earth, she realized, those mountains would be the Rocky Mountains under which Hassad had built Globe One, and the entrance to that underground city would be at the bottom of that cliff. This slope, then, must be where the aliens had found a portal—Point of Proximity—and their flight-craft must be somewhere near.

Now Lori found six of the aliens scattered in protected places on the slope. They were wearing the same uniform Oss Tiss was wearing and, like him, they carried weapons that looked like machine pistols but which, Lori knew, fired deadly purple rays. They seemed to be in a standoff situation with the Jassans, neither side daring to move, each side wanting the other to move first.

The hissing snap of a purple beam went close overhead, and both Oss Tiss and Lori ducked instinctively. The round was answered by two of the Ussir troopers lying in cover at their perimeter.

Now Lori understood the situation better.

The Jassans were trying to entice the Ussirs into attacking their position. But Oss Tiss, his green face intent, his yellow eyes showing growing tension, his red, forked tongue flickering constantly, wanted *them* to attack *his* position. It was a fundamental fact of war—those who attacked an emplaced position suffered the greatest casualties. And here, with the numbers so few, even two or three casualties could mean defeat. So they waited, each trying to entice the other into a fatal blunder.

A desperate game indeed.

Another exchange of purple bolts brought the peril of

her own position even more sharply into Lori's mind. If Oss Tiss and his trooper were killed, Tippi, Sam, and herself—and, yes, Hassad—would surely die with them. She couldn't have cared less about Hassad's life, but if he were to waken suddenly—

"Hassad could get us killed," she whispered.

"How?" Oss Tiss asked.

"He's a violent man. If I could wake him . . . tell him . . ."

He stared at her.

"I could interpret, give him your orders."

With sudden decision, Oss Tiss took a small case from a breast pocket of his uniform blouse. The case contained hypodermic vials. One would awaken a blank mind, he told her. But he was not sure why Lori would want to save him.

"It's my life, too," she said.

She began to crawl toward the grassy plot where Tippi, Sam, and Hassad were lying wrapped in blankets, staring mindlessly into the sky. It was awkward crawling, keeping her head down, dragging her round belly across the stony ground. She grunted away at it, cussing to herself, panting. A gray-eyed woman in a loose-fitting red blouse and black pants who wore her hair in a single waist-long braid, she was very feminine—arching brows, a clean, straight nose, a generous, easy-smiling mouth—but she was strong, too, the stuff of pioneers.

She stopped beside Tippi and Sam and gave each a careful injection. They awakened quietly, and she was able to control them, whispering a rapid account of their position. Then she went on to Hassad. After giving him the injection, she put a hand over his mouth and whispered quietly in his ear. "Wake up."

He did not awaken.

Because of his size, the drug would take longer.

He continued to stare up at the sky, his mind blank. Waiting impatiently for the drug to act, Lori lifted her hand to study his face. Ahmed Hassad. He had planned the murder of the human race, had tortured the injured Sam and had promised torture for Tippi and herself. And he was right here, at her mercy now.

She could kill him.

How many times had she vowed she *would* kill him? Dozens. Now all she need do was press a thumb on his carotid artery—just there in his neck—hold it for a few moments, and he would die without a struggle. Dead, he would go to where he surely belonged—to the very bottom pit of the inferno.

Yes! Kill him, then.

She put a thumb on the artery; she felt the pulse, strong and steady. She ordered her thumb to press down. Hard. Very Hard. But her thumb wouldn't move. It only touched the artery. It would not press down and take the man's life. She tried again and again, and still her thumb would not press.

She could not take a man's life in cold blood no matter how richly the man deserved it—that was something to discover about herself.

She didn't know if she liked it or not.

"C'mon!" she whispered, furious. "Wake up!"

And then he awakened.

She clamped a hand over his mouth and weighted his body with her own. She watched the giant that lived behind his eyes come alive to stare into her eyes from only inches away. Recognition, understanding—she saw both come, like coals turning to flame. But it was a controlled flame. Her hand on his mouth and her shaking head were all he needed to know there was extreme danger.

"Where are we?" he asked.

"In Jassa," she told him.

Then, quickly, as he lay still under her, his powerful muscles rippling to life, she told him more of where they were, how they had come to be here, and what the situation was. For her it was like watching a genie emerging from a bottle, turning from smoke to something enormous and formidable before her eyes. He was Hassad, after all; he had not grown from an orphan child to perhaps the richest man on earth without abilities beyond those given to most other men. He could listen, he could learn, he could act.

"Let me see," he said.

He crawled to a position beside Oss Tiss. With Lori there to interpret—to receive telepathically, to transmit vocally—he learned what the situation was and what their chances of survival were. They were sheltered behind rocks among stunted conifers on a gentle slope. Up that slope, at a distance of about a hundred meters, a sheltered swale concealed the flight-craft that had brought the Ussirs here. The flight-craft of the Jassan patrol had landed near it, and the soldiers of that patrol had deployed into cover below both craft and had all approaches in their field of fire.

"We want them to charge us," Oss Tiss said.

"And they want you to charge them," Hassad said.

"That's right."

"Something else..."

"Yes?"

"They'll get reinforcements soon."

The soft hiss of a quick breath said Oss Tiss agreed with him.

The Jassans must have caught some of the telepathy, for now they sent a series of deadly purple beams hissing close overhead.

"Nasty," Hassad said, ducking. "Very nasty."

"Cut a hole clear through you," Lori told him.

The Jassans taunted them telepathically, calling the Ussirs cowards and worse. Why didn't they attack? Why didn't they surrender?

"What would surrender mean?" Hassad asked.

"Death," Oss Tiss answered.

"Won't do," Hassad said. "Won't do at all."

He had lifted his head enough to measure the terrain, the distances, the comparative strengths. When he settled back, his beautiful, long-lashed dark eyes had that oily shine Lori had come to know so well.

There was evil coming.

"Tell him I'll take one of their weapons and climb the hill to the right," Hassad said to her. "He is to send four of his men down the trail to the left. He and his remaining two are to give us covering fire. Then I'll strike from above and clean them out."

Oss Tiss thought about it.

"They'll kill him," he said to Lori.

"Not if I know Hassad."

"He must be a very good fighter."

"That he is," Lori answered. "That he is."

The Ussirs had two weapons saved from their attack on Globe One. Hassad was given his choice. He took both weapons. He crouched then, his red silk shirt taut over huge, tensed shoulders, his tailored slacks taut on powerful thighs, his alligator slip-ons somehow looking like track shoes. And, crouched there, he looked as if he were only an instant from charging up the slope.

"Now!" he said through Lori.

Oss Tiss gave the order to his troopers. Four of them left their cover at once, running bent low. Oss Tiss and his two remaining troopers opened the covering fire as agreed. But Hassad did not charge up the slope as he had agreed.

He waited until the Jassans had concentrated their fire on the four Ussir troopers who had run to the left, cutting down three. Then, but only then, while the Jassans were busy trying to kill the fourth, Hassad charged.

He ran up the slope like the great Edwin Moses flying across high hurdles, incredibly swift, flowing power, beautiful to watch. And because of the safety gained by sacrificing three troopers, he made it to cover above the Jassan position.

"So *that's* how you do it!" Lori whispered in awe.

"Do what?" Oss Tiss asked.

"Get to be the richest man in the world."

The fire from the Jassans, aimed at the remaining exposed trooper on the left, suddenly stopped. And for good reason. From above them, striding down the slope like the wrath of Lucifer himself, a weapon spewing purple bolts under each arm, came Ahmed Hassad, in all his fierce, evil glory, fighting, killing without mercy. This was what Hassad was all about. Lori and Oss Tiss watched him destroy the last of the Jassans and, after he had destroyed them, go on to cut the fallen bodies to bits.

"What you see is what you get," Lori said to Oss Tiss.

"I couldn't have done it." Oss Tiss's telepathic voice was thin. "He used my soldiers as bait to save himself."

"He's the worst," Lori said.

"And the best for our need."

Hassad came down the slope, striding boldly, to give the two weapons back to Oss Tiss—a brave gesture if not for the fact they were empty. He showed Oss Tiss his beautiful teeth. "All it takes is guts."

"Very effective," Oss Tiss agreed through Lori, and she could almost taste the hatred and bitterness in that grudging admission.

Then Oss Tiss turned, and for her alone he said, "He is going with us. You are *not* going."

"But—" Lori began.

"I had an evil purpose in bringing you," he said. "But now I'm in your debt. I want you safe."

"What's safe?" she asked, suddenly plaintive and afraid. "We were with *you* when Jassans were killed! The Jassans will call us enemy—or spies. They'll kill us!"

The truth of that gave Oss Tiss reason to reconsider. "All right," he said after a moment with a difficult inner battle. "Perhaps I can keep you safe in my home."

"Good!" Lori said.

She turned quickly to Sam Barnstable and, with Tippi's help, began to get the huge young man to his feet.

"Easy, now, luv," Lori said. "Here, let me—"

"No!" It was Oss Tiss. "Not that one."

Lori and Tippi stared at him.

"There is no space for that one," Oss Tiss said.

"But I can't leave him. He needs medical help."

"You and the young one," Oss Tiss said. "But not him."

"I won't leave him. Damn it! We can—"

Oss Tiss turned away. He ordered his troopers out and motioned Hassad ahead of him. Before going, Hassad gave Lori a smile of amused contempt, then moved out ahead of Oss Tiss toward the Ussir flight-craft—he was, after all, where he had wanted to be and going where he had wanted to go. He had no further interest in the problems of others.

"Ma'am . . . Mrs. Borg!" It was Sam Barnstable, upright, pushing Tippi, who had been helping to support him, toward her mother. "I'll be okay, Mrs. Borg. Go—go with them."

"The hell I will!"

Lori was standing resolute, furious, glaring after Hassad, Oss Tiss, and his two remaining troopers. They were already away on the slope, climbing rapidly. She yelled after them.

"Go on! Go! We don't need you!"

"Your mother eats flies!" Tippi yelled.

A few moments later the Ussir craft lifted above the trees. Lori, Tippi, and Sam, standing together, watched it go. Lori shook her fist after it, yelling further imprecations, some of them quite profane.

"Wow!" Tippi said. "Shame on you."

"You should have gone with them," Sam said.

Only his enormous courage and great determination kept the big lad on his feet. His button-nosed face was gray with weakness and pain, and when Lori saw this, she forgot her anger.

"Oh, Sam. There, sit down. Get the blanket, Tippi."

"Ma'am . . . I'm sorry. I—"

"Shut up!"

She kissed him on his button nose and made him sit on a rock outcropping, a blanket wrapped about him. Then Tippi went to put her arm around her mother's waist. They were alone, the three of them, on the cold and windy slope of what would have been a remote part of the Rocky Mountains in their homeland, their only company now the bodies of the fallen Jassans and—

"Hey!" Lori said, her face suddenly alight. "Sam! If Tippi and I help you, can you climb that slope?"

"The Jassan ship!" Tippi shrieked.

"The one *they* came in!" Sam said.

"Right! I can fly it."

"I'll climb that hill." Sam was pushing to his feet.

It wasn't easy. It was a back breaker. Sam, even trying his mightiest, suffering in absolute silence pain almost beyond enduring, was a heavy burden. But they finally got to where the Jassan patrol craft waited, silent, empty, one hatch open wide, a few yards beyond the bodies of the Jassan police.

"Gosh, Mom—can you *really* fly it?"

"Sure, why not?"

Lori was not as confident as she pretended to be. She had flown Jassan craft when they had been in Jassa before, but all craft were different, weren't they? Police patrol craft and this ancient, battered vehicle, certainly. But she was going to give it her best shot—that was bloody sure!—when they had Sam safely aboard.

"Your left foot, Sam . . . a little more . . ."

Tippi coaxed gently, Lori pushed, lifted, and then the big lad was finally in the craft. He collapsed, his gray face dripping sweat. Lori raced around to the other side and got in behind the controls.

"You're the greatest," she said to Sam.

"And you're a liar, ma'am," Sam answered, his voice weak.

"For that—" Lori was learning the controls, finding the switches "—you're going to get—a hit—when I get time."

"You're *my* hero," Tippi told Sam. "That's for double sure!"

"There we go!" Lori said.

The craft had started the quiet vibration that meant the power unit was functioning. She tried the controls. All right! They worked! Now all she had to do was find her way cross-country to Guss's place, where they had stayed when they'd been in Jassa before.

"Mom!" Tippi's voice was stricken. "We've got company."

Looking up, Lori saw two Jassan police patrol craft approaching. They must have come in answer to a call from those now dead on the ground outside. One of the craft whipped in to hover directly over the fallen, mutilated Jassan patrol officers, and Lori found a cannon of some sort aimed directly at her.

"Whoo, boy," she whispered faintly.

CHAPTER 7

Guss knew how he had become lost.

He hadn't been careful. He hadn't thought. He hadn't watched where he was going. He had charged into the undergrowth that covered the ground beneath these great, tall trees, terrified he would lose his nerve and not go; and he'd not gone more than a few hundred meters, searching this way and that, before he realized what he had done. All the trees looked alike now. He knew up and he knew down, but that was all he knew. He didn't know which direction would take him back to the Trissnass and which direction would take him deeper into the forest where he might find Los Ross.

Nor was that the worst of it.

Behind any one of those giant trees there could be any number of filthy bassoe-meat traders waiting to strike him down. Calling out Los Ross's name—insane babbling, he realized all too clearly now—must have told them exactly where he was.

He turned slowly, rigidly, eyes wide, staring.

Any moment . . . any moment . . .

The short sword he had taken from Sissi was his only weapon, and he had little faith in his ability to use it. It might have conquered Harry's world for some tribe Harry had called Romans, but in Guss's hands it was probably

63

no better than a stick. Against an esso it would be nothing. Even against one of their primitive weapons it would be nothing. And if there were two or three of them?

"Osis," he moaned.

In another moment he would be afraid to move at all. His sudden realization of that shocked him into motion. He began running again, in the direction immediately before him, since it was no worse than any other. Branches whipped his lanky form and tore at his clothes. Wildlife fled squawking, and whether he was running to, or fleeing from, mattered not at all. He was not standing still, a target—that was the important thing. Moving, he would not be so easily killed. The vertical pupils of his golden eyes had become almost round with the forest darkness and with his fear.

He called again, "Los! Los Ross!"

Still no answer.

In a few moments he came to a well-worn path, and he followed it at a slower pace, searching, turning quickly, turning back, sword gripped tightly. He jumped a small stream, climbed a little hill, and then found an open glade. A small fire burned in an open pit here. There were crude eating utensils and sleeping robes scattered about.

And here, bound, silent and still on one of the robes, was Los Ross.

He ran to the little scientist, hysterically glad to have found him—to have found him alive, if unconscious— but even more frightened knowing his captors had to be near. He was able to kneel beside Los Ross only an instant before fear made him spring to his feet again, eyes bulging, to stare this way and that, to whirl suddenly, to whirl back. His forked tongue flailed, caught the scent of bassoe-butchers everywhere, but he could find none near. Now he bent to Los Ross again to fumble at the knots in the cords that bound the little scientist.

"Los. Los, wake up. Wake up!"

Los Ross remained limp, unresponding.

Guss had the cords on Los Ross's arms loose and was working on the ties that held the little scientist's wrists, when some fragment of motion caught by the corner of his eye made him jerk to his feet again.

They were here—three of the bassoe-butchers!

Two were as large as Guss, one smaller. Guss's wildly flicking tongue caught odors that told him they were filthy, and they looked it. Mud-caked, raggedly clothed, they gripped clubs in their hands, heavy clubs that could easily break bones. Three clubs against his sword. They parted, muddy yellow eyes fixed on him, tongues flickering at him. They were going to surround him.

His fear was like blinding pain. His mind was shrieking silently, "Run! Run! Run!" But he didn't run. He thought he was too frightened to move. But then he did move—not to run in mindless panic but to charge straight at the butcher in front of him.

He struck with the sword.

It was a mighty, flashing stroke, the very best he had. And it proved a good one. It sliced the head right off the bassoe-butcher's neck and sent it rolling. The torso dropped, to writhe and buck across the ground. Guss, too desperate to think, let the power of the swing turn him, took two long strides, and, with a reaching thrust, drove the blade through the second of the larger bassoe-butchers. The club in that one's hand, already swung, struck Guss on the shoulders and back and drove him to the ground. But Guss held on to his sword. He struggled furiously to pull it out of the dead body, knowing he was an easy target for the club of the last bassoe-butcher, but when he was finally able to get his bloody sword free, he found that one had disappeared.

"He ran off."

The telepathic voice of the little scientist was thin and weak as he struggled against bonds that still held him.

"Help me, Guss. Help me."

Guss was standing straddle-legged, panting, dazed. He looked at the bassoe-butcher he had beheaded. He looked at the bassoe-butcher he had run through with his sword. He looked at the sword he held in his hand, the bloody blade, the bloody hand...

"Osis, Osis," he muttered, unbelieving.

The gray inner lids began to close over his golden eyes. Darkness began to cloud his mind. He sank to the ground. He heard Los Ross calling as if from a great distance,

"Guss! Guss—don't faint now. Untie me, Guss! There is still another one!"

And then he heard no more.

Sissi had waited and waited and waited.

The bassoes had clustered close to the craft, peering in at her, baaing pitifully, pawing at the closed windows. They were hungry, she knew, perhaps starving. Two of the females carried babies close to sagging, empty breasts. Even mindless, the bassoes recognized her to be one of the kind who had always fed them. It was scoring her deeply to see them so needful, to see them begging, to have nothing for them.

"Slass, those butchers!" she swore.

To her torment of worry over Guss they had added this, those evil dealers in bassoe flesh! She had been sorry, deeply sorry, that she had taken the butchers' lives. But she was not sorry now, looking at the awful state the bassoes were in! Their soft gray fur would shine when cared for; their big brown eyes, long-lashed, loving, were usually bright, eager, friendly, trusting. Now their eyes were stricken, pleading, sunken. The masklike patches of skin without fur about their eyes were darkly shadowed. Their body fur was mottled, dirty; some even showed sores.

"Oh, liss," she moaned.

A herd-beetle had come out of the woods. When the giant insect saw the bassoes, who were always his charges, he came scuttling to them on six swift legs, fluttering his copper-colored wing shells, waving his antennae. The insect was anxious, concerned—that was clear. It seemed to want to do something to care for the bassoes, but lacking a Jassan herder now, it didn't know what ought to be done. The herd-beetle finally rounded them up close to the Triss-nass in which Sissi was sitting, then lifted itself to peer in at her with its many-faceted eyes, to squeak telepathically, questioningly.

"Name of Osis!"

This was too much! She hated the beetles enough to

have just killed one a few moments ago, but this one was pleading for the bassoes—it wanted help for them!

What next?

She had waited for Guss as long as she could wait. Fifteen minutes or not, she couldn't wait here a moment longer. Not a single moment. No matter what Guss might say.

She couldn't stand the waiting!

She pushed open the door, brushing the bassoes and the giant herd-beetle aside, and got to the ground. She straightened the camouflage uniform of the Red Flame Brigade, making sure the esso sidearm was secure in the holster, and then she was ready at last to face what had to be next—the dreadful task of going into that dark forest to search now for *both* Los Ross and Guss.

A half hour had passed since he had left her with orders to go without him if he hadn't returned in fifteen minutes. Go without him? Of course not! It was not difficult to make that kind of a decision. The big, stupid kess-ness! He should know she would rather die *with* him than die of loneliness without him.

He was all she had ever wanted.

She began running, and when she had run three steps toward the forest, the herd-beetle jumped on her back and knocked her down.

She screeched in terror.

Rolling, she tried to get the esso sidearm free to kill the nasty thing—and found the insect was petting her with its antennae, squeaking plaintively. Then she understood—it wanted her to tell it what to do with the bassoes!

"Oh, for liss sakes!"

She sat up, the bassoes gathering quickly to pat her with happy hands, the herd-beetle to lick her with antennae, to squeak eagerly. She brushed them all off, impatient but not unkind. "All right, all right! Let me *up*!"

On her feet, she straightened herself again. She was not sure, never having herded bassoes, what to do next, but she had to do something or they weren't going to let her search for Guss. She waved her arm, pointing a long finger in the direction she wanted to go—toward the forest.

"Go!"

It worked!

At least it was good enough for the herd-beetle. The insect rounded the bassoes into a bunch, and when Sissi ran, they all ran, first at her heels, then around her, almost tripping her, making her stumble, then ahead of her.

She hadn't had, she realized, the faintest idea of where to go once she entered the forest, but now, with a direction—a faint path that grew to a better path—decided upon by the herd-beetle and the bassoes, she went that way. And why not? It was as likely to lead somewhere useful as simple blundering—if not more likely.

Los Ross, exhausted from struggling fruitlessly against his bonds, lay panting, his face flushed beneath his almost comical helmet from which the knobs and antennae protruded, his forked tongue hanging limply from the side of his mouth. He lifted his head to look at Guss and called softly but urgently.

"Guss! Guss, wake up!"

Guss, the big brave coward, had never collapsed into so deep a faint before. His gentle reptilian face was turned toward the tree tops, his golden, vertically slitted eyes were closed, his tongue tips flicked out beneath his delicate nostrils, testing the air without concern—he slumbered peacefully.

At a time like *this*? With that last evil bassoe-eater lurking about, trying to get up courage to come in to attack again? Three times that one had begun an approach, only to lose courage at the sight of his two comrades—one beheaded, one gutted—lying where they had fallen to Guss's flashing sword.

And what a warrior Guss had proved himself to be! *Swissish! Stisss!* A head rolling, a belly opened.

There was the other one again!

"Guss! Wake up!"

Struggling frantically against his bonds, Los Ross watched the third bassoe-butcher sneak carefully, warily—first on tiptoe, then on hands and knees—across to where Guss lay in what seemed peaceful slumber.

"Guss! Guss!"

Los Ross's panic-filled telepathic cries were of no use. Guss slept on, dreaming of his success perhaps, reveling in his own invulnerability, while the ragged, smelly, evil-eyed bassoe-butcher came creeping on. Near enough finally, the bassoe-butcher reached out and carefully edged Guss's sword into his own hand. Once he had the sword in a firm grip, he leaped to his feet with a cry of triumph.

"Guss! Guss!" Los Ross screamed.

Guss did not move a muscle.

The butcher lifted the sword high.

Before he could drive it down and spike Guss to the ground, the first of the bassoes running ahead of the herd-beetle and Sissi burst into the glade, startling the bassoe-butcher and scaring him. Before he could recover his wits and drive the sword down into the slumbering Guss, Sissi drilled him with a purple beam. The sword fell from hands suddenly gone lifeless, and he fell on top of Guss, as dead as the other bassoe-butchers.

"Sissi! Sissi!" Los Ross squealed.

The cool scientist had suddenly become a joyous babbling idiot. Now Guss chose to awaken. He rolled and thrust the fallen butcher away, then regained his feet and the sword. He was standing, unsure how he had killed the third butcher but willing to accept the fact that he had, when he saw Sissi walking unsteadily toward him across the glade. Her esso was holstered again. She seemed barely able to keep her feet. Guss was shocked, alarmed.

"Sissi!" he yelled. "What're *you* doing here?"

"Looking for you."

"You disobeyed me!" Guss raged. "You should have left!" He waved his bloody sword, pointing. "You could get killed! Look! Look about you! *I* had to kill all these!"

"Oh, frass!" Sissi said helplessly.

Her knees buckled.

And *she* fainted.

"Fooss!" Los Ross said with some disgust.

If the truth, when Los Ross told him what had *really* happened, troubled Guss, it was not much and not for long. He untied Los Ross, and together they retrieved Sissi. And when she was fully awakened and something like her old self again, her first question was a shocker. "What are we going to do about them?" she asked.

"Them?" Guss's voice climbed. "Them who?"

"The bassoes, you dussil!"

"What about them?"

"They're starving—can't you see that?"

"Yes, but look—Sissi! We've got to get out of here— back to the hospital! We can get *shot* out here! We've got to—"

Sissi turned impatiently away. "I've got to find food for these poor things!"

The herd-beetle seemed to understand. It ran a little way down a path, then ran back. The bassoes gathered close to Sissi, baaing; the herd-beetle jumped at her, coaxing her.

"I'm coming! I'm coming!" she told the insect.

And with the insect leading and the bassoes bumping and jostling hopefully about her, she followed the beetle away down a hard-worn path.

"Sissi!" Guss's mental yell was plaintive. "Sissi!"

She kept going.

Guss and Los Ross exchanged helpless looks—and followed.

The path led them all to crude sheds with fenced enclosures attached. The gates of the enclosures were open, and the bassoes ran through them to gather at empty feed troughs. Their baaing held a note of pleading now. Sissi went directly into the building, where Guss and Los Ross found her searching through containers.

"Whew!" Guss said, appalled. "What a stinking mess!"

Still ignoring Guss, Sissi finally found containers that held meal of some sort. It was certainly not fit food for a Jassan, but the bassoes recognized the container, and when the meal was poured in a trough, they began scooping up the meal in their hands, burying their faces, eating ravenously.

"The poor things," Sissi said. "They *were* starving!"

"Seems so," Guss agreed.

He was feeling the same kind of sympathy for the poor creatures, but he was getting dreadfully anxious to get back to the Triss-nass and fly to the sanctuary of Siss State Hospital.

"Don't just stand there!" Sissi said. "Get them water."

"Great Essnia!" Guss said.

He turned hurriedly to search. There was a pipe; tracing it, he found a faucet, and turning the faucet, he let water into another dry and empty trough. It was the right thing to do. The bassoes paused in their eating to drink, sucking water up with their mouths, and then went back to eating. Watching them, Guss was glad Harry Borg was not here to see this. They were his species—they looked exactly like him, though fur-covered and smaller. If he were to find his kind treated like this, he would roar with fury. Not that there was anything he, Guss, or Sissi and Los Ross had done to bring the bassoes to this sorry state.

"We've got to get out of here," he scolded Sissi.

"Just a minute, just a minute," she said.

Los Ross put his helmeted head into the shed then. "There's really no need to hurry," he said tiredly.

"Why not?" Guss demanded, suddenly alarmed.

"Come see."

Guss and Sissi went out with Los Ross and saw a Jassan police patrol craft settle to the ground in an open area. As Guss, Sissi, and Los Ross watched, hearts sinking, two uniformed officers got out and advanced, automatic weapons ready.

A very cold, contemptuous telepathic voice spoke then. "Bassoe-butchers," the voice said. "Make us happy."

"Osis!" Sissi whispered.

"He means us!" Guss said.

"Who else is here," Los Ross asked, "on an illegal bassoe-meat farm, feeding bassoes?"

"Me?" Guss was suddenly outraged. "A bassoe-butcher?"

He had never been so insulted in his life.

A concert sissal-player of international repute, the idol of millions, revered, almost worshiped—they called *him* a bassoe-butcher? Guss's outrage became fury. They could shoot him, they could run him through a crissle, but no essan could so demean him. Golden eyes blazing, eight-fingered hands clenched into fists, forked tongue lashing, chest heaving with emotion, he strode straight at the offending police.

"Guss! No!" Sissi wailed.

The police were startled. How often did an intended victim stride at them, straight into the face of their automatic weapons? They held their fire—barely.

They looked at each other.

Then they looked at Guss, who had come to a straddle-legged, furious stance just before them.

"Guss! Guss!" Sissi was wailing, eyes closed now, certain she had lost him to the purple rays.

But they hadn't shot him.

"What do you want?" one officer asked, lacking anything better to say.

"An apology," Guss said.

"A *what*?" The officer looked at his fellow officer. "Did you hear that? He wants an apology—and I haven't shot him yet!"

The fellow officer stared at Guss. "It's *him*," he said suddenly.

"Him who?"

"The sissal-player!" the fellow officer said. "Guss Rassan!"

"Holy tiss! Really?"

Guss drew himself up to his most majestic height. "Really!" he said. "I am *not* a bassoe-butcher."

"Yes. I know. You play the sissal."

"I demand an apology!"

"Guss!" Sissi said. "For Osis sake!"

"It's all right," the fellow officer called to her. "He can have anything he wants."

"I can?" Guss said, startled.

"As long as you come with us."

"To be executed?" Los Ross asked.

Quickly, because Guss seemed on the verge of running, the fellow officer said, "No! Nothing like that. The government wants you. The whole police force has been looking for you. We need your help!"

"Help?" Guss's telepathic voice was climbing. "My help?"

"*His* help?" Sissi asked.

"Why?" Los Ross asked.

"To go back," the first officer said. "Back to Earth."

"No!" Guss said.

"What for?" Los Ross wanted to know.

"To get that Earthman Harry Borg."

CHAPTER 8

The clouds broke away like soft veils tearing, shredding off the tall spires, laying bare the ancient city, opening to the blue sky and the warm sunlight stone and mortar laid in times gone out of memory. The calling of birds began. The rich perfumes of jungle flowers, a witchery of fragrances, drifted on air stirred by the warmth of the rising sun.

Morning had come.

High on a tabletop mountain, thrust up from the green sea of tropical forest where no mountain should have been, Foss, the capital city of Jassa, was awakening.

The wide avenues were timeworn, the great buildings had the patina that only the passage of thousands of years can give, and when life came to them it was as if the Parthenon of Athens or Amon's temple of Karnak were still in everyday use. The citizens of Foss trod stones hollowed by eons; they went about affairs that had occupied ancestors long forgotten, as if those ancients had gone only yesterday and might return tomorrow.

The residence of Ros Moss, the elected leader of the Jassans, was a temple in appearance, and it dominated a rise to the north of the city. The road to it led through carefully tended grounds where lawns, lakes, fountains, and statuary delighted the eye, where fragrances beyond counting caressed the tongue.

At the top of a marble stairway, great carved-stone doors swung open silently to give admittance to a foyer where the floor was tile, intricately laid, and the walls were paintings of jungle beauty. In the center was a great fountain, where colored water splashed, exotic fishes swam, and lovely birds floated.

At the end of a main hall another pair of doors—not bronze but gold—opened to another foyerlike area with its own fountain, fishes, and birds. And just beyond this delight were the private quarters of Ros Moss.

He was an essan of considerable age, rather tall and bent, but he carried his years well. The flesh under his lightly scaled skin sagged only a little; his eight-fingered hands trembled hardly at all. His flickering forked tongue was still supple, questioning; his golden, vertically slitted eyes were sharp with knowledge and understanding. He was indeed a wise essan and as good as high political office allowed him, or anyone, to be. Robes were his choice in clothing, and on this morning his robe was blue, of a silklike fabric intricately patterned with gold thread. A turban of the same material, accented by a large sapphire, sat like a crown upon his head. A violet, intricately cut stone was suspended by a heavy gold chain about his neck.

Ros Moss hated the violet stone, and the turban even more—he was a creature of simple tastes—but they were badges of his office, and this morning was an occasion that certainly required all the trappings of office and authority. Dressed and waiting, he was restless, pacing about in the quiet, beautiful, softly scented luxury of his private quarters.

A young female bassoe, no more than fourteen years, human in all aspects except for the covering of soft, gray fur that made her lack of clothing seem no lack at all, followed his movements with very large brown eyes. The brown eyes were bright and lustrous, but they were without intelligence—her mind had been blanked at birth, as all bassoes had been before the law preventing it had been passed. She was, however, a cherished pet, now perhaps hoping for the tidbit that often came her way.

A dresser, worried about the drape of Moss's robes—Moss was annoyingly indifferent, even deliberately careless, at times about his appearance—hovered near, pushing in now and then to adjust this fold or that.

Ros Moss, all but oblivious to both pet and dresser, was seeking answers to most difficult questions: How did one admit a deficiency so great to the beings of a race so inferior? A race still raw, still new, still only at the threshold of learning? How did one admit weakness and still retain primacy?

How did one say to the humans, "We need you"?

How did one admit that the best efforts of one's own people were proving fruitless? That time was running out? That unless the humans could find a way to save them—and in the few short days left—the inhabitants of this planet would live in darkness for years to come?

With ceremony—this seemed to him the only way.

With ceremony that would make the truth less obvious, ceremony that would beguile them into believing that what they were being asked to do would be a favor to *them*, a chance for great profit.

A weak answer, but he could find none better.

"Your Excellency," a courier said to him. "If you are ready."

Ros Moss turned.

He gave the little bassoe pet a pat and a gentle command to remain where she was. The furred and naked little girl wriggled contentedly into the luxury of the cushion and watched with her large, luminous, and unknowing eyes as he left the room.

The humans were waiting in the Kassa.

The Kassa was an assembly area, a room of great antiquity, a place of memories. Murals larger than life told of Jassan scientists of long ago, of Jassan space travelers who had known distant galaxies. These scientists and travelers had the same reptilian appearance of present-day Jassans, but with a difference: They had a look of

strength, of boldness, the look of adventurers, even con-
querors, while the present-day Jassans were refined,
gentle, and retiring. Was the difference to be called the
result of decadence? Or was it the result of infinite
improvement? No matter. Whatever else the change had
done for them, or to them, it had robbed the Jassans of
the ability to cope with a present crisis, a crisis that might
not have given the Ancients more than a moment's pause.

Harry Borg was among those waiting here.

A far different man now from the one who had pun-
ished Cecil a short two days ago, Harry was clean and
sharp again. His dark blue eyes were alive with the joy
of life, his red-brown beard closely trimmed, the gold band
clamped to his left ear gleamed, and his powerful body
seemed to glow with barely controlled energy. At this
moment he was standing with his big right arm around
Lori's shoulders, proudly, possessively, even excessively
affectionate.

"Enough, already," she finally complained. "I gotta
breathe!"

She moved out from under his arm, though she reached
up to pat his cheek to reassure him. Sure, getting together
after all that time apart had been wonderful. Exhaustingly
wonderful, as a matter of truth. But the big bazoo did
everything the same way: totally. And total love from a
man who could leave bruise marks just petting?

Well...

She was looking lovely, fresh, and happy. Tall and gray-
eyed, she wore her blond hair in a single thick and shining
braid; her cheekbones reflected light. She had the bloom
pregnancy sometimes brings to women who love children;
her rich body strained the soft blue blouse, unbelted above
black slacks. In her fifth month she was still a vigorous
woman, still fully capable.

Tippi grinned at her as she escaped the overpossessive
arm of Harry. At thirteen, an innocent but very knowing
lass, Tippi enjoyed the spectacle of two grown-ups very
much in love. She had found her mother and Harry to be
kind of—well, *un*grown-up at times, more like a couple
of overgrown puppies than sober adults. She pulled her
mother's head down to whisper in her ear. "Is he still..."

"Tippi! Shame on you!"

Tippi dodged a swat and went to talk to Illia, the wife of Chad Harrison. A beautiful young bassoe, Illia had escaped mind-blanking and had proved to be not only very intelligent but very quick to learn—most things. She could speak English very well, she could do math, she could reason with the best, but she could not somehow learn to *like* clothing. Being a bassoe, she had the coat of shining soft gray fur, and what more covering was needed? Chad quite agreed with her that more covering only despoiled the already perfect, but convention required the concealment of certain areas, and he was delighted at the grace and style with which she wore the garments needed to cover those areas.

In Tippi, Illia had found a kindred spirit, and when they talked, Illia's huge brown eyes shone with a luminous glow. "I think they in love?" she whispered.

"Like yikkkk!" Tippi agreed, grinning.

Guss and Sissi were here, too.

As soon as Guss and Sissi had been able to establish that they were who they had said they were at the illegal bassoe-meat farm, they had been told they were indeed wanted, but not for purposes of execution, as they had feared. They were to be sent back to Earth to find Harry Borg and to return with him and his young warriors with all possible speed. Guss's plea of "In the name of Osis, not again!" had been answered with the word that if they did *not* go, they *would* be executed, and that had proved to be a persuasion difficult to resist.

"Is there no end to it?" Guss had moaned.

"I'm beginning to wonder," Sissi had moaned with him.

They'd had no trouble finding Harry. He had been standing close by the Point of Proximity they'd used when they'd left him and the others two days before—on a rocky hillside in the Arizona desert outside the Red Rock Motel. He'd been there, though the hour was long past midnight, face turned up to the canopy of stars, calling to *them* telepathically, pleading for *them* to come back because of *his* desperate emergency. The monitor Los Ross had left had guided the Jassans in, and Harry's yell of joy on hearing that Lori had been released by the green

Ussirs and had been found by a Jassan patrol—that she, Tippi, and Sam were safe and waiting for him in the capital city of Foss—might well have been heard in Tucson, a hundred miles away.

"That's my girl!" he'd bellowed. "That's my baby!"

And he'd hugged Guss and Sissi half to death.

Sam Barnstable and the cadre were here, along with the others. Sam was weak but, because of the medical skills of Sassan, the Jassan surgeon, the big young man was rapidly getting strong again and was suffering at the hands of his fellow cadre members. Chad, the white-haired, deeply tanned signal caller; Homer, the calm and capable center; Eddie, the black wide end; and Arnie, the knuckle-faced running back—they were all, with perfectly straight faces, apparently serious and deeply concerned about his ability or lack of it, asking questions.

"However in the hell could you do it, Sam?"

"Yeah? Up-futz at a time like that?"

"A simple duty!"

"Bodyguarding a beautiful lady—hey! C'mon!"

They had him snorting like a grizzly bear.

There was no stroke of a gong to begin the ceremony Ros Moss had thought the present need required. Sound to the essans, who were without hearing, was only an irritating vibration. A dimming of lights, a burst of fragrance—strange, earthy scents delicately blended with flowerlike odors and most probably impressively attention-getting to the essan tongue—was the way the ceremony was begun.

The attention of the waiting humans was directed to a raised platform, and after a pause, curtains suddenly parted to reveal a scintillating stage setting, vibrant with color, sinuously reptilian in line and form. A column of vapor, pulsing and crimson, erupted to tower in center stage, then suddenly cleared to reveal Ros Moss, splendid in blue robes and jeweled turban, arms outstretched in a dramatic gesture.

"Look out," Harry whispered.

"What d' you mean?" Lori asked.

"Something big is comin' down."

"Hush!" Tippi said.

They hushed. And they listened.

The President of Jassa was circumspect in the beginning, welcoming the humans, asking them to accept apologies for past treatment they might have felt was abusive, telling them this was the beginning of what would surely be a long and happy relationship. All this took a little time, since it was elaborately phrased, and when Moss had finished, Harry found he was more concerned than ever.

"Trouble," he whispered. "Double trouble."

"What d' you mean?" Lori whispered back.

"I know the guy."

"But he's saying we could get rich!"

"Sure. But he hasn't said how."

"I could stand being rich," Lori said. "Just once."

"Dead, you wouldn't like it."

"Shhhh!" Tippi whispered again.

And then came the snapper.

It was the old "Los Angeles is going to break off and sink into the Pacific Ocean" bit, and how many times had he heard that one? Only this time it was the President of Jassa telling it. And *believing* it! An island named Tassar, he said, was going to sink beneath the sea. And within seven days, give or take a few.

How about *that* for a yarn to tell your kids?

The tectonic plate supporting Tassar had, over a hundred million years, built up enormous pressure shoving against another. That pressure, their scientists had just discovered, was going to be suddenly released, causing one plate to slide fractionally beneath the other. That fractional movement, relatively small though it was, was going to cause the island of Tassar to drop a thousand meters almost overnight and sink beneath the sea.

"Like Atlantis!" Lori whispered, awed.

"What Atlantis?"

"The Greek island—or whatever."

"That's a myth!"

"A lot of people don't think so."

"A lot of people are nuts."

"Will you hush?" Tippi pleaded.

But if the island was uninhabited, as Moss had said, what did it matter if it sank beneath the sea? Who needed it? Only the entire population of the planet Essa—that was who needed it.

They needed it because the Source was there.

The Source, Ros Moss went on to explain, was the single most important device in the world of essans. The Source made the good life possible. Without it, all of Essa would fall into darkness.

The Source, as Harry came to understand it, was a computer-controlled device the Ancients had built many thousands of years ago on the island. It was a device that converted sunlight to pure concentrated energy through the use of an element called the Lassa Crystal. The energy, beamed to satellites, then back to all of Essa without favor, was then converted to electric power. Loss of the Source would mean the power would go off all over the planet.

"Bloody hell," Harry whispered.

"Their refrigerators!" Lori answered. "All their food!"

Harry gave her a look.

"Well, it's true! I lost a turkey last Thanksgiving—"

"Shhhhh!"

The island of Tassar could not, of course, be saved, Ros Moss went on. What he was going to ask them— Harry and his cadre—to do was to go to the island and turn off the Shield.

The Shield, Ros Moss explained, was an automated defense system installed by the Ancients to protect the Source. Computer-controlled, the Shield shot down everything that tried to approach—missiles, aircraft, essans, whatever.

"Star Wars!" Harry said.

"Star Wars?" Lori asked.

"Reagan's Star Wars," Harry said. "The Strategic Defense Initiative! He's saying the Ancients built a Star Wars defense system to protect the Source! And now they're stuck with it. Even they can't get through the damned thing!"

"Mom! Harry!" Tippi whispered fiercely. "He's waiting!"

And Harry realized then that Ros Moss had stopped and was waiting. Although the old essan could not hear Harry's voice, he knew Harry was talking to his fellow humans—they had turned to listen to him.

"Sorry," Harry said.

"There will be time for discussion later," Ros Moss said. "If I may have your attention for a few more minutes?"

"You've got it," Harry said.

The President's wince was hardly noticeable.

In a nutshell, what Ros Moss wanted—as Harry sorted it out—was for Harry to find a way to penetrate the Shield and, once inside, make his way to the control center, take possession of something called the Lassa Crystal, then turn off the Shield so that the Jassan aircraft could come in to rescue both humans and the Lassa Crystal before the island of Tassar sank beneath the sea.

There was more, but that was the heart of the matter.

"Lord a'mighty!" Harry whispered.

"Is it bad?" Lori asked.

"You better believe it!"

Rescue the Lassa Crystal and turn off this Shield before the whole damned island sank beneath the sea—in seven days or less!

That was the contract.

Sound easy? Sound like all it would take was a little Yankee ingenuity, a hard shake, a twist, a kick or two? No way. There were one helluva lot of bumps in this particular yellow brick road.

"Listen up."

The Ussirs, the green guys, had Ahmed Hassad, Ros Moss told them, and they were putting him to the same task. And they wanted him to get there first. Why? Because whoever got possession of the Lassa Crystal, now that it was up for grabs, would be the only ones able to build a *new* Source. And whoever controlled the new Source would control the planet.

"The other guys'd be slaves," Harry muttered.

"Slaves? Really?" Lori asked.

"When they got their light bill, they'd think so, anyway."

"Is that supposed to be funny?"

"If you can laugh at a hanging."

"Hoo, boy," Tippi sighed, despairing.

Nor were Ahmed Hassad and the Ussirs all of it.

There were also the Peacekeepers, the Jassan peace freaks.

The Peacekeepers would fight and kill to preserve what *they* considered peace, and they were, according to Moss, ready to kill to stop this whole operation. The way they saw the operation, it was a scheme made up by Ros Moss—and the Ussirs, too—as an excuse to get their war going again. They, the Peacekeepers, didn't believe a damn word of this story about Tassar sinking beneath the sea in seven days. Not a single damn word.

"How about that?" Harry whispered.

"What?"

"We've finally agreed on something—me 'n' the Peacekeepers."

"Such as?"

"I don't believe a damn word of it either."

But it meant he was going to have the Peacekeepers up his nose, trying to kill him, while he was turning off the Shield—and that was serious. Like all freaks, the peace freaks could get very, very nasty when they had something to be nasty about.

And another thing...

Why hadn't the Jassans—or the Ussirs, for that matter—penetrated the Shield and taken possession of the Lassa Crystal themselves if it was so damned important?

The answer was—and getting the answer was like pulling teeth—neither the Jassans nor the Ussirs have been able to penetrate the Shield in a week of desperate trying. Since they had learned the island was going under, they had tried everything they knew—battered at the Shield with missiles, aircraft, and personnel with staggering losses—and had failed.

Failed even to scratch it.

Though they were still trying.

When the Ancients had decided to build a Star Wars

defense system, they had built a good one. Good, hell—
it was impregnable! At least as far as anything the Jassans
or the Ussirs had been able to throw against it.

How, then, did they expect Harry—or Ahmed Hassad,
for that matter—to do any better?

Most didn't, as a matter of fact.

Ros Moss—and one or two on the Ussir side—were
about the only ones who felt that Harry and Hassad might
be able to penetrate the Shield. Moss had developed a
faith in Harry's ability to do the impossible, it seemed,
that verged on the religious.

Harry had only a very short time ago accomplished
the impossible when he had saved the Jassan race from
a life of slavery at the hands of the Ussirs, hadn't he?
And while doing it, he had saved Ros Moss's neck from
the exeuctioner's ax, hadn't he? And so, when Ros Moss
had found himself confronted with another impossible task,
wasn't it reasonable he would turn to Harry Borg again?

"Thanks a bunch!" Harry muttered.

While Ros Moss was going through some ceremonial
mishmash to end the proceedings, Harry gathered it all
together. He knew he had to take the contract. Ros Moss
hadn't gone to all this trouble to hear him say no. If Harry
tried to refuse, he and his people would be a long time
getting home.

He and the lads had to find a way through the Shield,
had to get to the Source, had to take possession of the
Lassa Crystal, had to turn off the Shield, had to give the
Lassa Crystal to the Jassans—not the Ussirs—while
punching their way past the Peacekeepers and fighting
their way past Ahmed Hassad and an army of Ussirs.

Had to or else.

How was that for a ball-buster?

Never mind the part about the island going under the
sea. Like Atlantis sinking out of sight, or Los Angeles
breaking off into the Pacific Ocean—that was a fairy tale.
In real life that kind of thing *never* happened. In real life
there was only one way to describe that kind of a story.

Horse puckey.

But the contract had a plus or two.

Say he and the lads were able to get the job done—

the pay would be better than straight time, that was sure. Or even golden time. They'd be able to write their own paycheck is what they'd be able to do. Trade with Essa, exclusive rights to any number of high-tech devices. Rejuvenation? How about that for openers?

Wall-to-wall money is what it could mean.

If they could live to spend it.

"Like you say," he whispered. "We could get rich."

Lori sighed. "A little of that never hurt anybody."

CHAPTER 9

The very first thing the Ussirs had done to Ahmed Hassad after Oss Tiss had delivered him in all haste to Koss, the capital city of Ussir, had been to provide him with a translating implant so they could communicate with him. And almost the first communication Hassad had made, using the implant, was a demand that Oss Tiss be sent back to Earth to get Soo Toy. Soo Toy was a female human, he had told the Ussirs, and a male human could not be expected to function in a strange land, populated by a species so anatomically different, without a female of his own kind to darn his socks.

Now, could he?

No, of course he couldn't.

They had understood the need, however Hassad had wanted to describe it, and Oss Tiss had been called in. He had accomplished the almost impossible feat of returning with Hassad, hadn't he? Then it followed, in the reasoning of his superiors, that he would be able to accomplish with less difficulty the lesser feat of returning with a female.

The reasoning of superiors is everywhere the same.

Oss Tiss had been sent.

And he had accomplished the mission.

But with considerable difficulty.

He had lost five more troopers and one very good

flight-craft, which, in the opinion of his superiors and in view of the need, were not unacceptable losses. Nor was the fact he'd had to mind-blank fourteen of the Globe One security guards, some perhaps permanently, of any importance. Or that he'd forced a large number of uniformed human soldiers—the National Guard, actually—to be called out. Or that he had frightened the tuss out of the entire state of Arizona.

If an omelet is to be made, according to an old Ussir proverb, a certain number of eggs must be broken.

The human female herself had been no trouble.

Oss Tiss had found the female, Soo Toy, to be a beauty, no matter the species. She had large, dark eyes that seemed faintly slanted; a wealth of shining black hair; a glowing, almost translucent skin, lightly colored; and a most alluring figure, if one could describe the human figure as alluring. More to the point, she had not been your usual kidnap victim, kicking and struggling in her own defense. No. She had not even required mind-blanking. It seemed that wherever her mate, the human called Ahmed Hassad, went, that was where she most desperately wanted to go. Rather than fight Oss Tiss and force him to mind-blank her, she had run ahead, preceding him to the flight-craft by at least a quarter of a kilometer.

And she'd had good reason.

With Hassad gone, Cecil, whose interest lay with the other gender, had been about to throw her out. And that meant she would have been deprived of certain basic necessities—her furs, her limousine, her servants, her Paris originals, her account with Cartier—essentials only Ahmed Hassad had been willing and able to provide. It didn't matter that Hassad would now be starting over in a strange world. She knew he would manage somehow to own the place in a few months' time.

And, indeed, it seemed he was well begun.

On the first morning after her arrival, she was finding that her accommodations wanted for nothing. Everywhere there was comfort and beauty—deep floor coverings, soft recliners, silken draperies, scented air, delicious food, a wardrobe full of garments, and bowing servants instantly at her beck and call. If the fact that the

servants were reptilian in appearance, with vertically slitted pupils, forked tongues, and eight-fingered hands, disturbed her, it was not apparent. Being a beautiful Oriental,
it followed that she would be, of course, beautifully
inscrutable.

And she was nude at the moment.

Nudity for her was not immoral. It was simply the way
she had learned to improve her means. No male had yet
been able to withhold from her anything she had asked
when given the possibility of being rewarded with those
amorous delights her nudity suggested.

Excepting the male Cecil, to be sure.

Now, safely with Hassad, she was humming to herself
as she laid out silk garments for both herself and Hassad
to wear. She was not in the least troubled about the future.
Whatever it was these creatures wanted from Hassad, he
would see they got it—and something more. Until they
had dealt with him, they had not learned what ruthless-
ness, cruelty, and avarice were all about.

And murder, too, should something of that sort be
needed.

At the moment, Hassad was in the bath, singing. He
had, he was discovering once again, a concert-quality
baritone. When his voice was bounced off the tiled walls
of this particular bath—a wide, high-ceilinged room where
a sunken pool large enough to be used for swimming was
filled with warm, scented sudsy water—the tones took
on a roundness and a resonance he had seldom been able
to achieve. One needed a Carmen to be a truly convincing
Don José, but all things considered, he was willing to
compare his performance now with the performance of
James McCracken on that famous opening night at the
Met in September of '79.

Modesty aside, he had to say his Don José was only
great.

His Pagliacci? Well, perhaps it *did* need a little work.

Naked, too, and up to his umbilicus in soapy water,
he was—at least in appearance—the most magnificent
Don José or Pagliacci ever to have graced a stage. Or a
bathing pool. His curly, dark hair topped the forehead and
face of a movie idol. He had large, almost shamefully

long-lashed dark eyes, a straight nose, a smile that made
women weak, and perfect teeth. All this atop a great body.
His neck was a column, his shoulders were wide, his chest
was deep and nicely accented with dark hair gone only a
little gray.

The Ussirs had told him what was wanted of him.

It seemed there was a protective curtain they called
the Shield—a sort of a Star Wars defense system left in
place by some ancient tribe—guarding an island somewhere that had to be turned off so they could take control
of something called a Lassa Crystal before the enemy,
called Jassans, could do the same thing.

A straightforward, get-there-before-the-other-guys sort
of an expedition, it had not sounded at all difficult. There'd
been some nonsense about the island sinking beneath the
ocean in seven days' time or less, but it had only been
their version of the Atlantis myth and not worthy of his
attention.

"Camel droppings" was the way he had described it.

Though not with quite that delicacy.

They had answered all his questions about personnel
and matériel available to him; and, by Allah! they did
have some marvelous equipment! Yes, all of it was very
old, and some of it lacked spare parts of any kind. But
the important thing was, for a man with an eye for business, none of it was protected by patents of any kind,
and they seemed blissfully unaware of that basic over-
sight.

They were assembling the personnel and matériel now.

What he had not been able to understand was why they
hadn't broken through the Shield themselves. Their answer
had been that they had been trying, and were trying right
now, desperately, and would go on trying, but they were
not at all sure they would be able to succeed in the time
there was left. Many in high places had thought that he,
Ahmed Hassad, being a human, might—just might—be
able to do what they had not been able to do.

Nor was that all of it.

The Jassans, it seemed, had a human they considered
to be a god, or at least the reincarnation of a god, whom

they had brought from Earth in the hope that *he* could find a way to penetrate the Shield.

And who was this god-human?

Harry Borg, no less!

Since the Jassans had the god-human, Harry Borg, a few of the top Ussir leaders had felt they needed a god-human also. Their research had discovered that Ahmed Hassad had been the only human adversary who had been able to compete with Harry Borg with any degree of success, and if that didn't make him a god-human as well, it at least gave them something close to parity.

"I'll buy that," he'd said. "Equal or better."

Better, if all he had to do was penetrate that strategic defense curtain and take possession of the Lassa Crystal. And he would do just that—they could be damned sure of it.

Because doing it would only be the start for a man with any sense of how to make money. Doing it would be like getting the key to the mint. Trade between Earth and Essa! Exclusive rights to no end of high-tech devices! The rejuvenation process! The rejuvenation process alone meant megadollars. If all he had to do to gain access to that kind of money was beat Harry Borg, they, the Ussirs, were the same as home free.

Borg would be no problem.

He was big, yes. And he was brave beyond belief. But he did have serious weaknesses. Among those weaknesses was the fact that he was a trusting oaf. The kind of an oaf who believed in childish things like honesty and fair play and patriotism and getting married. To a man who'd been raised in the lie-cheat-steal-or-die world of Algiers, Tunis, and Tripoli, men like Harry Borg verged on being silly.

They were believers, optimists.

Born to be plucked...

And easily killed.

"Toy!" he bellowed suddenly.

"Yes, Ahmed."

She appeared a moment later at the edge of the pool. Still wearing only the apparel she'd worn at birth, she was most certainly a delight straight out of the garden of Allah. Her voice was soft, caressing. "You wanted something, Ahmed?" she asked.

"Yes," he said. "Scrub my back."

CHAPTER 10

The island of Tassar was beautiful at dawn. Rising out of the bluest of seas, it struck the eye as a green jewel of enormous proportions, going far beyond the reach of vision as one drew near at lower elevations. The central peak, topped with clouds of its own making, thrust up out of long lava slopes that eventually descended into temperate land, then into jungle, and then into swamps where the land was flat and below the level of the sea.

A major island remote from any continent, Tassar had provided a perfect redoubt for the Source. There had been no need to approach the island once the Source and the Lassa Crystal had been put in place and were functioning unless assault was the motive.

The Shield amounted to a half a globe—a dome with a radius of two hundred kilometers—that covered most of the island of Tassar like a gigantic, inverted teacup. All projectiles, whether creature-controlled or mechanical, were destroyed the moment they touched the Shield by emplaced, automatically triggered ray-cannon of various powers.

No impulse—radio, mental, or any other—could penetrate the Shield. Thus, it was impossible to disarm the Shield from the outside, or for those outside, after so many, many centuries had passed, to know now what might be waiting inside.

The island of Tassar, having an irregular coastline, extended beyond the circumference of the Shield in a number of areas.

The Jassans, in their effort to penetrate the Shield and to rescue the Lassa Crystal before it was lost forever beneath the sea, were attacking the Shield in an area on the northeast side of Tassar known as Crass Head. They were firing rockets and bombing from a very high altitude with no noticeable result.

The Ussirs, on the southwest side of Tassar, in an area known as Kloss Reach, were using similar means with the same lack of success.

Harry Borg had chosen an area known as East Cliss.

If a way were to be found to penetrate the Shield, he knew it would have to be a way different from the rocket firing and high-altitude bombing the Jassans and the Ussirs were using, and to find that way, he had insisted that he go eyeball-to-eyeball with the Shield.

"I've got to *see* it," he said. "I've got to *feel* it—if it's possible to feel one without getting blown to hell and gone."

And that meant he had to know exactly where it was.

But the cartographers of Jassa proved to be of little help. They did not know the exact position of the outer perimeter of the Shield. All charts of the island chain, and of Tassar in particular, tended to be, as they delicately phrased it, imprecise.

Harry phrased it better. "Hell, you don't know within a half mile!"

But with stronger language.

And they had responded, with injured tones, that when measuring the domain of a god, one tried to be unobtrusive, which would almost certainly lead to inaccuracies.

"A god?" Harry had asked. "What god?"

And a whole new can of worms had been opened.

Yes, a god.

A god whose name was Uss.

Both Jassans and Ussirs believed the god Uss lived atop the mountain of Tassar, for what better way could

there be to account for the Source and for the continuing
supply of power that had come from the Source for so
many centuries—when the true origin had become
obscured in the mists of time—than to call it the blessing
of a god? And wasn't it better, then, to worship a god—
any god—than to doubt one existed?

Yes, certainly, it was. Safer, at any rate.

"They really think there's a god up there?" Lori had
asked.

"Some say yes, some say baloney," Harry had
answered. "But if there's a chance there *is* a god up there,
what's it going to hurt if they bow to it? Bowing now, the
way they see it, could mean the difference between a harp
and a coal shovel later on."

"What that's called," Chad had said, "is foxhole reli-
gion."

"Or coppering your bet," Homer had agreed.

East Cliss, the area Harry Borg had chosen for his
effort, was a sand and lava outcropping bare of any growth
and pounded unmercifully by seas that had rolled unhin-
dered across a great stretch of empty ocean. To reach it,
Harry and his crew were given the use of a small watercraft. The Jassans launched the watercraft from an
amphibious flight-craft, which they thought would be a
more stable launch-and-retrieve platform if it were maintained at a distance of thirty kilometers from the perimeter
of the Shield.

They were nothing if not prudent.

Harry was not about to argue with them. All he had
to do was remember the Iranian hostage fiasco to know
that if you couldn't get there, you couldn't get the job
done.

"And I'll get there," he had said. "Bet on it!"

But with the seas breaking over the bow and force-
seven winds knocking the tops off the combers, whipping
spume like buckshot into unprotected faces, and with the
watercraft bobbing up and down, getting there proved to
be something of a bother.

"I'll take the desert any time," Eddie yelled in Arnie's
ear.

"Why's that?"

"Drier, for one thing."

"Yeah. Yeah, you're right there."

Homer leaned close. "No sharks, either."

"Geeze!" Arnie said.

They reached the surf line mostly, they were to agree later, because their commander was determined to show the Jassans that the American soldier was one tough somebitch—that he could drown facing forward, that he had pluck, that he had grit, and that he just plain didn't give a toot if he lived long enough to write a letter home to mother or not.

Old Iron Balls was full of that kind of stuff.

But he was right in there with them—they had to give him credit for that. If he could have taken the craft in stern first, with him in front, they were sure he would have done it.

As it was, he drove them in, the jet going full bore, on top of a comber that broke a hellish thirty feet above the short stretch of black volcanic sand they'd called a beach. They shot off the top of the wave in a craft that was never meant to fly, and they landed like a shot-down piano in shallows that were racing back toward the sea.

"Hit it!" Harry yelled.

Then it was leap out, grab what you could lay your hands on, and drag it with you—knowing if you lost your piece, Iron Balls would damn well throw you back into the ocean after it—stagger through sand that sucked your feet, fall down, nearly swallow half the tide, stagger on, look back and see another comber coming, know you were never going to make it, and then hear, above the thunder of the waves and the squealing panic in your head:

"Come on! You're *Americans*! Fight it!"

How the hell had *he* gotten there already?

He was standing on the beach, waving the flag again, bellowing. His arms were full of twice the equipment anyone else could carry, and one hand was in the collar of a limp, unconscious Eddie, holding him out of the water. Arnie, on his knees as another comber sent a reaching, clawing surge of seawater boiling up around his chin, made a solemn oath that one day he would sneak up behind that big bazoo and clobber him with a two-by-four, just to show him he was as mortal as anybody.

A solemn oath he would die before he'd keep.

They all made it, finally. Chad had to go back into the surf to help Arnie, who, it turned out, was fighting with the stubbornness of a mad bobcat to save *two* packs of gear as well as his own pack and ray-rifle. When Chad got it all safely above the reach of the sea, he looked around, counted, and grinned at Harry Borg. "All present or accounted for, sir!"

Homer, lying on his back, panted, "I lost my American Express card."

"Call in," Harry said. "The very first thing."

Eddie regained consciousness, and aside from being a little dizzy at first and not believing that he'd been knocked out, he was all right. "Swallowed some water, I guess."

No one needled him.

They knew they'd all be lucky to have lived through what Iron Balls had rammed them into.

And this was only where it began!

"I don't see it, do you?" Harry asked. He was looking inland. Seawater dropped from his short beard, a drop of it on the end of his nose, and his dark blue eyes were staring, cold, challenging; the set of his jaw told his cadre that a long, hard day lay just ahead. "The map says it should be right there."

He threw a piece of lava at "right there," and nothing happened.

"So it's not right there," he said.

They were on the lee side of a black sand dune, sheltered from the wind. The beach stretched off to the left in a gentle curve, flattening under waves that caused the belly muscles of Chad, a surfer, to tighten. Twenty, thirty feet high, each one shaping a perfect tube.

Beautiful.

Straight ahead, the beach ended abruptly, giving way to a lava-coral outcropping, then to a line of palm trees. Beyond the palm trees they could see a mangrovelike swamp, then, distantly, green jungle growth, an uneven stacking of tall, mahogany-type trees, tops at fifty meters and more, vine-festooned, with giant fern and bamboo as undergrowth. More or less central on the island was a mountain, rising in the distance a long way off—and if those were inexact measurements, what else could they expect of a place gone almost mythical in the course of a few thousand years?

"You ever hear of a Greek measuring Mount Olympus?" Homer asked.

"Not with Zeus up there," Chad said.

"Big, that's all I care," Arnie said.

"And mean," Eddie agreed.

The mountain did have a threatening look. A volcanic cone, it had been battered and broken by time and weather. There were cliffs and outcroppings and long reaches of broken rock slopes. The top was lost in clouds.

"The Source is *there*?" Arnie's voice went squeaky in spite of himself. "On top of *that* mountain?"

"What they say."

"A volcano, ain't it?"

"Was a volcano. Been dormant fifty million years or so. Now it's flat on top."

"Great! I mean, that it's dormant."

"Hope it stays that way."

"Saint Helens didn't."

Harry Borg heard the lads talking, but his mind was on the most immediate problem: the damn Shield. Where the hell was it? He didn't doubt for a minute the Shield was there. Hell, the Jassan and Ussir air forces were busting their tails trying to crack it from a distance. And that was their problem: They didn't want to get anything like hands-on near it. Too scared. Not that he blamed them. It scared him, too. But their total lack of success told him he was not going to find a way to crack the Shield if he stayed at a distance.

"Can't crack it if I can't get at it."

And then they'd asked him how he was going to go about getting through if he *didn't* shoot at it from a distance, and when he'd said, "Some damn how or other!" they'd nodded their heads wisely, and it had taken him a while before he'd realized what they were thinking. They were thinking *he* was a god of some sort and that *he* had a lot of god-tricks up his sleeve, and all *he* had to do was pull one or two god-tricks out, and *zap,* he'd go right on through.

He hadn't argued with them. There wasn't time.

They'd said, when they'd put him ashore, that the latest information they had was that there were only five days left now before the island went under. Five days. And then she'd go. The whole island.

Well, horse puckey!

As far as he was concerned, the island would be here, just like it was, a thousand years from now.

What did limit the time he had to get the job done was the fact that the Ussirs were aiming Ahmed Hassad at the Shield, and if he busted through the Shield first, if he got to the Source first, and if he got the Lassa Crystal first, it would be all over for the Jassans.

And for a guy named Harry Borg.

He had to get through the Shield, get through the mangrove swamp, get through the jungle, climb the mountain, get to the Source, and get his hands on the Lassa Crystal before Ahmed Hassad could do the same thing or, to put it bluntly, it was going to be his ass.

He'd go home dead. Or broke.

Maybe both.

He threw another chunk of lava. Nothing happened.

"All right," he said. "I'll go up that beach and keep throwing things to see if I can find where it is."

"I'll go," they all said. "Sir."

"You'll stay the hell here," Harry told them.

"Sir!" they said.

They watched him stride off down the beach, arms swinging, feet slogging in the sand, a man going after an adversary he was going to beat the hell out of—if and when he ever caught up to him.

Mean and stubborn.

"He could get himself killed," Arnie said.

"Why he's going instead of sending you," Homer told him.

"Yeah, but mad like that?"

"Know what y' mean."

"He'd fight a tank bare-fisted."

"Might even win."

Homer watched Harry stop, pick up some object, throw it toward the jungle with no result, and plow on. Then he looked up to see Chad standing, tall and white-haired, swinging his cool gray eyes from left to right and back again.

"What's up?" Homer asked.

"Plotting an arc," Chad said. "If I use that mountain as the center and strike an arc that crosses right about there, I have to say Hard Balls is walking off on a tangent."

"Getting farther away from the arc every step."

"So he is," Eddie said.

"Should we tell 'im?" Arnie asked.

"Let me check first."

Chad had found a piece of driftwood, a wrist-thick stick about eight feet long. Holding the stick before him, reaching, searching with the point of it, he began to walk slowly inland. Ten meters . . . nothing. Another ten . . . still nothing.

"Keerist!" Arnie said. "Lemme do that!"

"Why you?" Chad asked over his shoulder.

"I can't stand watchin'!"

"Tough tussy," Chad said without sympathy.

He kept going like a very, very cautious blind man finding his way. He went another ten meters . . . and yet another ten . . . and then he found it. But not with the stick.

He felt it—

With his face.

It was almost imperceptible, as if he had broken glass as fragile as spider webbing, and the instant he felt it, he dropped to the ground. Only the fact that he'd dropped in a shallow depression saved his life. A purple ray flashed immediately above him.

"That's *it*!"

"Chad! For God's sake!"

"You all right?"

Chad, on his back, showed the palms of his hands to the lads. It was an urgent order to stay back. The movement also said he was unhurt—for the moment.

"Sir!" Homer yelled after Harry Borg.

"We found it!" Arnie yelled.

Harry looked back, saw them waving arms. "Blasted kids!" he swore.

He began a lunging, staggering run through the soft sand. Damn kids couldn't stay put, couldn't follow orders. Be some asses kicked—

Then he saw the Ussir fighting craft.

He hit the sand and tried to dig under.

The green fighting ship came in from the north, low over the seas, and started firing at the lads on the beach while still out of any sensible range. Seeing the lads and the landing craft on the spit of land had apparently persuaded the Ussir pilot that the Shield either did not exist or was far away. He cut his craft in an arc that carried him right overhead, firing purple bolts that sprayed surf and beach, tearing hell out of both but finding no flesh.

"Down!" Harry roared. "Dig in!"

He twisted onto his back and, holding his sidearm with both hands, neck cords stiff, mouth raging, tracked and fired at the racing green craft, missing every shot.

Chad, inside the Shield, could not move.

Arnie, Eddie, and Homer took cover, flattening into whatever scant protection they could find.

"Arnie!" Homer yelled. "Your ass's up!"

"Got rocks here!"

"Git another place!" Chad yelled.

Arnie scrabbled to a better depression.

"You, too, Homer!"

Out on the beach, Harry was scratching himself down below ground level like a groundhog gone crazy. It wasn't going to be any use, he knew that, but he had to do it. It was all he could do. The Ussirs had them cold.

That goddamn Hassad!

It was Hassad's work. Had to be!

The Ussirs couldn't have gotten their stuff together this quickly. Going for Harry before he went for the Shield—Hassad was some kind of a general, wasn't he? Whatever the hell else he was. And he, Harry Borg, he had been going to worry about Hassad later. Shoot! He wouldn't be alive later.

Here that sucker came again!

The pilot had made a looping, banking turn to the right,

flying that craft like an angel, swooping their way. He had them cold. Sitting ducks. Didn't even have to be a good shot. The power of those purple rays was enough to tear up a city block with every strike. Just keep coming, keep blowing holes.

Watching the Ussir craft come, Harry knew he was finished.

Gone . . . blooey . . . kaput!

A short life and a happy one.

Then he decided maybe not.

Then he decided hell, no!

He sat up in the sand to watch.

"How d' you like that?" There was nothing dumber than one of these lizard-types when they got an attack of the stupids. Of course, seeing all the lads on the beach right there had given the Ussir pilot reason to get eager, to forget what they were all here for. But none of that was enough reason to go completely dummy.

He was swinging too far to the right.

If he kept swinging, and if what the lads had yelled was true, and if what the Jassans had told him was true, that Ussir fighting craft was going to run into—

SCREEE-BOOM!

—the Shield right about now.

A direct dead-center hit.

Harry got up out of the hole he'd dug in the sand, watching the fragments of the Ussir fighting craft, blown apart by a purple ray fired from somewhere inland, flutter to the ground. Well, that answered a couple of questions for him.

There *was* a Shield. And it *did* work.

Worked fine.

"Beats wondering," he said.

Harry found the lads were scared half to death—not because of the fact they had damn near been blown away but because they had disobeyed his order to stay put. And worse, much worse, one of their own—his fair-haired lad—had his tail caught in one devil of a crack.

Be some hell raised!

After he'd been told what had happened, Harry stood

at a reasonably safe distance and glared fire at his pinned-down lieutenant.

"You hear me, son?" he asked.

"Loud and clear."

"You ever going to learn?"

"I'm young, sir," Chad said. "Got a lot of time."

"I'm not so sure."

"Well, now you put it that way..."

"How the hell can we get you outa there?"

"Couldn't say, sir."

"Or us in?"

Chad thought about it before he gave his answer. "Won't be easy."

CHAPTER 11

The security around the home of Guss Rassan the concert sissal-player was thought to be, as Harry Borg had described it, "tight enough to keep out rainwater."

There were high electrified fences. There were foot patrols, accompanied by free-roaming guard-beetles. There were flight-craft on twenty-four-hour watch overhead. And everywhere there were surveillance cameras transmitting pictures to a central control room where guards waited, fully armed, on a twenty-four-hour alert.

Harry Borg had insisted on these precautions.

"You want me to leave my wife, you've got to take care of her," he had said.

Not to worry, they had told him.

"I've had her back three days," Harry said. "That's all—just three days. After more'n a week of being apart and afraid I'd never see her again. We've got a lot of catchin' up to do. Unfinished business, y' know?"

They had assured him they knew.

"Anything happens to her," he had said, "or my little girl, or to Guss and Sissi, as far as that goes, and you folks are going to learn what trouble really is! This Shield problem'll be *nothing* compared to the fix you'll be in if I get back and she's gone again."

She would be there, they had told him. Safe and sound.

"Or it's your asses, believe it!"

They had believed it.

And they had done their best—every system and device known to them was in place and working around the clock.

But was she as safe as they thought she was?

Not quite.

The difficulty lay in the fact that the systems and devices were manned or operated by essans who, on the world of Essa, were no more immune to idiot ideologies than were the humans of Earth. And being of that sort—in the real sense only half bright—they were vulnerable to certain other persuasions. While offers of great wealth, eternal life, or even a life free from taxes were not considered in themselves to be enough to buy the average Peace-keeper, returns of this kind were considered to be acceptable as fringe benefits if they were to result naturally during the performance of regular duties.

And Peacekeepers were everywhere.

It was known that the Peacekeepers, thinking as they did, would do everything in their power to prevent anyone from reaching the island, let alone breaching the Shield and climbing the mountain to the Source. It was even thought possible they might stoop to a tactic so despicable as to infiltrate the security force protecting the humans who were also making an attempt to save the Source, and it was for this reason the security force had been most carefully screened.

What had *not* been considered possible—there had to be depths to which even a Peacekeeper would not sink— was that a Peacekeeper of long standing, working under cover, might have been the one who had done the screening and that he might have hired a few of his own. One had to observe at least a few rules of conduct, hadn't one?

Honor? Fair play? Sportsmanship?

Without them, where were you?

Dead, to name only one possibility.

Which was exactly the possibility that occurred for seven of the security guards, who were *not* Peacekeepers, late on the second night after Harry Borg had left Lori, Tippi, and Sam at the estate of Guss, the sissal-player.

There *had* been a Peacekeeper of many years' standing

serving on the screening board, and he had passed a small number who were as dedicated as he to the Cause. Moreover, since it had fallen easily within the scope of what they were committed to do anyway, they had agreed to perform a second task. While the second task was not truly a part of the first, it did provide a not-to-be scorned fringe benefit.

"The pregnant female bassoe," Les Koss had said. "I want her."

Les Koss was the head of a very important department at Foss State University, a very wealthy citizen and well worth listening to.

"The pregnant mate of the bassoe named Harry Borg— that female," he had said.

In the beginning, the mission of the Peacekeepers had been to kill Harry Borg, his staff, and any others who might be in residence and to burn the headquarters to the ground. But now, since they had missed their primary target—Borg and his staff had left without the several months of preparations considered obligatory for any expedition—they had only to destroy the headquarters. What could it matter, then, if they paused long enough to secure the pregnant female for Les Koss?

A simple task, a trifling diversion.

"I want her for my zoo," Les Koss had said. "I'll pay you well."

He had, of course, lied about wanting her for his zoo. He didn't *have* a zoo.

They knew his reason for wanting the pregnant female bassoe was quite different. Wasn't it—the *true* reason— a topic for debate in every high government circle? Indeed it was! Anyone who was anyone important was talking about it. But the reasons, true or not, were of no real concern. What was of real concern was that Les Koss had offered a substantial sum of money for the pregnant female bassoe's safe delivery. A deliciously obscene sum of money, in all truth, and obscenity of that kind can be so appealing.

Even to a dedicated Peacekeeper.

A little after midnight, on the second night after Harry

Borg had left, Lori Borg had found reason to be crawling over a huge chart she had spread on the floor of the recreation room in the main house of Guss Rassan's estate.

She had a pencil in her mouth, a calculator in one hand, and a rule in the other, and she had not the faintest notion that at that moment seven of the security guards assigned to protect her had just been killed and that five others who were Peacekeepers, dedicated to the cause of peace, were now masquerading as guards and were advancing toward the building where she was busy with the chart, advancing with great stealth and the most evil of intentions.

She had no reason to give the matter of her safety any thought. Hadn't Harry sworn a solemn oath that here, in Guss's place, surrounded by the most elite of guards, who were using the most advanced security systems, she was as safe as if she were in an innermost chamber of Fort Knox? Or in God's pocket, if she liked that better?

So what was there to worry about?

Her concern of the moment—and it was a very real concern, growing more real with each passing moment—was what the chart under her knees was telling her.

"There! And there! And there!"

Saying those words, with that emphasis, caused the pencil to fall out of her mouth. She put the pencil back in her mouth and went on crawling, growing more agitated with each move.

She cared nothing about her appearance, though had she given it any thought, she would have been the first to have said she was less than chic. She was wearing a loose-fitting yellow robe over a loose-fitting pink nightgown. Her feet were bare; her thick braid of shining, wheat-colored hair trailed on the map as she crawled. She was not even aware that as she crawled, her face close to the map as she studied topographical details, her behind was reared in a manner less than ladylike.

"As plain as the nose on my face!" she said. And lost the pencil again.

Convinced of the truth and the importance of her discovery, she pushed back on her heels, kneeling. Her gray eyes had grown large with her agitation, and now her anger; kneeling thus, she was a creature of rare beauty. She was an angry, pregnant female, which is thought by some to be one of the more beautiful though, admittedly, one of the more dangerous types of female.

"Hey, everybody!" she called suddenly.

They were all in their beds, sound asleep.

At that hour, what else?

Her own wakefulness had been the result of anger at Harry Borg. He had gone off on another of his heroic adventures, leaving her alone again—laughing loudly, as a matter of fact, at her suggestion that she go with him— and while staring at the ceiling, angry at Harry, she had seen a configuration of shadows that reminded her of something she had seen on one of the charts Harry had used, a something that had niggled at her mind, refusing to let her alone until she had finally, in absolute exasper- ation, gotten up and gone to the rec room, where the charts were still stacked. She had found the one she wanted, spread it on the floor, and begun crawling, nose down, behind high, rule in one hand, calculator in the other, pencil in her mouth, braid trailing, in search of the niggling something.

And she had found it—right damn there!

"Come on! Everybody!"

Since there was still no response, there was nothing for it but to go and get them. Sissi, then Guss, then Sam Barnstable, then Tippi, and then Illia, Chad's wife.

All but Sam Barnstable gave her an argument.

"Oh, please," Sissi moaned. "I just closed my eyes."

Guss didn't say anything. When Lori turned the light on in his bedroom, he jerked the covers over his head. When she jerked the covers off him, he covered his head with a pillow. And when she pulled on his pajama-clad leg, he held on to the bed as if it were a raft in a stormy sea. Then, sitting on the floor, he tried to look pitiful enough to be left alone, forked tongue lolling, gray inner lid across his golden, vertically slitted eyes.

"Come on, darn you!" she said. She could be very severe, even when using telepathy. "This's important!"

"Yisss," he groaned.

Sam Barnstable hadn't been asleep, after all. He met

her in the hallway outside Guss's bedroom, fully clothed and wide awake, his sidearm drawn. He had known she was up in the rec room, and he'd been drifting about the large establishment, making sure all was well while she was fretting at whatever it was that troubled her on the chart on the rec room floor.

"Chad is back?" Illia asked hopefully when awakened.

"No, love. It's something else," Lori told her, and crossed the room to the bed where her daughter slept.

"Aw, Mom!" Tippi groaned in her turn. "Y' know what time it is?"

"It's past midnight. And I still want you to get up and come see what I've found."

"Found?" Tippi asked sleepily. "Mice in the kitchen?"

"Smarty! C'mon, get up!"

"Mom—please?"

A whack on the bottom got her up, rubbing. "All right, a'ready! Y' don't have to beat a person!"

Illia smiled at Tippi. "She hit good!"

Lori finally got them all assembled, not fully awake but becoming so. When they had found out how agitated she was, they knew it had to be important, and they tried to give her wide-awake attention.

"Any of you ever hear of General Horatio Hooper?" she asked.

None had.

"At the Battle of Terryton? In the Civil War?"

Still none.

"What he did, what he became famous for," Lori said, "was he ordered his troops to attack, and *he* jumped on his horse and galloped off in *all* directions!"

They looked at her blankly.

"What I'm saying is," she said, growing heated, "that's exactly what our Harry Borg has done! Galloped off in all directions! He couldn't wait to do it right. He had to go right now!"

They still looked blank, though more concerned.

"He goofed!" she yelled. "Our lovable giant, every man's hero, has screwed up again—this time in spades!"

"You sure?" That was Sam's quiet voice.

"Mom! D' you know what you're saying?"

Guss and Sissi exchanged worried looks.

"It's right here on the map!" Lori said. "C'mon, I'll show you!"

She got down on her knees on the chart, motioning vigorously for the others to join her. They did so hesitantly—all except for Sam, who was too big. He remained standing.

"I can see all right from here," he said.

"Here," Lori said, stabbing the chart with her finger. "That peninsula right there is where Harry is going to start. See, there's the Shield edge where it crosses, that arc he drew."

They looked and saw the arc.

"Let's say he can get through the Shield," she went on. "I mean, if anybody can get through it, Harry can."

"He'll get through," Sam said.

"And Chad will help," Illia said.

Lori gave them both a look.

"So he get's through," she said. "Now look what he's got ahead of him. He's got two hundred kilometers of the worst kind of terrain ever, anywhere! See here. I plotted the best way possible, and it's a screamer—swamps, jungle, a couple of rivers, cliffs you wouldn't believe! And he's got to do it in—what? Five days now? Before it all goes under the ocean? If it's really going to go under?"

"It's going under," Guss said.

"You don't *know*," Sissi scolded. "For sure, I mean."

"It's what they say!"

"You shouldn't scare everyone with *they-says*!"

"All right. But I'll give you an *I-say* you can believe." Guss had become defensive. "And I say those charts are guesswork!"

"Guesswork?" Lori asked, suddenly appalled.

Guss retreated at once. "Well, mostly guesswork." She was still appalled. "Sort of guesswork?" Still appalled. "Not too dependable?" And then, rather weakly, because Sissi was glaring at him, "They're mostly okay, I guess."

That seemed to satisfy them.

"What isn't?" Tippi asked. "Only mostly okay, I mean."

"Chad very okay," Illia said defensively. The softly furred bassoe was very much in love, still new to being an acting member of the human race, still new to pretended pessimism.

"Sure is!" Tippi said, putting an arm around Illia.

Lori sighed impatiently.

"Whatever," she said. "But what I'm trying to say is he's not going to get there, walking, in five days. Superman himself couldn't do it!"

"He'll get there," Sam said.

Again Lori gave him a look.

"I know the man," Sam said stubbornly. "I've seen him work. He's harder to stop than a landslide."

"So you're loyal—that's fine. I admire loyalty." Lori turned her attention back to the chart. "What I don't admire is when somebody like Harry, when he gets in such a big hurry he can't take time to look for the easy way, goes galloping off in all directions."

"An *easy* way?" Tippi asked.

"There's one of those?" Sissi's golden eyes had gone wide.

Guss didn't say anything; he was afraid to.

"Well," Lori said. "Maybe not easy. Eas*ier* is what I should've said. Look here—and you'll have to get close to see it. There's an old, old trail right here." The others got their noses down and their rear ends up. "It must be one the Ancients used. It begins on *this* stick of land, on *this* side of the island. See?"

They saw.

"It goes right up that riverbank," Lori said. "Right up that canyon, across that flatland, through that little bit of jungle—and then walks right up the mountain."

"Quicker, I guess," Tippi agreed. "Winds around some, though."

"Not as much as the way old Superman's going!"

The young girl looked at her mother. "You're just sore because he didn't take you with him," she said.

"Who, me? Me? Sore?"

"Yes, you!" Tippi grinned her gamine grin and held her ground.

Lori gave in. "Well, okay—maybe a little sore."

Tippi's grin said that wasn't enough.

"Well, all right! A *lot* sore."

"But it *is* shorter," Tippi said, mollified.

"And easier!"

"Easier, too," Tippi admitted.

"And that," Lori said with finality, "is the way we're going!"

They were all shocked.

"We?" Sissi asked faintly.

"We?" Guss asked louder. "Who's we?"

Lori sat back on her heels again. "Us—all of us."

"You've got to be kidding!" Tippi again.

"This's nothing to kid about!" Lori said. "This is for real. You an' me, baby, and Sissi and Guss and Sam and Illia—us! We're going!"

They looked at her.

"I can't go alone!" Lori said. "And it's got to be done."

"What d' you mean *got* to be done?"

"If somebody doesn't push the button and shut off that Shield in time for the aircraft to get in there and get that Lassa Crystal, this whole country's going to go ka-put! Know what I mean?"

"All those fridges, right? All those turkey dinners?" Tippi asked.

"Worse than that!" She looked at them. "Hassad can get there first, you know. He's trying."

"Yeah, what about him?" Tippi said.

"He and the Ussirs'd take over the whole planet!" Lori warned. "And do you know what that would mean?"

"Turn it into a bunch of franchises?" Tippi asked. "Kentucky Fried? Taco Bell, sushi bars? On every corner?"

"You want that to happen, a nice country like this?"

"Gee, no!"

"Well, what d' you say? Will you go with me?"

Tippi shrugged. "Couldn't let you and Charlie go by yourselves."

"I go," Illia said promptly.

"Sissi?" Lori asked.

Sissi was startled, worried, and afraid all at once. But only for a moment. "We'll go," she said firmly then. "Guss and I, we'll go with you."

Guss's "Wait a minute!" was a telepathic yell. They all looked at him.

"We quit being heroes, remember?" he reminded Sissi. Sissi just looked at him.

"We swore off! We said no more! We said we'd done enough. We said—we said..." He lost strength under Sissi's unrelenting stare; his telepathic voice faded.

"I thought we did, anyway."

"Guss, so much depends on this!"

"I suppose it does."

"You don't want her to go alone, now, do you?"

"Well, no. I'd hate to see her do that."

"And you're going to give in sooner or later, aren't you?"

"Maybe not! Maybe this time I'll—" He tossed his hands in despair.

"You going?" Lori asked.

"When do we leave?" he asked wearily.

"As soon as we can get ready," she told him, turning away. "Sam—"

But Sam was no longer in the room. He had drifted out of the room, a huge shadow, moving silently, drawn by sounds the others hadn't noticed. Lori got up and went to the door to find Sam returning to the room, moving swiftly now. And he was carrying weapons. He tossed an esso to Guss and one to Sissi. And to Lori, Tippi, and Illia, he said, "Get behind that couch!"

"What's up?"

"We've got company coming," Sam said.

"What d' you mean company?"

"Peacekeeper company."

"The very *worst* kind," Lori said.

CHAPTER 12

Ahmed Hassad was furious.

He was murderously furious, but it didn't show. It was a basic tenet of Hassad that it was stupid to let others know how you felt or what you were thinking. To do so gave others a look inside you. It let them know what excited you, what upset you, and what filled you with a cold fury—it gave them an advantage.

To give others an even break was foolish, Hassad believed. To give them an advantage was unthinkable.

When Hassad was not angry, in fact when he was enjoying himself, he looked to be the most pleasant of all men—big, handsome, charming, with dark, curly hair, a perfect profile, great teeth, and a most engaging, dimpled smile. And when he *was* angry, he looked the same way—big, handsome, charming, with dark, curly hair, a perfect profile, great teeth, and a most engaging dimpled smile.

And so, even though he was murderously furious at the present moment, he looked no angrier than a politician seeking a third term in office.

"One craft," he said gently. "Just one?"

"Yes, just one."

Oss Tiss, the Ussir commander of the elite commando corps, who had been assigned—much against his will— to be the opposite number of Hassad, and in command, under Hassad, of the Ussir forces Hassad might need, could not understand why he was being treated the way he was.

So friendly!

In his world, when a mission failed, the one who had ordered the mission had the commander of the failed mission up before him and, with no preamble at all, began biting. Hard. Before the session would be over, the failed commander would be a bloody mess, demoted and lucky to be alive. If, indeed, he was still alive.

But it was not so with this bassoe.

This bassoe, this human being, Ahmed Hassad, smiled. His telepathic voice was gentle; his eyes held friendship and warmth. And Oss Tiss found that he was feeling embarrassed that his mission had failed. Even ashamed. But not frightened. Not frightened at all.

Very strange.

But then, the bassoes *were* an odd lot. One never knew quite what they would do or think in any situation. True, they had only recently come down out of the trees—ten million years ago, wasn't it?—and thinking was still relatively new to them. Ten million years might be enough to take the rough edges off their thinking processes, but it certainly wasn't long enough to have given them a polish. Their minds moved in elemental ways. Even brutish at times. Never predictable.

And *this* was the creature his superiors had put in charge, had given a responsibility so immense?

He, Oss Tiss, had proved himself, hadn't he?

Had there been another Ussir born since the time of the Ancients capable of doing what he had done? An Ussir with the courage, the planning ability, the military skills to have done what he had done? He had gone to a strange planet, Earth, braving uncounted hidden and unknown dangers to seek out, to capture, and to return with a single, specified bassoe. One special bassoe among many, many millions of bassoes! And he had done it not once but twice!

A heroic feat of the highest order, certainly.

And his reward?

A statue in the park? Certainly not! A victory parade? No. A banquet in his honor? No. A medal? No. A letter of commendation, perhaps? No. A handshake, then? A simple thank you?

Not even a day of R & R.

What he had been given was a new assignment.

But not the assignment he had hoped for, the one he had had a right to expect. That one, the most important assignment in the recent history of the Ussir nation, that one had gone to a bassoe—a *bassoe* for Osis sake!—and Oss Tiss had been ordered to stand under him.

He, Oss Tiss, whose military legacy was the best—his family went back three thousand years and included generals and admirals beyond counting—who had graduated from Toss Academy of Military Arts and Sciences with highest honors; he, that Oss Tiss, a young military genius—all false modesty aside—had been ordered to stand subordinate to a bassoe. A so-called intelligent bassoe, yes; but still no more than a food-animal with cunning.

Yes, he, Oss Tiss, had eaten many like this bassoe.

And now, standing before this one, he made a solemn vow that when this assignment was over, he would eat another bassoe.

This bassoe! This patronizing whisser!

"Under the circumstances," he said, "one seemed enough."

"What circumstances?" Hassad asked, still gently.

"We have so few aircraft capable of sustained flight at those distances," Oss Tiss answered. "That is to say, operable. Spare parts, you see. And there were only a few basso—" he caught himself "—my apologies, enemy to be eliminated. Those circumstances."

"Sir?"

"Sir."

"Say it. Those circumstances—"

"Those circumstances, sir!"

Roasted, Oss Tiss promised silently. He would have this bassoe roasted slowly on a spit over a charcoal fire. Then he would have him served with a tart cliss-au-vis sauce, with a few tolls and a light claris, or perhaps a red samiss—

"C'mere!"

Oss Tiss found his blouse front suddenly caught in a tight grip, found himself jerked forward, his feet barely touching the ground, his nostrils no more than six centimeters from the bassoe's nostrils, which were breathing something very close to fire.

"You miserable little cross between a snake and an ape."

The bassoe's telepathic voice was still soft, but it was no longer friendly. And his eyes had taken on a glitter that was—well, yes, it was frightening. The bassoe's true character had finally been revealed.

"I told you I wanted that man killed," Hassad said. "Man! You hear that? Not bassoe. *Man*! The next time you call one of us a bassoe, I'm going to take your head and stuff it up your—sleeve! That perfectly clear?"

"Yes . . . sir."

"And that man I sent you to kill is not an ordinary man. He's Harry Borg! A giant of a man. One of your ships couldn't kill him. I don't think ten could. You should have sent at least twenty!"

"I might be able to fly fifteen—"

"It's too late," Hassad said.

"But the Shield—"

"Damn the Shield! He'll be through it before you can gas your ships, let alone get there. Do you understand what you've done? You took our chance to get rid of our *worst* problem—far worse than the Shield—and you blew it!"

"Sir, I—"

Oss Tiss's feet left the floor as Hassad yanked him up to almost arm's length above his head before giving him a heave that landed him on his feet against a distant wall.

Alive on that spit, Oss Tiss promised.

And it was no idle threat. Oss Tiss's yellow, vertically slitted eyes had taken on a glitter of their own, not less frightening to those who knew his strength than the glow in Hassad's eyes.

Oss Tiss was no longer frightened.

"Don't touch me again," he said.

"And don't you give me any crap!" Hassad said.

They stared at each other.

"You gonna do what I tell you to do?" Hassad demanded.

"I am a soldier," Oss Tiss answered. "I obey orders."

"You damn well better!" Hassad said. "My order to you now is get your tail in gear! We're going to hit the beach on Tassar tomorrow morning at oh-four-hundred. Got it?"

"I have it."

"That task force better be there!"

"It will be there."

"Fully manned!"

"Everything as you ordered."

"Now—get out!"

Screaming on that spit, Oss Tiss promised. And left.

When Ahmed Hassad turned back to the room, he found Soo Toy standing in an inner doorway, smiling amusedly.

"You were severe with the little lizard, Ahmed."

He grinned, very pleased with himself. "Scared the hell out of him is what I did!"

"I suppose it was necessary."

"Very necessary." Hassad walked to a bar, poured a drink, sipped it. "Want one of these? Not bad. Got a nice little bite."

"Perhaps a small one."

He made one for her, then turned from the bar. Handing her the drink, he guided her to a couch before a window that gave them a view of the city.

"Authority," he said. "The iron fist of authority. Have to show them that if you want to get good work out of them. Lizards, men—it makes no difference." He sipped his drink.

"Women?"

He put his drink aside and cupped her fragile chin in a big, hard palm. "You better believe it, pussycat." His black eyes had suddenly taken on the shine again. She knew that shine well—she had suffered a broken wrist when his eyes had gleamed like that on a night early in their relationship.

"My chin, Ahmed," she said, *her* eyes gleaming.

"Only joking," he told her.

Her eyes had held *that* gleam the night she had hit him with a chair as he lay sleeping—two black eyes and a bloody nose was the price he'd paid for ignoring it.

"You're my treasure," he said. "My Star of the East."

She sipped her drink, looking out at the view. "I like this city, Ahmed," she said.

"Reminds you of Bangkok?"

"Angkor Wat."

"Even older. Much older. But better kept. The city's been here, what—five thousand, ten thousand years?"

"A very long time."

They could see great, tall spired buildings built of stonelike material, a rich, dark red, softened with the patina of great age, and wide avenues paved with use-eroded stone. There were parkways where trees were just coming into bloom, fountains and flowers that said a love of things natural had never been lost. Essan vehicles of all descriptions—the small personal kind, huge trucklike conveyances, passenger-carrying buses—were moving on the streets, but not in the numbers one might expect. The pedestrians moved at a leisurely pace.

"Run-down," Hassad said. "Half asleep."

"Peaceful."

"Who needs peaceful?" Hassad was impatient. "Life! That's what this country needs. Vitality! Drive! They go on like this, they'll go to sleep and never wake up."

"They've been this way a thousand years, Ahmed."

"Wasted years!"

"And you're going to change them?"

He laughed. "Watch! Give me a year—that's all I'll need. I'll have them up and going like a factory. Tearing down, rebuilding. Smoke coming out of chimneys. Whistles blowing. Trains roaring. Workers running. Prosperity! Money!"

"Dreadful," she said.

"What's dreadful?"

"What you just said."

"Soo! They're letting it all go to waste!"

"They're contented, happy. Happiness is a waste?"

"Happiness is taking life by the throat! Doing something with it! Shake it! Work it! Fashion it! *Mold* it! Make life into what *you* want it to be! Soo, I'm going to show these lizards happiness! I'm going to turn this country around. I'll have it booming in a year's time!"

Poor things, Soo Toy said—but she said it to herself.

One does have to stay in the good graces of one's protector, doesn't one? Particularly when losing that protector might very well result in your being eaten.

Hassad's effort against the Shield began the next morning on schedule. He had chosen a region known as Kloss Reach on the north coast of Tassar as the point where he would make his attack. There was enough land here, outside the circumference of the Shield, to provide a beach-head for a small landing force, and there was a safe anchorage offshore. And he found when he arrived that as Oss Tiss had promised, all was in readiness.

The Ussir high command had accepted his orders without dispute. But they had been, quite naturally, very curious as to how he intended to go about the task of penetrating a barrier they had thus far been unable to dent.

"Nothing to it," he had said.

Which did not satisfy their curiosity in the least.

Since the answer had been given with such absolute confidence, however, they had been impressed. Very impressed. And then, when he had refused to elaborate, defying them with smiling, even disdainful arrogance, they had been even more impressed.

For more than one reason.

His size—he did tower head and shoulders above their tallest—his personal magnetism, the inner force and drive that seemed to radiate from him like some strange light, had persuaded them finally that he was another of those bassoes like the one the Jassans had—a bassoe of supernatural powers, a bassoe who was the reincarnation of god. And since he was going to have to cope with the Jassan god, Harry Borg, and the god Uss, who was known to dwell on or just above the mountaintop, it was only appropriate that he, too, be a god.

Parity is so important.

Ahmed Hassad found he rather liked being considered a god.

As a god, he was given the kind of authority he favored most—total, unquestioned authority. More, if he were considered to be a god, he must then be considered to have the powers of a god, mustn't he? Mystical powers. Powers not granted to mortal beings. Most assuredly he must. And Hassad claimed those powers without a moment of hesitation.

Oss Tiss, however, did not believe in gods.

Neither did he believe in mystical powers.

But he was second in command. He was a soldier and therefore obliged to obey the orders of a superior officer—or lose his head for being mutinous in the face of the enemy. That would be a fate which would not only deprive him of his life but would also deprive his country of the only person capable of saving it in this hour of extreme need—himself. Oss Tiss. He *had* to stay alive at any cost. Therefore, he had to accept and to obey any order this false god Ahmed Hassad chose to give.

For the moment.

"Three craft," Hassad had told him. "In this formation and at these intervals. Be very careful about the intervals. The intervals are most important."

Oss Tiss had studied with great perplexity the diagram Hassad had given him. How could intervals be important? If the craft were to fly straight at the Shield and be destroyed, as they certainly would be, what possible difference could the interval between them make? These were questions Oss Tiss was not permitted to ask.

He could only send the craft.

The craft set out from a mother ship, three tubes of shining gliss, small against the towering slopes of a mountain, just lighted by a rising sun. Brave ships. Oss Tiss, standing on a gently shifting deck, almost lost them as they crossed the surf line, then found them again against the dark green of the jungle.

His heart was with those pilots, aching. Good essans, those. Young. They'd had faith in him. They'd believed him when he had said the bassoes had mysterious powers and knowledge mortal beings did not have. Keep that interval, he had told them. You will be safe.

Beside him now, an arm around his female, the enormous bassoe-god was watching with him. A curious vibration was coming from the beast, a contented, untroubled vibration.

Hassad was humming to himself—that was what was causing the vibration. Everything was going fine for him. He had control. He had these smart-ass lizard-types right where he wanted them, doing exactly what he told them to do, and doing it without question.

Gullible little beasties.

He a god? The opposite number was more like it!

Using his normal voice—one the Ussirs couldn't interpret—he said to Soo Toy, "This little sucker next to us is going out of his skull. He *knows* those craft are not going to make it."

"Do you know that?"

"Hell, yes, I know that!"

"They are going to be killed?"

"If that Shield is what they say it is, they're going to be blown to hell and gone any second now."

"Then why did you send them?"

"It's the way I'm going to break the Shield."

"I don't understand."

"You're not supposed to understand. I'm a god, remember? I work in mysterious ways my wonders to perform."

"Bull-hockey," she said.

The craft found the Shield just then.

A sudden purple beam from somewhere inland flashed, turning the first craft into a ball of white flame. A second purple beam caught the second craft in the same way, with the same result. The pilot of the third craft, flying at the ordered interval, a full kilometer behind the first two, did not alter his course in the slightest. He flew straight on, trusting Oss Tiss, trusting God, only to be met in his turn by something far more substantial than an article of faith—a flashing purple beam that caused him to disappear forever in a white ball of flame.

"All right!" Hassad said, pleased. "It works!"

Soo Toy was mildly shocked.

Oss Tiss could not say anything. He needed all his forces to reholster his sidearm, which had somehow become half drawn.

CHAPTER 13

"Y' know what that is?" Harry Borg asked. He was standing at a reasonably safe distance from Chad, who was lying flat on his back in a slight depression, stiff, afraid to lift his head. And with good reason. The purple bolt he had drawn when he'd broken the Shield had zipped at him close above the ground.

Sure death. Beautiful but sure.

"The Shield?" Chad answered.

The answer was tentative, because Chad thought the question was probably rhetorical. Iron Balls did that sometimes—asked rhetorical questions at the damnedest times. He considered himself a thinker. Came up with some beauties.

Homer said nothing. Neither did Arnie or Eddie. They were all feeling somehow to blame for the predicament Chad was in. And equally at risk—danger to one was danger to all. One of them was not going anywhere without the others beside him—and that included into the Great Beyond if it were to come to that.

And it looked like it was going to come to that.

Iron Balls was not about to leave Chad there, flat on his back, unable to move anything but his eyeballs and his fingertips for fear of being blown away. Leaving one of his men was not his style. Head down, shoulders

123

bunched, legs driving, going straight in after him—that
was his style. But he wasn't doing that, either. He was
just standing there, spraddle-legged, a black scowl on his
bearded face, his dark blue eyes almost black with fierce-
ness, staring.

"That's nothing but a damned Maginot Line!" he said.

Arnie looked at Eddie, strained. "Geeze!" he whispered. "What's *that* mean?"

"Or a Siegfried line," Harry said. It was almost a curse.

"A fixed defense," Chad said, catching on.

"Right!" Harry said. "You can't build a fixed defense
and hide behind it. You've got to deal on an intellectual
level. You've got to win the *minds* of your adversaries.
Otherwise they'll find a way to penetrate—or go around—
your fixed defense, your Shield, your Star Wars canopy,
your S.D.I.!"

"Hadrian's Wall?" Chad said. "Second century A.D.?"

"Right! The Great Wall of China?"

"What about the Berlin Wall?"

"Won't work either. Not in the long run."

Arnie couldn't stand it. "I think you're both bats!"

Harry Borg's dark blue eyes came to bear on his young,
obviously very distraught soldier.

"Why d' you think we're bats, son?"

"Talkin' history?" Arnie's voice was shrill. "At a time
like this? Chad lyin' there in stuff up to his neck, and all
you can think to do is talk history? You gotta be bats!"

"We learn from history," Harry said. Surprisingly, a
faint smile blemished his ferocious stare. "That's what
history was put there for. If you impatient little squirts
would realize that, you could stay out of a helluva lot of
trouble."

He turned back to Chad and drew a couple of cartridges
from his weapons belt. "Keep your head down, son," he
said to Chad. "Gonna be some fireworks."

He threw one of the cartridges toward the screen, high
and to the left. At a distance of perhaps thirty meters, the
cartridge was met by a purple beam, small but adequate
to the need. The cartridge vanished in a sudden flash of
light.

"Kee-rist!" Arnie whispered.

"Some kind of radar in there," Homer said.

"Some kind of quick!" Eddie said. "It got itself greased!"

Harry threw a second cartridge high and to the right. That cartridge got the same reaction, even faster. As Eddie had suggested, the mechanism that did the firing from within the Shield, unused in a millennium or two, must have overcome its rust.

"All right," Harry said. "Let me think."

He turned and walked away toward the beach again. His cadre watched him go, their faces aching with worry and despair.

"Sheee-it!" Eddie said.

And that seemed to say it all.

They watched their leader walk away a couple of hundred meters, kicking sand, cussing, hitting a fist into a palm, talking to himself. They saw him stop finally to stare fiercely at nothing. Then they saw him return, unbuttoning his shirt.

Unbuttoning his shirt?

They couldn't believe it. But that's what he did. And he took the shirt off. Then he went to stand at that reasonably safe distance again. After examining his shirt, every inch of it, as if he had never seen it before, he wadded it in a ball, hauled back, and threw it at the Shield. The shirt penetrated the Shield just as the cartridges had, and, just like the cartridges, the shirt was zapped into nothingness.

"Holy mother," Arnie whispered, growing more frightened.

"Steady," Homer said. "He's on to something."

On to something? Throwing his shirt away, and now taking off his pants, he was on to something? He'd lost an oar was what he'd done. They watched him lay the pants aside, then stand and take off his underwear, a standard pair of jockey shorts. Bare-ass naked, he walked a little closer to the Shield.

"Loony," Arnie whispered. "Bonkers."

Harry Borg was standing there like some big-league pitcher on the mound—bases loaded, two out, the count three and two in the last of the ninth and a one-run lead. He had the shorts wadded into a baseball size. He juggled that ball, stared at it, thinking. Then, finally, he got a foot on the rubber, so to say, reared back to make the pitch—and then he balked.

"Damn!" they heard Harry say.

Then he wound up again, this time a stubborn, determined kind of a windup, and he threw the balled-up underwear—a ninety-five-mile-an-hour fastball, a strike—straight at the Shield.

Nothing happened.

Not a damn thing—to the underwear.

"Jumpin' jiminy Christmas!" Arnie said.

The underwear, untouched by any purple beam, had gone through the Shield to land on Chad's chest. Chad didn't move. He couldn't move. He could only stare at the undamaged underwear as if it were a snake, suddenly coiled on his chest. Then, when realization came to him, he stared at the undamaged underwear as if it were a gift of gold. He lifted his eyes to his leader.

Harry smiled. "How about that?"

"Why didn't I think of it?" Chad asked. "I carried the stick."

"Hard to think when you're nervous."

"I was *scared*!" Chad said. "Still am."

Eddie, his black face shining with the sweat of his anxiety, his almond eyes wide, said, "Whatever in the hell are you dudes talkin' about? First history, then underwear? What's goin' *on*?"

"Organic," Homer said. "The radar doesn't see things organic."

"Anything metallic, you're dead," Harry said, pulling the gold band from his left earlobe.

Then he had his boots off and, stark naked, he stood erect at that reasonably safe distance. Right here it was go or no-go. He had to test his theory the only way that mattered—with his own bones, flesh, and hide. He used a moment to take a deep breath, to gather his forces. Then, head down, shoulders bunched, legs driving, he went straight in after Chad—just as his men had known he would. He didn't hesitate when his face broke the cobweblike edge of the forcefield. He didn't even flinch.

He cringed—inside, where it didn't show.

And then he was standing above Chad, unharmed, smiling down at him. When Chad was finally able to breathe again, he used his first breath to breathe reverence:

"You are one brave son of a bitch—sir."

"Frightened, you want the truth."

Then Harry knelt beside Chad. "Let's get you out of those clothes," he said. "Brass buttons, insignia, zippers—metal of any kind, and you'll get hit. Any fillings in your teeth?"

"None."

"Should be safe. C'mon, now, easy does it."

Working very, very carefully, they got Chad stripped down to his underwear and Harry back into his. Then they both got to their feet. They had to take a moment to stand there, to revel in their newfound safety. They waved their arms to test that safety to the limit, to do a little war dance. Then they grinned at each other, shook hands, turned, and walked back through the Shield to join the others.

The others were going loudly bananas, yelling.

"Way to *go*!"

"Y' did it! Y' did it! Y' did it!"

"Yeah! Wow-weeeee!"

Eddie had even run down to the water's edge to do a war dance of his own and to throw water into the air. They were all so occupied with joyful nonsense, making so much noise, that they didn't hear the rumble. It was a distant rumble at first, hardly loud enough to be heard above the steady roar and pound of the surf.

The rumble had no exact source.

It seemed to come from everywhere, left, right, above, and below, growing louder and louder and louder still. Then the ground beneath their feet came alive. The ground trembled. Then the ground shook. Then the ground heaved insanely, furiously. It dropped from beneath their feet, leaving them weightless, only to drive up again, knocking them down. Flat on the ground, they found themselves hanging on for dear life, with the ground gone mad and thunder in their ears. The insanity lasted only a few moments, though it seemed much longer. Then the ground stopped heaving, subsided into tremors, then into stillness.

"Holy Mary, Mother of Christ, save us." It was a whispered prayer from Arnie.

They all got up cautiously, as if any sudden movement might make the earthquake start all over again. And they were all very sober.

"Seven points," Harry said. "Maybe eight."

"I'll go ten."

"What d' you mean?"

"On the Richter scale."

"The needle went clear off the paper."

"I was in L.A. when that earthquake hit the valley," Eddie said, his black face drawn. "Knocked down the freeway overpasses, the hospital. Remember? Bush compared to this one."

"Major league, this one," Harry agreed. "Real badass."

They looked at him.

Homer was the first to put it in words. "Sir, do you think there might be something to it, what they said?"

"Is the island going to go under in five days?"

"Or less."

Harry's answer came slowly. "We just had one helluva an earthquake," he said. "No question. But think of the size of this island, lads. It's as big as Maui. Maybe bigger. A place this big, been here millions of years, going under? I hardly think so. This island'll be here long time yet."

"Glad to hear that," Homer said. "Be scared as hell if I hadn't."

Harry stared at Homer hard.

"Sir," Homer said, but he didn't back off.

"All right," Harry said. "We've got reason to worry, I'll go that far with you. Right now we've got something more immediate—tidal waves. We better get our butts to high ground."

"Double time!" Chad said.

He grabbed up his spare set of clothes and began stripping them of metal—brass buttons, insignia, belt buckles, anything and everything that could possibly draw fire.

The others did the same. And as they worked with great urgency, realizations came.

"Our weapons—they're metal!" Eddie said.

"Holy smoke!"

"We got to go bare-handed?"

"Or go home."

"What about boots? There's nails in these heels. Eyelets!"

"Gimmie that knife—I'm not goin' barefoot, that's for sure!"

They worked at a furious pace. Anything questionable was tested by throwing it through the Shield to be picked up later if it passed, forgotten if not. The purple rays sorted the organic from the metallic with a devastating infallibility. They were left finally with what had to be called bare essentials—uniforms tied together with string, boots heelless and eyeless, packs with knotted straps. The food in the packs was wrapped in cloth, not cans; they kept plastic canteens, plastic pill containers, plastic cups.

Harry, Chad, Homer and Arnie, working right beside Eddie, hadn't noticed that he was breathing heavily, that his black hide had become drenched with sweat, that his almond-shaped dark eyes had grown wide. They hadn't noticed that he had set aside a screwdriver. When they were all ready to go through the Shield, Eddie held back.

"Can't go," he said. "Not like this."

"Whatta y' mean can't go?" Arnie demanded.

"Wouldn't get through the Shield."

Arnie was outraged. "Color don't matter a damn!"

Eddie managed a laugh. "You *are* a dumb sucker!" he said. "But there's something you gotta do or I can't go." He handed Arnie the screwdriver. "Homer, you've got to hold my head. Chad, you sit on me. Arnie, you're just dumb enough to make a smart dentist."

"What're you talkin'?" Arnie asked, horrified.

"I've got a couple of gold crowns."

"You mean you want me to—"

Eddie was relentless. "The butt of your piece'll do for a hammer."

"Eddie! Geeze, I can't—"

"The hell you can't!" Homer said suddenly.

He took Eddie's head between his big hands and sat down, dragging the black youth down with him. He clamped Eddie's head firmly between powerful knees.

"Come on, damn it!" he said to Arnie. "Show some guts!"

"He's my *buddy*!" Arnie moaned. "He's—"

Harry Borg stayed out of it. Could they do it? Or could they not? It was a trial by fire, certainly. He wanted to know, needed to know, if they could or not; there was a lot worse coming.

But it was hell to watch.

"Godamighty," Arnie yelled.

He knelt suddenly across Eddie's chest.

Homer, with Eddie's head caught in the vise of his knees, thrust a thumb inside Eddie's cheek, forced the cheek aside, drawing the lower jaw down. Arnie placed the screwdriver, hit the handle a crack with the butt of his handgun. It didn't matter that tears were streaming down Arnie's face.

The tooth was gone!

Gold crown and all!

A twist of the head, a second blow, and the other tooth and crown were gone.

"There, damn you!" Arnie swore. He jumped up and threw the screwdriver into the sea.

Eddie got up, spitting blood.

He grabbed Arnie, who was facing away from him, and slapped him on the side of the head.

"Cut it out!" he said. "Y' gutless honky!"

"Nigger!" Arnie swore at him, turning, eyes full. "Yuh black bastard! Make me do a thing like that!" He grabbed Eddie, hugged him. "Hope you bleed to death!"

"C'mon!" Harry said. "We've got miles to go!"

They followed him through the Shield.

CHAPTER 14

Worst kind of company or not, Lori was not going to hide behind any cockamamy sofa. She had her own piece—she was never farther than a long grab away from it anymore, not since the last couple of days of getting shot at all the time—and it was right where she'd left it on Guss's sissal.

"Careful!" Guss cried, then groaned.

The scratch she left on the sissal, a most treasured possession, an instrument centuries old, handcrafted of rare woods, capable of fragrances of rare beauty, was hardly noticeable—to her in her cold excitement.

To Guss, it was as if she had scratched the very flesh of his heart.

He could scarcely believe the sudden change he was seeing in this female human. Her gray eyes had suddenly taken on a hard shine, her rather attractive chin had thrust forward in an expression of great determination.

She looked dangerous!

"Mom! For gosh shakes!" Tippi said. "Remember Charlie!"

Lori patted her stomach. "Charlie's all right," she said. "You get behind that sofa!"

Tippi didn't take orders any better than her mother. Nor did Illia. When the exasperated Sam took them into

131

the hall to disperse them, Tippi and Illia were on Lori's heels. And in the room where they were concealed, Tippi armed herself with one of Guss's swords, decorative though quite lethal if used as a weapon, and Illia took another.

"We hit them?" Illia asked.

"Bet your bippi!" Tippi said.

"You two stay back!" Lori ordered.

Sam Barnstable, looming like a dark mountain, and Guss, frightened stiff, were waiting silently in the doorway at the end of a hall the Peacekeepers had to traverse to reach the inner part of the building from the rear. Sissi, Lori, and Tippi were in a room beyond them, accessible only over the dead bodies of the males.

Guss, hanging in but trembling, whispered telepathically, "You sure they're coming?"

"Dead sure," Sam answered.

"But how do you know, for Osis sake?"

"They forgot something."

"What something?"

"Shhhh."

The Peacekeepers came straight on into the darkened hallway being watched by Sam and Guss, the shooters of the deadly purple beams in their eight-fingered hands, the pupils of their vertically slitted eyes gone round in the dark, their long, forked tongues flickering in and out, catching the strong scents of the human bodies and the lesser but still recognizable dry-earth odors of their own kind. Confident their attack would be a total surprise, they had no fear. Neither the humans nor the essans would expect an attack from their protectors, now, would they? One of them had described their task nicely:

"No more difficult than stepping on a bissel."

"Now!" Sam said.

He touched a switch that lighted the end of the hall, backlighting the intruders. There were three of them, essos in hand, caught in silhouette, startled. Before they could react, Sam had cut down two of them with carefully placed bolts. Guss, equally startled, missed badly with two shots but crippled the remaining Peacekeeper with a third. That one threw his esso aside on falling and threw his hands up in a plea for mercy. There'd been a crash in the inner room, and Sam turned immediately that way in careful haste.

"Stay with the cripple!" he ordered Guss.

The crash had been caused by the remaining two Peacekeepers, breaking through a window to enter the house from the front to execute the standard military maneuver of hitting the enemy from the rear. They had expected total surprise. What they found, instead, were four very alert and very prepared females, one of them pregnant, two with essos and two with swords.

"Banzai!" the smaller human female yelled.

The older two females fired their essos, the purple beams lashing out like evil fingers across the room, hunting flesh. The Peacekeepers fired essos in return, but they fired while dying, pierced by the purple bolts from the females, their own purple bolts going wildly astray.

Then darkness again, then silence. Deep, pervading silence, the kind only death can bring.

Then a sobbing, telepathic wail from Sissi.

A comforting "Come here to me" from Lori.

"Mom—Mom, you and Charlie?" a small voice asked.

"Scared, both of us. Scared as hell, that's all."

"We showed those suckers!" the small voice said.

"That we did, honey. Showed 'em good."

When Sam touched the switch that brought light, he found the females unharmed, clutching each other, hugging, searching for nonexistent wounds, and crying.

"You all right, ma'am?"

"Yes, Sam," Lori answered. "You? Guss?"

"Okay. Sorry I couldn't have been here."

"Only one of you—and we managed."

"Yeah, you did!" Sam turned and was gone again.

He did not return until he'd made sure the grounds and the buildings were secure in the control of genuine security personnel, who were abjectly ashamed personnel, to be sure. They could not believe, much less understand, how such a thing could have happened.

Guss meanwhile had a long talk with the wounded Peacekeeper and gathered some startling—and frightening—information. But he would not reveal it to Sam until they had gone outside, away from the females, and Sam had answered his question of how he had known the Peacekeepers were going to attack.

"You psychic or something?"

Sam chose to show him, not tell him. The answer was readily at hand.

"These cans," Sam said. "I don't know what you call them, but we call them tin cans. And this fine thread. When the Peacekeepers tripped this thread, I knew they were coming."

"But how?"

"Humans can *hear*!" Sam said with only a little smugness. "The Peacekeepers forgot that. Or never knew. When the thread was tripped, the cans jangled together. They made a racket, a noise, sound! All your high tech is fine, but there's nothing wrong with making sure with a home-made burglar alarm."

"I'll be twissed!" Guss said, amazed.

"Now tell me what you got."

Guss sobered at once.

The telling was not going to be easy. After all, it was going to put his kind in a very bad light. He was, to say the best, tentative, hesitant, circumspect.

"They wanted to kill us, yes," he began. "But that was, well—only part of what they wanted. The least part."

"The most part?" Sam asked.

"They wanted—they wanted Harry's mate. Lori. They wanted her alive. Well, no, they didn't actually want *her* . . ."

The difficulty Guss was having became so obvious that Sam felt the need to put a big hand on the back of Guss's neck. It could have been thought of as a steadying hand. Or it could have been thought of as a hand about ready to unscrew the head. Guss thought the latter was closer to the mark than the first. But it also steadied him.

"They want her child!" he blurted.

"Her baby? It's not even born yet!"

"No matter. Her baby is being talked about in—well, very, very high circles. And—I don't like to say this, but it's true—a lot of money is being offered for it. Double if it's a male."

"For the love of God, why?"

"You—you said it, right there."

"Said what?"

"For the love of God—that's why!"

"Why what? C'mon. Make sense!"

"It's the love of *a* god." Guss was very distressed now. "How do I say it? You know intelligent bassoes are most unusual—like yourself, for instance—but Harry Borg is so unusual, many think—many are *sure* he's a god. The reincarnation of a god, anyway. The God of the Red Flame. That—that's why *he* was asked to—why he was thought to be our only hope to penetrate the Shield and save the Source. Don't you understand?"

"We're not talking about Harry," Sam said. "You said it was Lori's *baby* they wanted! You said—" His telepathic voice stumbled. He said, "Holy Mother!" in his normal voice as a realization began to grow. "Like the colt of a great racing stallion."

Staring up at Sam's shadowed face, Guss knew Sam was beginning to understand—the grip on his neck had slackened—and took heart.

"The child of a *god*," Guss said. "You see?"

"You really mean it?"

"Beyond all value—wouldn't such a child be?"

"If you believe in that kind of nonsense."

"They—we—believe. And it's not nonsense to us."

"But the kid's not even born yet!"

Guss could hardly find strength enough to put into telepathic words what he had to say next. "They don't have to wait. They have means. They were not going to wait."

"They'd kill her if they took it now!"

Guss moved his head in a helpless gesture.

"Would they *really*?" Sam asked in disbelief.

"The child—to have it, to keep it, to worship it—that is their only concern. Their *first* concern."

Sam suddenly threw Guss to the ground, then towered over him, a raging bull of a young man. "You miserable lizards! Kill a woman to take her child for some freak reason. God freaks! Damn you! You're rotten crazy!"

He raged for long moments.

Guss knew—though he could only receive the vibra-

tions, not the words, of Sam's fury—that he was as near
death as he would ever come and still live. The vibrations
finally slowed, then faded out. A big hand reached down,
took him by the front of his clothes, and lifted him back
to his feet as easily as if he were a toy.

Then a big hand brushed his clothes.

"Sorry." Sam was using telepathy again. "I know you
wouldn't do it. You'd give your life for her first. I know
that. I—I just I lost my temper."

"It's all right," Guss answered.

"No need to tell *her* about this," Sam said.

"I agree."

"We'll see it doesn't happen. You and me. Okay?"

"Right on!"

Sam stared at him. "You're beginning to talk like us!"

He put a big arm around Guss's shoulders, and they
turned back to the main building.

They knew that the dead Peacekeepers had been taken
away by the security forces and that the females had been
working to bring the premises back to order. What they
didn't know, however, or perhaps had not yet learned was
that in the minds of females, the more things change, the
more they remain the same.

"Where've you been?" Lori scolded. "We haven't much
time."

"Time for what?"

"To get our things together before we leave! And
there's so much to do!"

Leave? Do?

And then Sam and Guss were reminded forcibly that
Lori wanted to go to the island of Tassar on her own
mission to push the button that would shut off the Shield—
if such an enormous task could be described in those
simple terms.

Wanted to go, nothing!

She was damn well *going* to go!

"Whoo, soss," Guss sighed helplessly.

Sam looked at him. "Couldn't agree with you more."

They both were then drawn into preparations, and,
once begun, they proved to be a pair of powerhouses.

"If we have to do it, let's do it right," Guss said.

"You got it!" Sam agreed.

"And doing it right," Lori said, taking charge, "means we're going to travel light. We've got to walk a long way, remember."

"And it's all uphill," Tippi said.

"*If*," Sissi said, trying to sound cheerful in the face of what seemed to her a calamity, "we can get through the Shield."

"Whaddayuh mean *if*?" Lori demanded. "You think I'm going to let that Shield stop *us*?"

"It's stopped everyone for thousands of years."

"We're not everyone. We're something else!"

"That I'll drink to!" Sam said. Under his breath.

Lori and her group approached the island of Tassar through light rain that was soon to become a downpour. For them it was the beginning of a perilous journey reached only after a most arduous beginning.

Obtaining a flight-craft with the range, speed, and load capability needed for the trip to the distant island had been their first and biggest problem. They had given it to Guss, and Guss had solved it in a simple and direct fashion.

He had stolen it from the military.

Evading the military had then become their next biggest problem. They had been able to solve that one, they were sure, only because they had been extremely clever and the government completely stupid.

Not so.

What they hadn't known was that the government, including President Ros Moss, had been aware of what they had been up to from the very beginning and had done everything in its power to further the appearance of its own stupidity.

As the government saw it, any effort in this hour of great national need was not only permissible but greatly desired.

"But an effort by a pregnant female bassoe?" an aide asked.

"It couldn't hurt," the president had answered.

Had Ros Moss known, however, how Lori intended to penetrate the Shield, he might have responded with something other than a borrowed phrase. He might even have been appalled.

Guss certainly had been. "Dig under?" he had asked in pain.

"You got a better idea?" Sam had been pretty belligerent with that question, because Guss had given such a pained response to Sam's simple request for shovels.

"But—*shovels*?"

"All right, so it's nutty," Sam had said. "But you got a human female, and she's preg, and you don't get her what she wants, you've got a problem. I mean a *big* problem!"

Guss had not been sympathetic. "We have nothing like that with our females in their egg-laying phase."

"Can't change the system, now, can we?"

"No, I suppose not."

"Shovels?" Sam was still belligerent.

"We have something similar," Guss said resignedly.

The question, to dig or not to dig, however, became moot almost at once. The eastern shore of the island was lava rock and coral, which put digging out of the realm of possibility. Once Sam had established the outer circumference of the Shield by throwing bullets at it, they had taken turns, while standing in the pouring rain, suggesting alternative possibilities for penetrating the Shield, none of which were better or more practical than digging under.

And that gave Guss reason to hope. "I have a concert day after tomorrow," he said casually.

"So what?"

"I can get you all free tickets. Very good seats—"

"Forget it," Sam told him. "This lady won't quit."

"Neither will this one," Sissi put in.

She and Lori went off together to exchange ideas. They could see the faint trace of the old trail, the trail of the Ancients, just as the charts had described it to Lori's observant eyes, just there beyond the reach of the surf, a scant hundred meters inside the Shield.

"Gotta find a way," Lori said.

The trail traveled along the bank of the little river as promised, a pretty little river that reached the sea inside the Shield on the left, spilling out of jungle growth of palm, fern, and vine-draped trees, then led enticingly toward the mountain lost for the moment in rain clouds. So near and yet so far beyond reach.

Sam and Guss stood disconsolately, wiping rain, hoping this idiot expedition would be abandoned soon.

Tippi and Illia walked away by themselves.

They were quite a pair. A small thirteen-year-old, mod, in her J.C. Penney high-school-age clothes—waist-tied pants, a jacket of off-white sheeting, and a nice sweater—and the native essan, a huge-eyed young lady who wore a coat of rain-slicked, soft gray fur as well as the bikinilike wear conventional modesty required. They were both blowing bubble gum, both anxious. They stopped on a lava rock above the pounding surf to watch the seas, to feel the wind.

"Look over there," Tippi said. She pointed to a cliff face half a kilometer away, where seabirds nested. Illia watched with Tippi as the birds dropped off the cliff face to sail out to sea and feed, while others from the sea swooped up to feed young in the nests with fish they had gathered.

Realization came to both of them at once. They looked at each other, eyes big.

"How about that!"

They turned and hurried back to the others, running, hopping from rock to rock, faces shining with the rain and excitement, hair blowing.

"Hey, Mom! We got it! We got it!"

"Got what?"

"How to get through the Shield!"

"You being a smarty?" Lori asked.

"Being serious."

Sam and Guss came over.

"So go ahead," her mother told her. "Be serious."

Tippi and Illia grinned at each other knowingly. Then, with some triumph, Tippi said, "Look at the birds."

Lori turned to watch the seabirds on the cliff face, dropping away, swooping back. She wiped rain from her face, scowled, puzzled. "So I'm looking," she said. "So what about the birds?"

"Mother! They're flying *through* the Shield!"

"Well, so they are!"

"If birds can do it, we can!"

"Fly through the Shield?"

"Get through it! Walking."

"But of course," Lori said, suddenly understanding. "And we're flesh and blood, just like they are!"

And she turned, as happy as if she had good sense, and hurried toward the Shield. Sam stared at her. It took a moment for his thoughts to percolate, but once they had, he leaped in pursuit of Lori and caught her just before she reached the perimeter.

"Hold on!"

"What in the world—"

"Ma'am! Those birds are wearin' feathers!"

"So?"

"The bullets didn't get through! It must be that if it's metal, it draws fire! We shoulda seen that from the start. Here, lemme try my cap—it's got gold braid on it."

He tried, and the cap got zapped.

Lori's eyes went huge and her legs weak. "You saved my life, Sam," she whispered.

"Wearin' metal, right?"

"You know it!"

Her wedding ring was gold. There was silver in the brocade on her blouse. Nor was that all. There were metal snaps in her clothing, a clip here, a zipper up the side . . .

"The clothes we're wearing," Sissi said weakly. "The cloth has metal woven in it."

"Mine, too," Guss said.

"I no need clothes," Illia said.

"I'm dead—a walkin' junkyard," Sam said.

"I'm okay. Brought my clothes from home," Tippi said.

Then, when she saw the way her mother was looking at her, she almost shrieked. "Mom! Come on, now! You can't do it. No way! You can't be serious! Not really!"

"Sorry, hon."

"But I'm size nine!"

"I'll manage somehow."

"Mom! I'd be practically naked!"

"But you're just a little girl," Lori said. "And I'm a mother."

CHAPTER 15

A thundering storm of rain with lightning and wind, a vertical downpour sluicing out of a sudden, massive gathering of dark clouds, had halted Ahmed Hassad's assault on the Shield over an hour ago. But Hassad had not written the hour off as wasted. He had used it instead to strengthen his position as a god.

This was a deluge of his making.

So he said.

Who else but a god could command a flood so fierce from the heavens?

Immediately it had begun, he had strode out on the open deck to stand with his arms wide, his head thrown back, roaring his order for more and yet more. Lightning ripped and tore in the heavens, thunder boomed enormously, rain poured down. And there he stood, exulting, water streaming from his face, his silken shirt plastered to his magnificent body, a striking, heroic, powerful figure.

If not of a god, what then?

The Ussirs, who were mortal, cowered in shelter, abused and afraid, and when the downpour ceased as suddenly as it had begun, few were able to say it had not stopped the moment Hassad dropped his arms.

Hassad thought he had timed it about right.

"Behold!" he roared then. "I am here!"

He paused a dramatic moment to be sure there was not an Ussir in range of his telepathic thundering who would fail to receive him, then he delivered an ultimatum to the god Uss, who most of the Ussir were sure lived on the mountaintop.

"Because you are evil, I am here, O Uss!"

The rich green complexion of many of the Ussirs paled. To call a god evil was to ask for a strike of lightning right on the spot, wasn't it? That the lightning did not strike Ahmed Hassad down just then was proof to many that Hassad's powers were as great as the powers of the god Uss.

Perhaps even greater.

"I shall overcome you, Uss!"

He shook both huge fists at the mountaintop.

"I shall smash you down!"

And he went on like that at some length.

A great performance.

Hassad could not remember ever having done better. Or anyone else ever having done better. He looked about at the Ussirs, who were staring at him transfixed, their forked tongues hanging out in what could only be translated as awe. A few fell to their knees, bowing to him, arms outstretched, worshiping.

"Fools," he said aloud as he made holy gestures over their heads. "Idiots! Clowns!"

They could not, of course, hear him. They assumed the vibrations meant he had blessed them.

Oss Tiss, the commander of the Ussirs, was not on his knees. He was glowering, his yellow, vertically slitted eyes beaming hatred. He did not believe in gods. But he did believe in the military convention which required absolute obedience to superiors, a convention almost as ridiculous as a belief in gods and certainly as binding.

Soo Toy was trying not to laugh. Crossing to her, Hassad growled out of the side of his mouth. "One giggle," he said. "Just one, and see what happens."

"I get hit in the face, right?"

"Try me."

"But Ahmed! It's such dreadful baloney."

"They believe it."

"Why?"

"Because they *want* to, you dummy!"

And now, with the weather rapidly clearing, it was time to resume the effort against the Shield. Yet another flight plan was handed to Oss Tiss. This one called for six craft to fly at the Shield in a formation that would cause them to reach the Shield at specified intervals. One was to lead. The second and third were to follow at an interval of two kilometers. Then a fourth and fifth were to go in at a higher altitude. And finally, a sixth at a lower altitude. The plan made no sense to Oss Tiss. None at all.

"They will be killed," he said to Hassad.

"You question my authority?"

"Only the method, sir."

Hassad might have been amused. "The method of a god?"

Oss Tiss's telepathic voice was an expressionless monotone. "I see the wreckage of eleven ships. I know after these six are gone, we will have but two left."

"Send them," Hassad said.

The ships were sent.

Hassad and Soo Toy watched from an upper deck.

Oss Tiss watched from a deck below.

Hassad thought it only sensible to have that distance between himself and Oss Tiss when these ships began crashing. Even a dedicated soldier has limits of self-control, and Oss Tiss had very nearly drawn his weapon and assassinated his commander when the last ships had died.

"Are these going to be destroyed?" Soo Toy asked Hassad.

"Probably," he answered.

The ships went out as bravely as the others had gone before them. Three of the pilots who flew the ships had seen the bassoe-god reveling in a storm he had himself wrought, a storm that had exceeded any other they had ever known in the ferocity of the thunder and lightning and in the fall of rain. They had seen him order the storm ended, and the storm had ended at his command.

Such a god could be trusted. Certainly obeyed.

Soo Toy watched the first craft, a brave and shining tube against the deep green of the forest, suddenly burst into a white flame. Then the second and third. The charred remnants fluttered down to join the others. Even though the pilots were essans—not human but reptilian—the spectacle of their lives being extinguished in an attempt so cold-blooded, so futile, was devastating.

"No, no, no," Soo Toy whispered.

Her beautiful, inscrutable Oriental face had somehow become very scrutable. Pain was there, and tears were in her large, almond-shaped dark eyes; her lips trembled.

"Gutless wimp," Hassad chided her.

"Beast!" she answered.

He laughed softly.

And then the fourth craft burst into white fire, tumbling.

But not the fifth!

And not the sixth!

Hassad yelled his triumph. "There y' are!"

"What happened?" Soo Toy asked.

"They're through!" Hassad bellowed. "Look at 'em go!"

The craft were indeed well through the Shield, wheeling in turns above the distant jungle, coming back unharmed. The chorus of telepathic cheering from every member of the expeditionary force was mind-bending. Various articles of clothing, mostly headgear, were being thrown into the air in an excess of jubilation. Arms were waved, eight-fingered hands clenched in gestures of victory.

Soo Toy was staring at Hassad. "You knew that was going to happen!"

He smiled. "Had to happen. The question was when."

"But *how* did you know?"

"I'm a god, remember?"

"Horse-doo!" she said.

"That's irreverent," he said mildly. "Even profane."

"But you're full of it!"

"Maybe a little," he conceded. "I'm also smart."

"So make me smart."

He lifted her chin with a finger. "A fact of war," he said. "There is no such thing as an inexhaustible supply of ammunition for any weapon. Even ray-guns can be emptied."

"And you emptied those by sending planes at one spot until—"

"Simple, wasn't it?"

"But you might have killed hundreds, thousands!"

He shrugged. "Whatever it took." And he smiled, pleased with himself.

"Monster," she whispered.

"Just so," he agreed.

He was still smiling, still pleased with himself, when he went to the deck below to enjoy the adulation of the crew, some of whom, to be on the safe side, again prostrated themselves facedown on the deck.

"Hassad, Hassad." The moan was the ultimate in reverence and obeisance.

Oss Tiss did not prostrate himself and did not moan. He could only stare with hatred at the huge, triumphantly smiling bassoe who had somehow managed to do the impossible. Not for a minute did he credit the beast with supernatural powers. How, then, had he broken the Shield that had turned back every attack for three millennia and more? Oss Tiss had no answer. But he did understand with absolute clarity that all one needed to be instantly confirmed a god was such a happening, a seeming miracle.

"Hassad, Hassad."

"You don't believe I'm a god?" Hassad asked Oss Tiss, needling him.

"No, I do not," Oss Tiss replied.

"All right." Hassad was beginning to like this stubborn green lizard. "You don't have to believe. What you do have to do is what I tell you to do. Or I'll have you shot."

"*That* I believe."

Hassad smiled. "You see? We've made progress."

They had not, of course, broken the Shield.

One of the pilots of the remaining flight-craft, an adventurous kind, more daring than sensible, tested the canopy at a greater height and was promptly blown into extinction. Another tried the airs at a lower elevation farther inland and suffered the same fate. Oss Tiss had grounded the remaining two. Two land-craft were put ashore, and they immediately proved to be of no practical value, since they could not operate in swamp or jungle.

"We're going to walk?" Soo Toy asked, pained.

"What else?" Hassad answered.

The party was assembled quickly. Seventy-five of Oss Tiss's Elite Guard, carrying full packs and such supplies as were considered essential to the comfort and well-being of a god and his delicate consort, made up the main body of the expeditionary force. They took ropes for climbing, machetes for clearing, small inflatables for the crossing of streams, tents for shelter, and weapons enough to protect against every conceivable danger.

Excepting the god, Uss, about whom they had only minor misgivings at this time.

Hadn't they their own god to safeguard them? The bassoe-god, Hassad, who had demonstrated his powers by calling down a storm of unprecedented proportions and who then had stopped the storm with a mere gesture of his arms. Hadn't he solved the problem of the Shield? What was there to fear, then, but fear itself?

There were no paths in the beginning. Beyond the beach lay a kilometer of swampy tideland. They waded, sometimes chest deep, through mud infested with all manner of detestable snaillike, wormlike, eellike, sucking, biting, flesh-drilling creatures that stuck, sucked, whined, and stung.

Soo Toy crossed this area riding on Hassad's wide shoulders.

Steaming jungle followed swamp, and here enormous vine-festooned trees soared high above a lesser canopy of fern and bamboo; huge butterflies flounced and bounced from enormous flower to enormous flower; reptiles exactly in the form of earthly snakes, though hugely longer and thicker, slowly coiled and squirmed through branches, looping, hissing; mammalian species, some with prehensile tails, some with leathery wings, some with great ears, some with eyes of incredible diameters, flew or swung branch to branch, booming, squeaking, calling raucously—the jungle was a green paradise where superfertility had created such an overabundance that beauty had become pestilential.

There seemed to be no end to it.

A day was spent in this clinging, cloying over-abundance, this beautiful morass, this perfumed hell.

Then another day.

And another.

Three days of their allotted five were gone. Three days passed, and they had not reached the nearest ridge.

Beyond the ridge, they knew, must be more cannon with unused, undiminished stores of purple ray and more jungle and more ridges, and if all this weren't enough to break the resolve of even the most determined, there was still more.

There were earthquakes.

The earthquake that had shaken Harry and his troop when they had reached the island had come and gone before Ahmed Hassad and the Ussirs had reached the shores of Tassar. This task force had experienced the tidal wave that had resulted from that quake while still at sea; they had waded through the tidal flats that had been hugely flooded and strewn with debris by the wave.

But nothing more.

They had been told there would be earthquakes. They had been told the earthquakes would be quite severe, growing more severe with each occurrence. And they had been told that within a stated number of days—five as the possible maximum and any lesser number as the minimum—the entire island was going to sink beneath the sea with a measured suddenness.

The part about the earthquakes they had believed.

But not the part about the island sinking beneath the sea.

It had not seemed to them a sensible notion that an event of that dimension could possibly occur outside of legend. Perhaps a small portion, a reef, a beach, could drop a meter or two—something like that. But not an enormous landmass the size of the island of Tassar. The scientific community had been rather certain about it, to be sure, but then, scientists were not always right about everything, now, were they? Weather forecasts, for example. How often did they get those right?

The first tremblings did not alter opinion.

The tremors were presaged as usual by a faint rumbling, distant, deep, and only faintly disquieting. Few of Oss Tiss's Elite Guard gave it serious notice. They were vibrations, after all, not *sounds* to the reptilian receptors. And the reptilians were deep in a hot and humid sarcophagus of green plant life where *all* vibrations echoed themselves into sinister proportions when those first vibrations came.

"Ahmed!" Soo Toy wailed. "What's happening?"

"An earthquake," Hassad answered. "Hang on."

"To what?"

"Me, if you like."

The faint rumbling built into a booming that came from everywhere at once as the ground beneath their feet became alive. As the ground surged with growing madness, the booming became an enormous boiling caldron of racket—creaking, cracking tree limbs, then a thundering crashing as shallow-rooted trees lost grip, tottered, and tore their way through the limbs and vines toward the ground, as birds screamed their fear and monkeys howled.

The ground heaved enormously, becoming suddenly a living thing, a monster of gargantuan proportions shaking in furious, crazy determination as if to rid itself of some infestation that had come upon its back to cause great pain.

The first contortion was followed by a second, then a third, each greater and more exaggerated than the one before, each more devastating, and it went on, and on, and on . . .

A happening so vast could not be of mortal design or deal alone with material things, soil, rock, water and air, or even stars; it could only be the work of a god who dealt with the all of everything.

A god angered beyond any mortal understanding.

A god with wrath so blazing, he had taken up the universe and had shaken it until all living things lay utterly destroyed or shivering in abject terror.

What god had such power?

Only one.

And it was not the minor god, the bassoe named Hassad.

The god Uss alone had the power to do such things.

And if he did such things, after being beneficent for years numbered in thousands, then he must have been angered hugely. And what had angered him? His place, so long revered, had been desecrated—that was what had angered him.

Mortals had dared set foot on holy land!

What could save them now, these violators?

Only departure, swift and immediate.

So they went. All of them, in great haste.

And then there was silence.

"Where did everybody go?" Soo Toy asked when she was finally able to lift her head out of the shelter of her arms and discovered that only Ahmed Hassad and the indomitable Oss Tiss were anywhere in sight.

"Took off," Hassad said. "Just plain cut and ran." He was looking at Oss Tiss with enormous contempt.

"A little earthquake," Hassad said, and his telepathic voice held a contempt equal to his stare. "And they ran. They ran back the way they came. A pack of yellow cowards."

"Green cowards," Oss Tiss corrected.

His telepathic voice was thin. He was stricken, bitterly ashamed that of his kind, only he had remained steadfast after the giant earthquake had ended. That he had remained steadfast had not meant he had not been equally terrified; it had meant that he had been held by a force even greater than terror. He had been held by hatred. Hatred of Hassad. He had not been able to run and, by running, admit that he was less, less in any way, than this damnable bassoe, Hassad.

Rather, he would remain until his soul blackened.

"Can you get them back?" Soo Toy asked.

"No."

"Then what are we to do?"

"We'll keep on," Hassad said.

He was still looking directly at Oss Tiss, his large, long-lashed brown eyes shiny with evil intent, finding and holding the huge, slitted yellow eyes of Oss Tiss, challenging, daring, questioning.

Oss Tiss did not blink.

"We must," Oss Tiss said. "We must go on."

CHAPTER 16

The one they called the god Uss had not caused the earth to convulse, the land to shake, the trees to fall, the waves to build and crash on every shore. He made no such pretensions. He knew he had no such powers. He knew he was not a god at all.

He was Old Mind.

He did not even live.

He existed.

In circuitry, in measured pulses of electrical energy, once powerful and crackling, now trickling glimmers of force grown feeble with the inexorable ravages of time, with the disintegration, the reversion to the randomness that must come to all things ever ordered, to pulse, to record, to think ever more slowly.

Which is not to live.

Existing, Old Mind was a thing of great ingenuity. He knew that to be true. He knew he had been constructed by creatures of keen intelligence and left to mystify those creatures whose abilities would be diminished, to be feared by those lesser creatures and therefore to be worshiped; to be credited with all manner of powers great and small.

And this amused Old Mind in a quiet, uncaring way.

If the creatures of the planet Essa, or of the planet Earth, chose to give him godly powers, let them. Perhaps when he was gone beneath the sea, as he would be soon, life would be given him. And if that life were no more life than the life that existed in a single cell—the power to become two cells, to reproduce—he would feel he had been exalted beyond any god.

He had tried once, himself, to create life.

The creatures of Essa had children, small reproductions of themselves that grew into creatures like themselves. Then why could he not have children? He could make them. He had made them. And he had made them not in his own image but in an image he thought better suited to the life he had wanted them to lead, an image called human. With arms and legs and heads with eyes and hearing and mouth parts, and minds that held the programs of children. Programs of games. Programs of joy and laughter.

They had given him delight. They had run and played as children.

They still ran, they still played, they still filled the woods with laughter—but they would never grow, never make others like themselves.

They were not alive.

They existed.

They were machines.

And he had made adult kinds. He had fashioned them in the same form, as if the children had grown. He had programmed them to be wiser, to occupy themselves with pursuits most common to the adult living creatures—and they still so occupied themselves.

Exactly, endlessly.

For they, too, were machines, not living things.

And he had made beasts of many kinds, in forms and shapes of beasts living and beasts long dead, to inhabit the waters and the forests, and they moved even now in their appointed ways, doing all things beasts had ever done. All things but one—they did not themselves make beasts of their own kind.

For they were not alive.

They, too, were machines.

And so was he a machine, not any kind of a god.

The true living creatures were the creatures of Essa,

the creatures of Earth. They had penetrated the Shield only now. Three groups, each led by creatures of Earth who had come to Essa bearing within them the spark, the fire, the will of the Ancients, a life-force of rugged strength, a willingness to challenge, to dare. And now they had but a few days to reach the Source, to end the Shield, if the wisdom of the Ancients was to be saved.

Each group would be tested—tested severely. Would they survive the tests that awaited them? Did they have the courage, the good sense, the will to overcome?

Would they succeed?

Old Mind thought not.

But then the thoughts of Old Mind were not really thoughts at all. They were only digits, zero through nine, arranging and rearranging themselves in infinite variety . . .

CHAPTER 17

After Harry Borg and his young men had crossed the first several hundred meters of land inside the perimeter of the Shield, they found themselves on the shore of a swamp. Here huge trees reared out of tidal waters, standing on great knees of root that arched like temple-roof supports, founded in sucking mud and lapped by tidal wavelets.

Odd, long-beaked, storklike birds picked daintily through the shallows. Strange booming, groaning sounds echoed out of the dark turns and spoke of other hungers.

"Seen better lookin' nightmares," Chad Harrison, at Harry's shoulder, said quietly.

"Nightmare is right," Harry said. "Only this nightmare is alive."

He stepped off the lava rock, dropping into water up to his chest, and started wading.

The water was warm, oily; the bottom was soft. Using his big arms much like oars, alternating strokes from side to side, Harry Borg powered his way across the first open stretch. Sometimes he sank until the surface reached his bearded chin; sometimes he reared out, streaming water, until he was only waist deep.

The strength of his drive pushed up a bow wave; he left a wake.

Chad dropped in immediately behind him. The others followed.

They had never seen trees of such height and girth or roots that tangled above their heads like columns supporting roofs, or waded in waters where swimming creatures rushed at them, nipped, and rushed away, where long-bodied insects hovered on transparent wings like giant hummingbirds sipping flowers.

They were strong young athletes, yet they were made to pant heavily with their efforts. They flinched when stung by poisonous plants; they swore when slime-coated globs of living matter boiled out of the sludge and stuck to bare skin with hideous blood-hungry kisses. They yelled their anger when slipping feet caused them to drop from sight.

Visions of dragons filled their minds.

Lesser fears tormented them: alligators; schools of pirhanas, razor-toothed, flesh-tearing; gape-mouthed hippopotamuses; water moccasins; electric eels. They saw none of these, yet these creatures were no less frightening unseen. They could be waiting just beyond the next great root.

Within a few more steps.

And then, with solid ground in sight, one of the giant roots proved not to be a root but a half-submerged length of giant reptile—in all reality, a dragon. The reptile suddenly lifted a huge head out of the yellow water, streaming, dripping swamp vine from opening jaws. Turtlelike, it had slitted eyes, a beaked mouth. And when the mouth gaped open, it stretched wide enough to engulf a man.

That man, Harry Borg.

The mouth descended on Harry Borg, the long forked tongue laving out toward him, the throat, a writhing pit, already working. Weaponless, condemned to hands-only combat by the Shield that had stolen their weapons, Harry Borg, dark blue eyes gone black and blazing, yelled a furious defiance and lunged.

Not away—straight forward.

Chad and Homer, somehow instantly at his shoulders, with Eddie and Arnie just at his back, lunged forward with him. Harry drove his big right arm deep into the gaping maw of the reptile, ironlike, grappling-hook fingers seeking flesh to grip. Chad's arms went over the ugly snout, and Homer's arm went under Harry's arm, wrapping the lower jaw in a wrestler's lock.

A hoarse roar came from the reptile. The great head shook.

Trying to rid itself of what had gripped it, the head thrashed the water into foam, going deep, then rearing up high to find that two more humans—Eddie and Arnie—had fastened on, tearing, gouging, ripping. Shake as it would, the giant reptile could not rid itself of the humans it had thought to eat. The head bounced the men on the water. The head flailed the men against arching roots. The head held them under the surface, grinding them into the muck. The entire body rolled and writhed and coiled. But still the humans clung, yelling in fear and anger.

Harry Borg's arm was sunk to his shoulders in the maw of the reptile, his own great muscles straining, his mouth contorted with effort, the cords of his neck rigid bars. Homer dragged the lower jaw down as if bulldogging a steer. Chad, back arched in a powerful bow, pulled the upper jaw back. Eddie and Arnie, each at an eye, tore at lids and clawed at pupils.

Flesh gave finally, deep in the throat of the reptile, with a suddenness that spilled Harry Borg back free.

He went under the surface of the roiled water, then burst into view again, draining, shouting triumph, holding aloft the reason for his triumph—the bleeding two-meter length of the forked tongue of the beast, torn out at the roots, still writhing and lashing in his fist.

"Let 'im go!" he yelled.

The others let go of the giant reptile, dropping off.

That creature, now a purposeless mass of convulsing coils, rolled away, seeking deeper water, safety, and an end to torment.

Harry Borg stood with chest heaving and threw the length of tongue after the beast.

He and the others looked at one another.

They howled.

They roared.

And when at last they went on wading, they were no

longer afraid. They had proved to themselves, and to any
that might have seen, that in this swamp or on any land
there was no greater terror, nothing to be more feared,
nothing more ferocious than the beast they themselves
became when they fought together.

Reaching solid ground, they plunged into jungle.

Here trees soared high above their heads. Looking up,
they saw levels of life layered among the limbs and leaves
and vines, like the strata of an ocean. Some life, high up,
flew and called raucously; some, lower down, swung
branch to branch on long furred arms and prehensile tails;
some, just at eye level, crawled or coiled; some, on the
ground, simply fed on lesser things.

And it was hot, steaming, humid.

They went on through the morning.

In the afternoon it rained. The downpour roared on
the leaves, spilled and splashed and soaked, and then
suddenly was gone. Suddenly, as if it had lingered beyond
its time onstage, a stage needed now for the earthquake
that was to follow.

The ground heaved and bucked, and trees fell. The
men moaned, clinging. And the sound of the quake boomed
like many cannon.

But it finally passed, leaving the men to understand
once again that they were not enormous and powerful,
after all, but only weak and human when weighed on the
true scale of things.

When night came, they reckoned they had come no
more than five kilometers away from the sea. Seven at
best. And there had to be still a great many yet to go.
And another day was gone. Another precious day out of
the beggarly few allotted to them.

At night they rested under a giant, arching fern.

"Couldn't be blacker 'n this inside a goat."

Thus had Harry Borg described the darkness when it
had come down on them with tropic suddenness. There'd
been no possibility of going even a few more strides after
the darkness had come: It was total. Groping for one
another, they had formed into a unit in the shelter of the
giant fern, communicating in the dark with disembodied
voices.

"Got a glob of somethin' here that sure as hell ain't ham on rye, but it's filling."

"Try some of mine."

"You want potato chips?"

"Got any?"

"Hell, no. Just askin'."

"Turkey!"

"That swamp water's fulla protein, y' know that?"

"Been strainin' it through my teeth."

"Like a baleen whale?"

"Only it ain't krill I'm eating."

"Trick is, don't get sick."

"'Fore we git to the top o' the mountain, anyway."

"Hey! Anybody want a piece of pie?"

"What kind?"

"Git him!"

"Offered pie, and you want a choice?"

"Sure."

"Here?"

"Anywhere."

"How come?"

"Only pie I eat's banana cream."

"There ain't no pie, y' dummy!"

"I know that."

"Then why not say you'll take coconut?"

"I don't like coconut."

"There ain't no coconut."

"No banana cream, either."

Voices in the dark. Talk to fill the blackness, the long and scary hours . . .

They broke out of the jungle on the third day, the heavy undergrowth giving way to a sea of grass that cut like saw-edged swords and grew head tall.

"Eddie, shinny up a tree and keep us on line."

The umbrella, acacialike trees grew at scattered, random intervals. High in the limbs, Eddie could see his comrades wading through grass, over-their-heads deep for the most part, and by yelling he was able to keep them going straight. When they had gone a half kilometer, Arnie took over from another tree, and Eddie caught up, following the trampled-down trail they'd left.

Time was slipping away.

Each quake, when it came, came sooner than the last and lasted longer. They were on a slight knoll, trying to recover from the terrors and the shaking of the quake just gone, trying to get some strength back.

"We can't do it this way," Harry Borg said.

He was lying flat on his back, staring at the sky. His chest was naked now, his shirt stripped into rags in the jungle and lost. Pants legs cut off. Boots tied with broken laces. Skin scored by thorns, hairy, oiled with sweat, but still covering muscles that were coiled power.

The young men waited, looking at him.

The bearded chin pointed to the sky, stretching, flexing. He opened his mouth wide, skinning his lips back from strong white teeth, and blew a powerful blast from his lungs. Then he sat up.

"From now on," Harry Borg said, "we make haste more slowly."

He got to his feet.

"Double time?" Chad asked. "Instead of a full gallop?"

"That's about it," Harry told him.

He led the way at a fast jog. "Got a long way to go and no time to get there."

They were out of the grass in another hour, and because they'd climbed in elevation, they were in a more temperate climate. The green jungle was behind them, as were the swamp and the sea. They were in foothills, broken country where steep-walled canyons became gorges and whitewater rivers ran furious and cold. They could see the mountain rising into clouds, and it seemed to move tantalizingly away as they fought to gain on it.

The first indication that they were not alone came in the form of a stone cairn, then a path that did not meander. A paved path.

"People built that," Harry said.

"Some kind of people," Chad agreed.

"Not supposed to be any here. It's inside the Shield."

"Who's been inside here to look?"

"Nobody. In a couple of thousand years."

"So they don't know, do they?"

"Could be anybody—anything."

"Wasn't fuzzy little animals, that's sure."

"Intelligent beings."

"Damn!" Harry Borg exclaimed.

They lost the path, found it again, and it became a narrow roadway. They walked carefully, searching ahead. Five men, half naked, all their faces bearded now, hair uncombed. They carried clubs and long sticks shaped into spears.

"Hold up!"

The late afternoon sun was slanting off a cliff face up ahead when Harry saw the first movement in the low trees. It was a furtive movement, not a fleeing one; a stalking approach. He waited motionless. The others, drifting into cover, waited behind him.

"Somebody up there," Harry said.

"I count two . . . three," Chad said behind him.

"They look human."

"Yeah, they do."

After watching for a few minutes, Harry Borg and his young men were able to agree that the creatures were more human than anything else. They were about the size of men, and they had the same general configurations— heads, arms, torsos, legs, feet. No hair. No noses. They had eyes, glinting and round, which meant sight. And hearing, for there were trumpetlike extensions on the sides of their heads which would qualify as ears. They wore no clothing, at least not clothing in the usual sense. What they wore, if anything, was skintight, shining, metallic.

And they were armed.

"Those are rifles of some kind," Homer said.

"But they don't fire bullets—our kind of bullets."

"Better'n our clubs, whatever they are."

"That's for sure."

"At ease," Harry said softly.

Then, after a few moments of silence and hard listening, he asked, "Any of you hear any talk between them?"

"Nothing," Chad said. "Nothing telepathic."

"They've got ears—maybe voices?"

"We'll see." Harry lifted his voice. "You, up there! We

come in peace. We don't want trouble. We don't want to harm you."

His big voice echoed off the walls of the canyon. And it did cause some reaction, a startled kind of twittering among them. Telepathic twittering. And it did reveal three more of the creatures, because these emerged from hidden places to look at the humans. But they still made no overt action.

"Will you let us by?" Harry called. "That's all we want—just to go past you and on up the mountain."

No answer.

"We're in kind of a hurry," Harry said.

Still no answer.

"Shoot!" Harry said. "They wouldn't know our language!"

He tried again, this time expressing the same thoughts telepathically. There was more twittering, and finally some movement. They did not approach. They moved strangely. They crossed the road to opposite sides. Then they crossed back again. They kept looking at Harry and his men, peering, swaying.

"Make up your minds," Harry muttered impatiently.

"I'll help them," Chad said.

He stepped out without asking Harry's permission and began striding up the road in the direction of the creatures. His approach caused immediate twittering, as if the creatures understood they were being challenged.

"Hold it, son!" Harry said.

Chad stopped.

"Give them a chance," Harry told him. "See what they'll do."

After a moment, one of them lifted his weapon and pointed it at Chad. There was no sound of a shot. There was no flash of light, no beam of any kind. The creature lowered his weapon, and Harry breathed a sigh of relief.

"Thought he was going to shoot you," he said to Chad.

"He did," Chad answered.

"What d' you mean?"

"He shot me. I've been hit."

"Say again," Harry said in sudden alarm.

"I've been hit. I can't move."

It was only then that Harry realized Chad was communicating telepathically. "Can't move? What the hell?" He went forward at once and reached Chad, who was standing motionless in the center of the narrow roadway, to find the young man staring fixedly ahead, suddenly not a man but a carved statue.

"God almighty Christ!" Harry swore.

He reached out to take hold of Chad, an instinctive movement, a need to shelter the lad somehow, and when his arms were at full length, his hands just touching Chad, he saw out of the corner of his eye a weapon in the hands of a creature level at him.

He didn't feel any pain. He just lost control.

"Hell!"

His movement had put all his weight on one foot, and under normal circumstances this change of balance would have required the shifting of his other foot, but he could not move that other foot, so he tipped and fell into Chad like a tree falling, arms and legs and everything else frozen into position.

Eddie, Arnie, and Homer yelled and charged.

And they were caught in midstride and frozen, too.

They fell however their movement and bodies required them to fall when all muscle mobility was suddenly locked. Now all five of them were lying on the road and off it like knocked-over carved statues.

Statues with telepathic voices.

"What the hell's goin' on?"

"Zapped us!"

"Those little buggers."

"Some kind of pieces. Shoots nuthin' at you."

"Nothing? You call this nothing?"

"I'm good as dead."

"But you ain't dead."

"All right! But I can't move!"

"You ain't dead!"

"Then I'm the next thing to it."

CHAPTER 18

The children were so cute!

Five, six, seven years old. Boys and girls about even in numbers, though it was hard to tell which were boys and which were girls, because their clothing varied only in color and they were so alike in most other ways.

They had huge, round, violet-colored eyes, laughing eyes, in sweet and happy faces. "Elves" was the word that came first to mind. They had pointy little ears that peaked out of red curls, four-fingered hands, and feet encased in calf-high boots of soft leather. They wore green velvet shorts with biblike fronts and shirtwaists brightly colored. And there were little silver bells fixed to the peaks of their caps that rang sweetly as they ran.

Twenty of them. Thirty? Perhaps more.

How could they be counted? They were never still.

They had come suddenly out of a sunny patch of woodland, running eagerly to meet the group trudging up the trail of the Ancients; they came with happy cries, the sound of silver bells, and joyful laughter. Suddenly they were everywhere about, a wonderful greeting for tired eyes, tired minds, and tired bodies.

Sam Barnstable, walking point a hundred meters ahead of the others, heard the silver bells and held up a hand for the others to delay until he had sorted out this new sound.

And when he saw the children, a sudden smile warmed his face.

How could one not smile, not laugh, with so much joy and happiness spilling everywhere?

Lori Borg, walking second, hurried up to join Sam, and they stood together among the little creatures—they had to be children, hadn't they?—extending their arms to take the eager gripping hands that reached out to them. Some offered flowers that were marvelously fragrant; some offered fruit that was like great purple grapes in delicious clusters, sweet and juicy, so welcome to hungry mouths.

"Good heavens to Betsy!" Lori said. "Sam, what are they?"

"Beats me," Sam said, smiling. "A welcoming committee?"

"So many of them!"

Tippi and Illia hurried up.

"Like school's out someplace," Tippi said. "Or maybe there's a picnic, and the parents are near."

Sissi and Guss, who came up last, were baffled.

"They look like human children," Sissi said.

"On Essa?"

"They're not bassoe young."

"What can they be?"

"I have no answer."

They stood among the little ones, who ran about constantly, pushing at one another, jumping over each other, tumbling. Sitting down finally to rest, the humans—including Illia, the fur-covered native of this planet, Essa—ate hungrily of the grapelike fruit that was brought them.

Sissi and Guss did not eat. Their taste, more reptilian than mammalian, found the sweetness of the fruit unappealing, and perhaps, since they were reptilian, they were less enthralled by the drove of what seemed to be offspring of some mammalian species. They stood together, apart from the others, not for a moment resenting the chance for rest and amusement that had come to the humans so unexpectedly.

"They *were* tired," Sissi said.

"Hungry, too," Guss agreed.

These two had managed to forage on small creatures, caught and eaten along the way, but the humans had fared less well since they spurned insects and required meat to be cooked.

They had reached this plateau early in the morning. It had been on their third day from the sea, their third day inside the Shield. The agony of the swamp—that thigh-deep morass of muck and weeds and steaming heat that had confronted them once they had gone a kilometer into the island—had been a nightmare.

Nakedness had been a problem.

More for the males than the females. Sam had been most severely distressed when given the choice of divesting himself of almost all clothing or remaining behind, and for him the waist-deep mucky water had been a welcome covering. Guss, too, had been severely tested. All of his clothing had contained metal threads in the weave, and that had meant he had to go bare through the first day and a half—at a distance from the others.

"Don't be a shiss!" Sissi had scolded him.

"I am not a shiss," Guss had responded from behind a tree. "I just don't think it is proper to make a public display of myself."

"If we have to, we have to!" Sissi said.

"I don't have to," Guss had answered. "Not as long as I can find trees to hide behind."

"You don't see me cowering in false modesty, do you?"

"But you're a female," Guss said. "You're nice to look at."

"Oh, foss!" she answered, pretending more anger than she felt.

Illia, with fur, had never felt the need of clothing.

The young human female, Tippi, had been very embarrassed when forced by the greater need of her mother—or had it been the seniority of her mother?—to yield her clothing to the older woman, who had managed with great ingenuity to fashion the teen-style slacks and shirt into covering for a pregnant woman. But mischief had soon overcome Tippi's embarrassment.

"You looked!" she had chided Sam, whose face had been a constant flaming red in those first hours. "I saw you look. Out of the corner of your eyes."

"Hell, yes!" Sam had answered, furious. "I looked! I looked! You're so damned cute, I can't help it!"

Tippi's eyes had sparkled. "It's all right if you look— once in a while."

And after the swamp came the jungle.

In the jungle there were leathery leaves to provide almost adequate covering when sewn together with thread-strong vines. And the need of any covering at all became secondary compared with the real necessities: food and clean water, protection from enormous insects, carnivores, pouring rain, and earthquakes that seemed determined to shake the jungle trees down about their heads. Then, as they gained altitude, they had climbed out of the jungle along the trail of the Ancients and had come finally to the plateau and the delightful children.

"Sure seems good to sit down for a while," Sam said, sighing heavily and contentedly. He had found a place to sit on comfortable turf in the shade of a large tree. Lori sat with her back against the same tree. Tippi and Illia were close by, Sissi and Guss at a distance. The humans and Illia were making a much-needed meal of the grapes the children had brought them. Sissi and Guss shared carefully rationed meat of their own liking at a little distance from the others.

"Those are not the young of any bassoes I ever saw," Guss said again.

"No," Sissi agreed.

"Harmless?"

"Apparently."

The happy children ran and laughed and played about the humans, a milling little throng that gathered to a dozen or more, then thinned to number only one or two as some ran off to the sunny woods in search of some pleasure of their own.

"I can't read any intelligence in them," Guss said. "No words. No conversation."

"Buzzing," Sissi said. "That's all."

"Are they communicating?"

"With each other? I don't know."

"They seem to be. They respond to something."

"Move together. Like a flock of birds."

"Birds don't communicate."

"One moves, they all move—something like that."

"I'm waiting for the adults to show themselves," Sissi said.

"Adults," Guss said thoughtfully. "These juveniles are all about the same age. Means the adults would be the same."

"Very strange."

"The adults could be dangerous."

"Let's hope not."

But no adults came in an hour.

Lori Borg, sitting with Sam against the tree, her hunger satisfied for the first time since their adventure had begun, had never felt better, she decided, than she felt right now. It seemed to her that all her aches and pains—those due to her pregnancy and those due to unaccustomed physical exertion—had all decided to take some time off: She didn't hurt anyplace.

"Y' know something?" she said to Sam. "I feel good."

"Same with me," Sam said. He smiled at her, his button-nosed face relaxed, content. "Funny what a little food will do for you. I mean, you get a full stomach, you get a whole new outlook on life."

"Those grapes are filling," Lori said.

"Have to take some with us when we go."

"Let's don't go for a while."

"No need to. We can use some rest," Sam said.

"I agree."

"An hour or so. What's the harm in that?"

"Do us good in the long run."

"We've got the time."

"How about you, short stuff?" Sam asked Tippi. "How're you doing?"

"Never better." Tippi was lying on her back, watching clouds go by. "Just resting."

"Illia?"

Illia was lying beside Tippi in the soft grass, her great coppery-brown eyes dreamy; she was holding a large and fragrant flower against her nose.

"Me, too," she said. "I'm fine."

"She sounds like Chad," Sam said to Lori. "Illia, I mean. Fine is a word Chad uses a lot."

"Figures," Lori said dreamily. "Married to him and all. That she'd talk like him, I mean."

"And they said bassoes didn't have any smarts."

"Sure they do! Illia's as smart as anybody."

"Got a permanent mink coat, too," Sam pointed out.

"And that's not such a bad idea." Lori had edged her back lower on the tree trunk, then lower still, until she was finally extended full length on the soft turf. She cradled her cheek on her arm and sighed comfortably. "I could use a little snooze," she said.

"You earned it, ma'am."

"Forty winks?"

"Take all you want."

"Tippi," Lori called, her eyes closed.

"Yeah, Mom?"

"Take a nap. While we've got the chance."

"Just what I was gonna do." Tippi closed her eyes. And so did Illia.

Watching the humans fall asleep one by one, Guss and Sissi were surprised but not concerned. The humans had been getting very little sleep these past three days. They needed the deep rest if they were to have enough strength to get to the top of the mountain in the next day or two.

The little children seemed to have lost interest. They had fluttered away like a flock of birds searching for new interests once the humans had fallen asleep. And Guss and Sissi, in the silence and the warm sun, found it hard to stay awake.

"You sleep, I'll watch," Sissi said.

"No, I'll watch," Guss told her. "You sleep."

Sissi watched as the gray inner lid finally closed over his eyes; then the outer lids closed, and he fell asleep in spite of his good intentions. The air was warm, the breeze light, the grass soft, and they were all so very . . . tired . . .

Sissi felt her eyes close.

The earthquake awakened them with the great booming of unseen cannon, the lifting of the ground, the dropping away, the deep shaking. For Guss and Sissi, the old terrors came back with their sudden awakening. Was this the final quake? Was this the one that would drop the island beneath the sea? When they were awakened, and when they clutched the convulsing ground that heaved and bucked like some insane animal, they were sent almost out of their minds with fear.

But for the humans it was different.

Tippi yelled happily, "Hey, Mom—a Magic Mountain ride!"

Lori agreed. "And it's free!"

Sam and Illia joined in the fun, riding the shakes, calling out their enjoyment. Though the humans were vocalizing, Guss and Sissi could not fail to understand that something had gone very wrong with their companions. They were enjoying the quake! Their faces were smiling; the vibrations of their vocalizing were those the reptilians had learned were associated with laughter.

"Lori!" Sissi called telepathically. "What's wrong with you?"

"Wrong? Nothing's wrong!"

Another great shuddering of the earth brought more vibrations from the humans—peals of laughter from the females, a side-splitting, knee-slapping roar from Sam. Guss and Sissi looked at each other, a new terror in their wide, golden eyes.

"Guss—they've lost their minds!"

"Osis! They *are* mad!"

Did a massive overload of fear affect humans in this way? Did some inner safety mechanism trigger insanity so that the human mind was spared the awful reality? This quake, far the worst yet experienced, could well signal the end of the island, the end of their lives, and yet instead of crying out in terror, they were riding the giant tremors with expressions of joy.

"Wheeee!"

"That was a big one!"

"Eeeeek!"

"Ride 'em, cowboy!"

"Whoops!"

"Hey, Mom! Look at me! Wow!"

"Hang on, hon! Here's another—one! Oh, good heavens!"

"Yah . . . wow . . . wheee!"

And while the giant tremors lasted—thundering, booming, causing trees to topple and great rockfalls on distant cliffs and dust clouds to rise enormous, ballooning—the humans rode the quakes with shouts of laughter and yells of pretended fear like riders on some gigantic roller coaster. When the violence finally ended and the ground became still again, they lay about exhausted from their merriment, panting, hiccoughing as laughter drained, giggling, silly.

"Goshawmighty, what a ride!"

"You can't find rides like that one in Magic Mountain."

"No way!"

Guss got to his knees, shaking his head; his long, forked tongue hung limp as he fought to control the panic that had all but consumed him. When he could trust himself to stand, he crossed to take Lori's chin in his eight-fingered hand, to tip her face up so he could look into her eyes.

"What happened to you?"

She met his concerned stare with amusement in her wide gray eyes. "Guss! Come on! Nothing happened to me! What's wrong with *you*? Can't you enjoy life anymore?"

"Enjoy life!" His telepathic voice was almost a yell. "That was death! Death staring you in the face!"

"Oh, bosh!"

"That was fun!" Tippi giggled happily. "Oh, golly!" She had laughed so much, her side hurt.

Illia was shaking her head weakly.

Sam said, "A gas . . . a triple-plated gas—that's what it was!"

The little children returned then.

"Hey, kids! Kids! C'mere!" Lori called.

A flock of the children, perhaps ten or more, had come

out of the sunny woods, running, the silver bells tinkling, their faces bright with happiness. Tippi and Illia met them, caught little four-fingered hands in their own, and began dancing in a joined circle.

"C'mon, Sam!" Lori cried, getting to her feet. "Let's join them!"

"Right with you!" Sam got eagerly to his feet, caught up two of the little children, set them on his shoulders, pranced, and sang. They circled for several moments, then Lori stopped them.

"I know what let's do!" she cried. "Let's play run sheep run!"

"What's run sheep run?" Tippi asked.

"It's a game. Come on! I'll show you."

Before Guss and Sissi's unbelieving eyes, Lori Borg, the big and beautiful human female, the female who had devised a scheme even better than the one devised by Harry Borg, who had had the wit, the strength, and the determination to get them this far, had quite suddenly become a happy child and was now leading them all into the sunny woods, running, skipping, and laughing joyfully.

"Lori! You can't!"

"Come back, Lori!"

But Lori and the others went on, unheeding.

CHAPTER 19

The pterosaur snatched up Soo Toy late on the fourth afternoon.

She was alone when it came. The ordeal of the swamp, followed by the jungle, had reduced her to what she thought of as a smelly, unsightly little blob of yukkk—a far cry from the exquisite jewel of femininity she had always prided herself on being—and when a clear pool in the higher elevations beyond the jungle had offered a chance to make repairs, she had insisted she be allowed at least an hour alone to tend to her personal needs.

She was sitting on a rock in the open after bathing, working her waist-long jet-black hair into braids, when the pterosaur came upon her from behind, extended two giant, clawed feet, clamped them about her waist, lifted her, and carried her away.

Screaming.

Now the huge, leathery-winged, long-billed creature with a wingspan of at least fifteen meters was gaining height slowly but inexorably, flying toward distant cliffs.

"Aaaaaiiieee!" Her scream was of pure terror.

The ground was dropping away.

The great clamping claws held her securely, easily, without breaking her bones or even penetrating her skin. She looked up and saw a huge head with a long, serrated

beak and enormous eyes; she looked out and saw the
skin-covered, bony, featherless wings, the tips so far away,
beating slowly up and down in long mechanical strokes.

"Ahmed! Ahmed—Help! Help meeeee!"

She saw Ahmed Hassad, Oss Tiss, and the few returned
Elite Guards frozen by the fire, staring up, growing distant, dwindling as the great creature gained altitude.

"Soo! Damn! Good Christ!" Ahmed's cry was startled,
then raging—both vocal and telepathic.

"Help me, Ahmed!"

"Bloody hell!"

What could he do? She was out of reach.

He was helpless, furious.

He had snatched up one of the spears he and Oss Tiss
had been shaping by hardening the tips of long sticks in
the fire, but he was too late to do anything but curse and
watch her go.

"Why didn't someone watch her?" Hassad stormed.

"You said no!" Oss Tiss replied.

"But from a distance—aw, hell!"

There was no use railing at the Ussirs; he, Hassad,
had been equally to blame. As he watched now, the creature caught a thermal updraft, stiffened its wings, and
rode effortlessly upward, spiraling toward a distant cliff-
top aerie.

"She's gone!" Oss Tiss said. His moan held finality.
And self-rebuke. He felt the loss as much as Hassad,
though in a different way. His loss was the mark it made
against his military prowess, his ability to keep all near
him safe, while Hassad's loss was one of a personal kind,
the loss of a loved one.

At least a valued one.

"Should have watched those birds!" Hassad swore.

They had seen the pterosaurs perched high on the cliff
the moment they had reached the ridge top after clearing
the jungle. Since the creatures had shown no interest in
them, they had lost interest in the creatures—certainly
there were many more immediate problems close at hand
that required immediate solutions.

The making of weapons, for example.

As they watched now, the pterosaur carrying Soo Toy

gained enough altitude to enable it to glide in on a vacant aerie identical to those being used by two others and, with a series of quick wing beats, settle there.

"Ahmed . . ." Soo Toy's telepathic cry was clear enough.

Hassad sent a telepathic call back to her. "Soo . . . Soo! Are you hurt?"

"Damn. Yes!"

"How bad?"

"Scratched to hell. Bruised . . ."

"Bleeding?"

"Not—not yet! Just—scratches."

Although Hassad and Oss Tiss could not see Soo Toy at that distance, her telepathic messages seemed to be telling them she had not yet been seriously hurt. Frightened almost beyond sanity but not crushed, not torn, not bleeding.

"Don't fight it!" Hassad told her.

"Fight it—what are you saying?"

"Is it—"

He wanted to say, "Is it going to eat you?" but he couldn't bring himself to it. Instead he said, "What's it doing?"

"Just standing on me."

"The others?"

"Doing nothing, just standing."

And from the distance, as nearly as Hassad could tell, the other two pterosaurs were ignoring the first pterosaur and the meal it had brought. One might have expected there would have been a squabble, a contest for the meal, but there was none.

"Are you in a nest?" Hassad asked.

"Don't know what it is—smells awful. A great pile of bones—that's what it is!"

"Bones? You mean sticks?"

"I mean bones!"

And they were bones.

Soo Toy, pressed down into a pile of stinking putrescence by a great claw across her torso, was beginning to think rationally again now that her initial, mind-burning terror was subsiding.

"Oh, my God . . . oh, my God."

"Soo Toy . . . Soo Toy." Hassad's telepathic voice, full of helplessness for the first time she could remember, came through to her, trying to comfort her.

The great beast had folded its wings. She looked up a massive, powerful leg with faintly scaled skin to a big, boat-shaped breast, then to a long neck that looped back, folded down on itself in repose, and finally to a huge, wedge-shaped head out of which a beak at least two meters long was thrust. Large, milky, violet-colored eyes stared off into nothingness. As she watched, a gray, thin-skin inner lid closed across the eyes like a curtain being drawn. A rickety, clickety, satisfied purring sound that came from inside the breast of the creature slowed, then stopped.

"What's it doing?" Hassad's telepathic voice asked, full of anguish.

"Nothing," she replied.

"Nothing?"

"Gone to sleep, I guess. Like the others."

"What d' you mean, gone to sleep?" Hassad was angry, incredulous.

"It closed its eyes. It quit purring."

"*Purring?*"

"Ahmed—please!"

"I'm sorry."

"All I know is what's *happening*." Soo Toy's telepathic communication degenerated into a continuous wail of fear and despair.

"It brought me here—it's standing on me—in this stinking god-awful mess—forgot me—went to sleep—eyes closed . . ."

"Don't wake it up!"

"Get me out of here! Ahmed, get me out!"

"I will! I will!"

Soo Toy, panting in terror, tried to control herself. She had been almost nude at the moment of her capture, and lying now under the foot of the enormous beast, crushed into the rotting slime, she looked, and felt, especially violated. Even desecrated.

"Oh, yakkkkkk!" she gagged.

She was on a pile of decaying corpses—she could see

that now. Animals of all kinds, victims like herself, captured and brought here. Some recent, some old, some ancient. An enormous pile. Looking across a short distance, she could see that the other monstrous flying reptiles were standing on identical heaps. There were decaying carcasses at the top of gigantic piles, turning to bones. As her eyes traveled down, the heaps became crumbled bits and pieces of very old bones, then dirt, then rock.

Meter upon meter upon meter . . .

Centuries of victims rotted away . . .

Victims like herself . . .

She screamed wildly, silently.

After they had penetrated the Shield, after the giant earthquake had sent Oss Tiss's Elite Guard running in terror of the great god Uss, Ahmed Hassad, Soo Toy, and Oss Tiss had gone on.

Soo Toy had ridden on the back of Hassad when the tangle underfoot had become so deep that her short and slender legs had been unable to stride properly, so she clung with her arms around his neck and her legs clamped about his waist as he tore his way through the deep ferns, ripped aside vines, and stripped fronds that barred his way, seemingly unaware of her presence.

Oss Tiss had sometimes taken the lead, giving Hassad a breather, and though he had chosen his way with greater finesse, he had been no less determined and had maintained almost an equal speed.

On the third evening, as they had crouched beneath a sheltering fern, eating fruit, the first of the Elite Guard who had deserted in such panic during the monster quake had begun to filter quietly in along the back trail, joining up again and bringing with them what gear and supplies they had not lost in their panic when they had fled. Soon there had been three, then five, then, finally, eleven.

Hassad had made no comment. His curled mouth, his look of disdain had said enough.

The solution to the problem of the deadly purple rays had come about for Hassad and his party much as it had for Harry and for Lori—the fact that organic material was unaffected became obvious after a time, and they found in their turn that they could move at will if they divested themselves of weapons, supplies, communication gear, and all that was metallic.

Which meant they, too, had to go bare-handed.

Then, after they had worked their way out of the jungle and to higher ground, with a measure of safety at last, and with the need to feed themselves, to rest, and to make some kind of weapons, they had stopped to build a fire.

The site was near a pool of fresh, clear water.

This was where Soo Too had bathed—and where the pterosaur had found her.

Hassad was standing in the late-afternoon sun, head thrown back as he stared at the distant cliffs. His red silk shirt had been torn all to ribbons, leaving his big chest and his muscular arms bare. His fist gripped a fire-hardened spear so long and heavy that the strongest of the Ussir Elite Guard could have managed it only by using two hands.

"I'm going to get her back," he said.

But how? Oss Tiss wondered silently.

True, the human was formidable. But he was no god— Oss Tiss would not concede him that. He was as powerful as a half dozen essans, certainly. But there are some things even the most formidable of creatures cannot do.

"Those cliffs are impossible to climb," he said quietly.

"I know that," Hassad agreed.

"And we have no time to spare for your female."

Hassad threw back his head and laughed. "We've got the time, bucko! And we're going to take it!"

They heard a telepathic wail from Soo Toy, distant, pleading. "Ahmed, please!"

"Hang on, sweetheart! I'll save you!"

Oss Tiss could not believe what he had just heard. The human was here, far away from the cliff-top aerie where the female human was being held, presently to be torn apart by the long, swordlike beak of the creature, bit by bit, and gobbled down, and the human had told her he was going to save her.

Ridiculous!

And yet the human seemed so sure!

The human hefted his heavy spear, found it too clumsy for his purpose—whatever that might be!—tossed it aside, then ran to the rock where Soo Toy had been sitting when she had been taken by the flying monster.

Hassad stretched himself out there, as if offering himself as a sacrifice.

"You're mad!" Oss Tiss's telepathic voice was both furious and appalled.

"I'm going after her," Hassad answered.

"That beast won't come after you!"

"Want to bet?"

"If it did, you'd die!"

"I'm a god, remember?"

"You are not!"

"Hard to kill, anyway!"

Hassad was lying flat on his back on the top of the rock, watching the distant pterosaurs and flopping his arms to attract attention.

"If I don't come back, you're in command!" he told Oss Tiss.

"I'm in command now!" Oss Tiss screamed. "You've lost your mind!"

A sudden, frightened, moaning telepathic cry came from the Elite Guard at that moment. They had seen the pterosaur that had taken Soo Toy lift its head and stretch its neck. Now the enormous wings opened, and the creature lifted from the aerie, wings beating, seeking thermals. Finding one, it wheeled, sailing, and began a long glide that would bring it on the same path it had used to snatch Soo Toy from the rock where Ahmed Hassad was lying.

Soo Toy's screech came faintly to Hassad. "Ahmed, he left me. He flew away."

"He's coming after me," Hassad told her.

The pterosaur was indeed following the same glide path it had taken before. At a distance of several hundred meters from the rock, the creature lowered its enormous clawed feet to reach for Hassad. The giant wings lifted, slowing the great beast to a near stall, the clawed feet extended.

"Yah . . . woweeee!"

Hassad's yell was vocal, an excited cry.

He raised himself to meet those giant, reaching claws. He leaped at them, avoiding the filth-covered points, finding a purchase around the ankle, and clung there as he was swept away. His greater weight was almost too much for the giant creature. The huge wings had to beat hard to keep the beast from crashing into the ground beyond the rock, but weight was finally overcome, height gained, and a slow ascent was begun.

"On my way!" Hassad sent that telepathic message to Soo Toy.

The message was received as well by Oss Tiss and his Elite Guard. They had watched with amazed horror as the human had given himself in sacrifice to the evil demon. If there had been any reservations regarding Hassad's status as a superbeing, they were gone now. No mortal could possibly do such a thing. Oss Tiss, who did not believe in superbeings, could only curse.

He watched the human, Hassad, small in the distance now, clinging to the legs of the winged monster, being carried upward toward the aerie of bones atop the cliff.

Gone now, lost certainly.

And the mission was finally his.

CHAPTER 20

In the capital of Foss, in the palace, behind the golden doors, there was a "war room," hastily constructed to serve in this time of extreme emergency. Here Ros Moss, the elderly leader of the Jassan nation, was now spending all his waking hours.

One entire wall had been given over to a graphic representation of the island of Tassar. The Shield appeared as a nearly opaque dome that covered the island almost entirely, with only small areas of land extruding beneath the edges at various places around the outer perimeter.

The interior of the island, that area that lay beneath the dome, was indicated in faint outline, because the cartography was, as Harry Borg had discovered, inexact. The mountain plateau, the ancient buildings that housed the Source, and, of course, the Lassa Crystal were depicted by lines Ros Moss knew to be only approximations, since the positions had been taken from maps many centuries old.

There were lights to indicate the areas where assaults had been made and were currently being made. Blinking blue lights in two locations near the top of the dome told Ros Moss that his missile corps were hurling explosive devices at the Shield in a continuing effort to rupture it and that flight-craft were dropping bombs from very great heights with the same intent.

Neither the missiles nor the bombs were very powerful, because the very powerful varieties had been outlawed by the Jassan and Ussir nations a very long time ago. Of what use a war if there were to be no survivors? And certain care had to be taken in rupturing the Shield, if indeed the Shield could be ruptured. Of what use was a broken shell if the contents were hopelessly scrambled?

The blinking green lights indicated areas in which the Ussirs were engaged in the same sorts of attacks, with the same sorts of results.

The red lights indicated areas where the humans had made their effort. Those lights did not blink. The male human Harry Borg and his young warrior males had been put ashore at the South Cliss, and the last reports that had come to Ros Moss had indicated they had attacked the Shield at once and had been lost at once. The red light had been left on only as a reminder.

"You are certain they were killed?" Ros Moss had asked.

"The Shield is still intact, and they are gone," Os Riss, his portly field commander, had answered, with a satisfaction barely concealed. A veteran, heavily medaled, he had been against using the humans from the very beginning, and he was satisfied they had not succeeded where he seemed to be failing.

"No word at all from them?"

"None."

"But I am told communication from within the Shield is not possible."

"That is correct, Your Highest."

"How, then, do you know they are dead?"

"A kliss of our very best Elite Troops—all volunteers—were sent to investigate, and they were vaporized immediately upon encountering the Shield at that same point on the South Cliss."

"The humans, then, were vaporized?"

"That is our assumption."

"And the female human?"

"The party of the female human, which included the

sissal-player Guss Rassan and his consort, Sissi, has most certainly suffered the same fate."

"Nothing of them was found?"

"Nothing, sir."

"Outside the Shield?"

"Outside. It was not thought necessary to sacrifice more troops by sending them against the Shield at this point, though volunteers were available."

"And what do you know of the efforts of the human the Ussirs used on Kloss Reach? Ahmed Hassad, I believe he was called."

"We have learned they did achieve a penetration. But it was only for a short distance and of short duration. Survivors who managed to return reported the balance of the party was destroyed. That would certainly include the human known as Ahmed Hassad."

"And our efforts with missiles and bombs?"

"They continue."

"With what success?"

"None at this time."

"You are aware that we have been given only this day and one more before the island will sink?"

"I am, sir."

"Do you think you will be able to demolish the Shield or at least force an entry through it in that length of time?"

What could only have been intense anxiety widened the yellow eyes of the old soldier and caused his hands to tremble. "I am certain we will succeed," he said.

"And I am certain you are lying."

Now, at this moment, staring at the steadily glowing red lights, remembering that report, Ros Moss seemed to grow older, more weary, more bent. His bony shoulders sagged; his gray, lightly scaled skin had the unhealthy pallor of an old man who has worked too hard, too long. But there was still an unyielding fire in his large yellow eyes, only slightly scored by the narrow vertical line of the pupils; his tongue flicked, tips curling.

Yes, he had known from the beginning that sending the human Harry Borg and his young warriors had been a desperate measure with no real hope of success. The same had held true for the human female, the mate of Harry

Borg, though Moss had pretended not to be aware of her effort. The emergency had been—and still was—so great that *every* effort had to be made.

And though he had, from the very beginning and in all honesty, expected that the humans would die in their attempt, he had felt no real guilt about it.

He was fighting a war.

He was fighting a war against darkness.

A makeshift Source had been built that would provide energy after a fashion once the Source on the island of Tassar was lost beneath the sea if—and this was indeed a big if—the Lassa Crystal could be saved.

If the Lassa Crystal could not be saved or, perhaps even worse, if it were to fall into the hands of the Ussirs, all of Jassa would suffer years of the most severe tribulation.

To lose soldiers, human or essan, when fighting such a war was not only to be expected, it was to be accepted willingly, as long as the losses were shared equally, and he was sparing his own kind not at all. Every essan whose death might possibly improve the chances of the Jassans' gaining control of the Lassa Crystal would be sent to die.

But were the humans dead?

What real proof did he have of their deaths? They had tried to penetrate the Shield; they had disappeared. Others who had attempted the same thing had been seen to die. But then, the others had not been a human named Harry Borg. Or his mate for that matter. While Ros Moss did not quite attribute supernatural powers to Harry Borg or to his mate, there was something about those humans that made him believe that the impossible, for them at least, was perhaps not impossible at all.

What was it Harry Borg had said about the impossible? "It only takes a little longer."

While good sense told Ros Moss that Harry Borg had failed, as expected, and that his female had most certainly failed in her effort, and that most certainly the Ussirs' human, Ahmed Hassad, had also failed, Ros Moss realized that he had not given up on them entirely.

Very far back in his mind there was still hope.

A fool's hope? An idiot's dream?

Perhaps. Or, to be honest, almost certainly. But at this time what else was there to sustain him but the hope of fools and the dream of an idiot? The best efforts of both his military and the military of the Ussirs were going to fail.

He knew that with absolute certainty.

His forces, the forces sending the missiles and bombs against the Shield, were continuing their efforts, but they were now going about it in a hopeless, desultory way that meant that while they were continuing to try, they had already accepted defeat.

They knew they had lost.

And wasn't that the reason his kind—both Ussir and Jassan—had declined from the once-great nation of the Ancients to little more than effete tribesmen, incapable of sustained, concentrated, determined effort, lost in aimless disputes, in purposeless contentions?

His kind sought defeat, Ros Moss was sometimes sure.

For them defeat meant the end to the struggle, whatever that struggle might be.

Defeat meant rest.

Defeat meant ease at last.

But it was not so with Harry Borg.

For Harry Borg defeat was not an acceptable outcome of any effort. Nor was defeat an acceptable outcome to his female. Nor, in all likelihood, was it acceptable to the human Ahmed Hassad.

For the humans, only death was an acceptable alternative to success. Only death could defeat them. Knowing this deep in his heart, remembering the resourcefulness he had seen the humans display, Ros Moss found he was not ready to accept that they were dead and their efforts ended. He knew he would go on harboring this faint thread of hope until the island of Tassar, the Source, and the Lassa Crystal were finally and irrevocably gone beneath the sea.

And there were still two days.

This day and one more.

CHAPTER 21

They weren't dead.

They could blink their eyes, they could breathe, their internal organs went on functioning, but they couldn't change the position of their arms or legs or turn their heads.

"Very selective," Chad Harrison said. He was communicating with telepathy.

"What're you talkin', selective?" Arnie asked.

"This paralysis," Chad answered.

They were lying as they had fallen, frozen in position, like statues in a formal garden knocked over by vandals. Helpless.

"I can breathe, blink my eyes, my heart goes on beating."

"Same here."

"Like we'd been shot with tranquilizing darts."

"Kind of 'em. Real humane!"

"Be in a helluva fix if we couldn't do *anything*."

"Y' think we *ain't* in a helluva fix?"

Harry Borg was listening but not taking part. Lying as he was, he could see the sun, and he had been watching the slow progress it was making toward the cliff.

"It could be worse," somebody said. "Could be a lot worse."

"I don't know how," somebody else said.

"Try being dead once."

"No, thanks."

"What d' you see, Eddie?" Harry asked then.

"Nothing, sir," Eddie answered.

Eddie was the only one who had fallen with his head in a position that allowed him a view of the road ahead, and he had been watching the movements of the strange little manlike creatures who had paralyzed Harry and the others.

Nothing was going on right now.

There had been moments of absolute terror, certainly. To be utterly helpless, incapable of any defense, is the worst possible of all predicaments. Anything can be done to you. Anything at all. And when caught in such a position, the mind will supply all manner of unpleasant possibilities.

"There's one now!" Eddie said.

He had seen one of the strange creatures rise up from the rocks that had concealed him, stare for a moment at the fallen, motionless humans, then cross the path to disappear again.

"Same deal as before," Eddie said.

"Just one side to the other?"

"That's it. Takes a look, goes out of sight on the other side."

"Weird."

Harry and his men knew the rocks were concealing at least six of the creatures, because they had been able to count that many before the attack. Six strange creatures, not human though built in the human configuration, and armed with riflelike weapons that Arnie had named stunguns.

"Just looked?" Harry asked. "And that's it?"

"That's it," Eddie said. "Wants to see if we're still down, I guess. He'll do it again, going the other way in a little bit."

"Bloody hell."

"Beats havin' 'em cut us up, don't it?"

"Sure as hell does."

How long had they been like this? Harry, watching the

sun, thought it had been at least an hour. In a few more minutes, possibly ten, the sun would reach the cliff, and then shadows would race out toward the men who were lying on or near the narrow roadway. Darkness would follow not long after, and then what?

Were the creatures waiting for reinforcements?

Surely they knew the humans were helpless. Then why, having rendered them helpless, hadn't they gone on to some next step? Why hadn't they taken the humans captive? Or killed them for whatever purpose killing them might serve—food, loot, whatever?

Unable to move, the humans would soon die.

And it was not going to be a case of rotting flesh falling away from old bones. The whole damned island, like the fabled Atlantis, *was* going to sink beneath the ocean. They believed that now.

One more earthquake like that last one was all it would take.

A real shaker and banger that last one.

Lying paralyzed, they had been heaved around like popcorn in a popper. An enormous thundering had come up from below. The ground had rolled. Great hunks of the distant cliffs had again broken free to avalanche down, sending up the usual storm clouds of dust. It had been enough to make a believer out of anybody. No island could stand that kind of treatment long. It had to fall apart, had to sink.

"Couple of more days," Harry had said. "We're gone, the whole island's gone—you can take it to the bank."

Now he watched the sun reach the cliffs and begin to drop behind them, watched the shadows race out from the foot of the cliff. Darkness was going to be pure hell, he thought. Lying paralyzed like this in the dark would drive even the strongest—

"I can move," Chad said quietly.

"Oh, for Pete's sake!"

"How much?"

"Hands, arms, legs—everything. It's all gone, or going." Chad's telepathic voice was very quiet, whispering.

"How come you and not me?" Homer asked.

"I was hit first."

"Chad's right," Harry said. "I was hit second, and now I'm beginning to get movement back. A little at a time."

He took a moment to verify the fact of movement, testing his limbs very carefully without changing his position. Hands, arms, legs, head—control was coming back to his entire body.

"Me, too," Eddie said. "I can move."

"Stay still!" Harry's command was low, flat, intense.

"It's wearing off all of us," he said then, whispering. "Don't know if *they* know we're getting loose or not, but let's don't tell 'em. When you've got full movement again, report."

After a few tense moments, their whispering voices answered.

"I've got it."

"I'm stiff but moving."

"Gonna break in half, but can do."

"I'm loose."

Harry Borg turned his head carefully to bring the rocks that concealed the strange creatures into his view. He could not see any creature or any movement at the moment. He waited, breathing quietly, sweating, for long moments. Nothing. The shadows from the cliffs had reached the rocks, darkening the area, cooling it.

"Can't just lie here," he said. "We'll have to go at them while we can still see what we're doing."

"On your count." Chad's telepathic voice was quiet, immediate.

"Homer? Eddie? Arnie?" Harry asked.

"Any time," they said quietly.

"Go!" Harry said.

And they lifted up from their frozen positions, five statues suddenly come to life, running. Harry ran two long strides in front of the others, hollering, trying to be as frightening as possible. There was not in any one of them, truthfully, any real hope they would survive the charge. How could they? They were all but naked. They had no weapons other than sticks and stones. The creatures had weapons that paralyzed at the very least, that killed at the very most.

Yet they went up the road, running and hollering.

"Full bore."

"Brave as hell."

"Like soldiers storming the barricades."

"Bare-handed."

They said those things later, when they could laugh about it. But while they were doing it, it wasn't funny. While they were doing it, they were scared as hell. Witless. Harry stormed over the top of the first big rock to find the six creatures standing motionless, frozen, and he fell like a storming devil upon the first one that came within reach, to tear the riflelike weapon from the creature's grip, to reverse the weapon into a club, and to swing that club against the side of the creature's head and feel the weapon shatter and the satisfying crack as the head broke and its contents splattered.

Contents...

Brains?

No!

Electronic parts! Wires, chips, ceramics, whizzits, pips.

Harry stared at the mess with stupefied amazement. "Robots!" he yelled, incredulous, almost angry.

"Hell's fire!"

"You're right!"

The others were making the same discovery.

Each had attacked the first creature he had been able to lay his hands on only to discover he was not attacking a live creature or even a functioning mechanical creature. The objects they were attacking did not fight back. Did not struggle at all. They were unresisting devices. They did nothing. They were like toys with run-down batteries.

Harry stood holding the pieces of the robot he had attacked. The riflelike weapon had been a part of the hand and arm, and when he'd torn the weapon from the hand part, he'd ripped wires loose. Now he saw that the positions the robots occupied were worn, mechanical places, probably put there centuries before, and he saw that there were tracks where the robots crossed the road and crossed back, tracks worn deep with centuries of use.

"I'll be trampled to death by a duck!" Harry said in awe.

"Make that two of us," Chad said.

"They were turned off," Homer said.

"Shut down for the night?"

"Not runnin' now, anyhow."

Eddie, who had been raised in his father's radio-TV repair shop, was rummaging, fascinated, even delighted, through the wreckage Harry had made of the head of the device he had attacked.

"Would you *look* at this," he said.

Homer looked. "IBM, eat your heart out."

Harry snapped out of his awe with the suddenness of a man hitting ground after a long fall.

"Fall in!" he yelled as he threw aside the pieces he had been holding.

"Yo!" they responded at once.

"Double time—march!"

They followed the trail that led upward toward the still distant mountaintop. While they ran, they kidded each other about the fact that they had been waylaid by robots. Six robots! Robots programmed to act out a single simple-minded cowboys and Indians routine. Robots powered, to the best of their understanding, by sunlight and heat. Robots that stopped when shadows and coolness came.

"Correct name'd be androids, wouldn't it?"

"Whatever."

"They had that one thing to do."

"And they did it."

"That's all they did."

"If something moved, it was an enemy."

"See an enemy, shoot it."

"That's all—just shoot it."

"Nothin' about takin' captives in their programs."

"Too much to write in a program."

"Some program, though."

"Ever try to write one? A program?"

"Couldn't write one like that."

"Couldn't even come close."

"Love to have me one of them stun-guns."

"And carry the whole robot under your other arm?"

"Be unhandy, that's for sure."

"All hooked together."

They ran on, following the ancient roadway at a steady double-time jog, climbing into the cloud cover, going higher and higher. Night came. They waited out the darkness, trying to rest.

Two more earthquakes, another pounding rainstorm. What rest?

Daylight, and being able to run again, to get warm again, was a blessing almost beyond counting. An hour after dawn they reached the top of the mountain.

"Whoo, boy!" someone gasped happily. "We made it!"

The top was a plateau, more than a square kilometer, its edges indistinct because of the gray mist of the cloud covering and the light, almost constant rain. They ran on through the rain, and the rain stopped. A wind came up and tore away the clouds.

And there it was.

The Source!

Built of some black, obsidian material, the enormous buildings were squat, solid, half buried in lava rock, a stack of great, dully shining cubes. Beautiful. Formidable.

The many faces were unbroken.

"Hell," Harry said. "There's no way in!"

CHAPTER 22

They ran, they laughed, they played.

All the joys of being very young had come to Lori Borg, Sam Barnstable, Tippi, and Illia again. They had no cares at all. They were as free as butterflies. By some happy chance their feet had become dancing feet: They could sing. Time was nothing to them. There was no end, no beginning. There was only now, this beautiful moment to enjoy.

They began the game of run sheep run, but the game dissolved, the intent of it lost in only a few moments, their minds unable to keep attention fixed. They joined hands with the elflike children; they danced in circles.

Guss and Sissi, agonized, followed where the little children and the humans went, watching with a kind of unbelieving and growing horror. Being reptilian and not being absolutely certain they knew every human vagary, they weren't sure what to do. Was this a normal kind of thing? Was it a thing of only a few moments? Would it end with the next moment? Surely the madness—it had to be madness, it was so lacking in form or pattern—would cease as quickly as it had begun!

"Lori! Lori! For Osis sake! Stop it!"

"Sam! You're not a child! Come back!"

The frantic telepathic calls of both Guss and Sissi went

unheeded; all their demands were laughed away. It seemed
the humans were answering calls from the strange little
children—and no other calls at all. And they did not get
better as time went on. They continued running into the
sunny woodlands, running out into the fields again.

It must have been an hour that Guss and Sissi followed
the aimless dancing, running, and playing before Guss
saw something strange in the behavior of one of the strange
little children. Running then like a cheetah in pursuit of
prey, Guss cut the fleet-footed little one down, and then,
holding it down, learned the little one's secret.

"Sissi!" he yelled. "Come look!"

She came, and she looked. And then they talked rapidly, quietly.

"If it isn't these little children, it's the fruit," Guss said.

"The fruit is a narcotic," Sissi agreed.

"We must be careful."

"They could be dangerous—without meaning to be."

"Yes."

"Let me try with Sam first. I can run faster than he
can."

"Be very careful."

Guss caught up the little child and ran to the edge of
the sunny woods, where Sam Barnstable was lumbering
about, one of the small elflike children on either shoulder,
singing.

"Old MacDonald has a farm . . ."

"Sam! Look here!"

When Guss was sure he had Sam's attention, he took
the little child he had by the heels and swung it like a
club against the nearest tree. The head burst like a melon
with the force of the blow.

"Hey! Damn you!" Sam roared furiously.

Outraged, savage, Sam dropped the two little ones he
had been carrying and charged at Guss like an angry bull,
bent on violent punishment. Guss tossed what remained
of the child he'd killed into the air so that Sam had to
catch it.

"Look at that!"

Sam looked at the broken body, his big, tough face
contorted with grief as well as anger now. A great sob

shook his shoulders. He held the broken body in his big hands and sobbed again.

Then he stared with growing disbelief.

The broken head had held electrical parts!

"What the hell is *this*?"

"A robot!" Guss answered.

The shock of learning that what he had thought were little children were not really little children, not really *living* things, but mechanical devices brought a measure of sobriety to the big human. But, still under the influence, he was not quite ready, or able, to fully accept what his senses were telling him.

"How come? I don't get it!"

Sissi ran up to join forces with Guss.

Then, while Sissi held Sam's attention, Guss caught the two little child-androids Sam had been carrying, tore their clothing, then twisted and tore at their mechanical limbs until the inner workings were exposed. He carried them to lay before Sam.

"Poor little things!"

What at first glance seemed to be awful butchery of children was shock enough to break the deepest hold of the narcotic that Sam had ingested with the fruit. Then the realization that they were not children after all but devices stirred his intelligence back into working condition. His eyes began to clear.

"What happened—what happened to us?" He looked for Lori with real concern.

"That fruit was narcotic," Sissi said.

Sam hit himself on the forehead, trying to speed the clearing. "Must've been! LSD—something like it! Holy smoke!"

He turned. "Mrs. Borg! Tippi! Illia!"

They seemed not to hear him, nor to care.

Sam looked at Guss and Sissi. "Gonna need some help."

"No time to waste!"

Sam, Guss, and Sissi spent the rest of that afternoon catching the joyfully struggling Lori, Tippi, and Illia and tying them so that they could not exhaust themselves further. The three captives accepted their bondage as some kind of a new game, joining in with high spirits and pretended fear, laughing themselves into exhaustion—and then, slowly, returned to sobriety.

"My God! What happened to me?" Lori asked.

"You got high on those grapes," Sam told Lori. "We all did."

"The little children did *that* to us?"

"Those little critters are robots," Sam said. "Don't ask me who they belong to—I don't know. But they were just doing what they were programmed to do."

"How long've we been out of it?"

"Four, five hours—something like that."

"Oh, Lord! We've got to make it up."

"Yeah, we do!"

They started out again.

Lori, five months pregnant, led the way. She set a fast pace, bending her body against the hill, walking hard, sometimes running.

"Mom!" Tippi moaned worriedly. "Think of Charlie!"

"Charlie's lovin' it!" Lori said, panting, red-faced, but absolutely sure in her heart that what she was saying was true. "He wouldn't have missed this ride for the world!"

Tippi watched her mother's rump bobbing ahead of her.

"Can't believe it!" she panted to Illia, who ran beside her. "She's thirty-two! She's an *old* woman. And look at her!"

"Too-moozing!" Illia, the fur-covered bassoe girl, gasped.

"What that mean?"

"Means—she—must—have—magic."

"I'll—buy—that," Sam panted.

Whether with magic or not, Lori held the pace through the rest of the day. Early the next morning, after enduring the same series of violent earthquakes and the same heavy rainstorms Harry and his group had endured, they in their turn finally achieved the top.

Streaming wet and bone weary but elated at their success in making the climb, they stood looking at the randomly stacked cubes of black obsidian buildings that housed the Source.

"Looks scary," Tippi said.

"Scary ain't the problem," Sam said.

He was fighting a sudden surge of disappointment. All that way, all that struggle, to finally come to this: The trail of the Ancients led to a blank wall.

"The problem," he said, "is something worse."

"There's no way in," Lori said. "That's the problem."

CHAPTER 23

From the edge of the stinking pile of putrescence that was the aerie of the pterosaur, Soo Toy had been watching when the nasty creature had taken its second victim.

Ahmed had *let* the monster carry him away.

Deliberately!

He was brave.

Oh, sure!

But who needed brave?

What help was he going to be to her, to himself, *to anybody*, dead and eaten up? What good was it going to do either of them if they were both picked to pieces, yelling and screaming, and gobbled down into those nasty insides?

"Ahmed!" she had screamed telepathically. "You idiot!"

"Comin' at you," he had answered.

She could see him now as the great bird-of-a-snake-lizard soared on the wind currents drawing closer . . . going above now . . . circling . . . Ahmed caught in the claws—

No, Ahmed was not caught!

He was *riding*!

He had straddled his legs, catching the claws and pulling them together until he could use them like a saddle. He had wrapped his arms around the legs to hold himself secure. He didn't look scared—or even worried. She could see the flash of his white teeth.

He was smiling! The crazy man. He was *enjoying* himself!

Like some darned kid on a merry-go-round!

They were going to be eaten up by a monster flying beast, and he was *enjoying* himself?

She was going to get sick and throw up.

The giant, leathery, flying dragon-thing came around in a landing circle, then, right overhead, it swooped its wings several times, blowing up a storm of wind, and settled down to the pile of rotting flesh. Just before those giant claws crrr*unch*ed down, Ahmed jumped off and stood aside to watch.

"Ahmed!" she screeched at him.

"'S all right, baby," she heard him say.

He was looking up, watching those great wings fold and the long neck of the nasty creature double in on itself, watching the long, horrible beak come in and the huge eyes of death close.

He just stood there.

What in the name of Buddha was wrong with him?

At a time like *this*, he went bongo?

He had his head tipped, and he was listening as the evil monster stopped purring, as it decided to sleep again before gobbling them both down.

"How *about* that?" she heard him say.

He was looking across the way at the other two monsters, sleeping on their roots.

"They must be rusted," she heard him say.

He *was* mad!

Soo Toy, frightened out of sight now, bedraggled, battled her way across the rotting flesh and bones to his side. She grabbed on to him as if he were the last palm tree standing in a hurricane.

"Ahmed! It's going to *eat* us!"

Hassad looked down at her clinging to him, smeared and crying. "Whew! You stink!"

That made her mad. She let go and swore at him.

"You don't *care* if it eats me?" she asked then.

"It's not going to eat anybody."

"It'll eat you, too! It'll—" She stared at him. "What'd you say?"

"I said it's not going to eat anybody."

"It brought us here! To this stinking nest! It—"

Then, staring again, she squeaked, "It isn't?"

"Only living things eat people," he said.

"It's living! It's only sleeping! It's—" She stopped suddenly. "It's not sleeping?" she asked faintly.

"It's not alive, my smelly pet. It's a robot."

"Robot," she said vacantly. *"Robot?"* she squeaked.

"A computerized piece of machinery," Hassad told her. He was looking up at the creature, studying it. "It was programmed to pick up any living thing that got into that target area and bring it up here. And that's all it does. After doing it, it shuts down and waits until it's triggered again."

"What're you talking?" Soo Toy shrieked.

"I'm talking robots," he said reasonably.

"Robot?" She was outraged. "This great nasty beast is no damn robot! It's a—a—*really*? A *robot*? Ahmed, stop it! I'm scared witless! I smell like death! And you're talking robots—"

Her chattering ceased as she looked up at the creature, as a realization began to grow, as belief came. "I'll be darned!" she said in awe.

"What?" he asked absently.

"I said, 'I'll be darned.' It *is* a robot!"

She moved to fling her arms around his neck and kissed him vigorously wherever she could land her lips in a hysterical kind of joyful relief.

She wasn't going to be eaten, after all!

He peeled her loose and held her away. "You *do* stink, you know."

That made her furious. "You bastard!" she yelled at him.

He patted her on the head. "Down, baby."

She kicked his ankle.

It didn't hurt—her foot was bare—but he looked pained. "After all I've done for you."

A large hand in her face, a not too gentle shove, caused

her to sit down suddenly. She lapsed into weeping. He ignored her.

"Oss Tiss!" he called telepathically. "Do you read me?"

"Yes, I do," came the answer immediately.

Oss Tiss's telepathic voice was thin, choked with a mixture of anger and disbelief. And with good reason. He had been driven to his wit's end. Was there something, after all, to this ridiculous god business? Certainly the luck that befell this human being exceeded all mortal limits. If, as the human said, the creature was indeed a mechanical device and not alive and was not going to devour that great bassoe of a human, then the great bassoe of a human was still in command, and he, Oss Tiss, had still to take his orders.

By great god of Miss, when this was over—

"Now hear this!" Hassad's telepathic voice was like a whip being laid across Oss Tiss's bare back. "Now hear this!"

Name of Osis!

When this was over, Oss Tiss promised himself, when sanity had returned and all was normal again, this great bassoe, Hassad, was going to be cut in small, bite-size pieces, perhaps sautéed with mushrooms, then pickled in a spicy red wine.

"Go to that rock," Hassad was saying. "Lie down there. I mean all of you. One at a time."

That great bassoe had gone insane!

He wanted them to—

No! Absolutely not!

Let that nasty device pick him up and fly him to that nest?

Never!

After the giant mechanical pterosaur had transported Oss Tiss and his eleven-man Elite Guard to the aerie— and after two of the guards had been detailed to escort Soo Toy to a stream some distance back from the cliff so that she could become once again her usual sweet-smelling self—Ahmed Hassad proposed another task Oss Tiss thought must have been conceived in the mind of a devil, not a god.

"Utterly impossible," he said. "Sir."

Hassad grinned at him. "Mind telling me why?"

"Not at all."

With considerable dignity—and with a certain relish, to be sure, because proving to this human he was badly mistaken was a rare privilege—he told Hassad why. "The Ancients possessed wisdom no ordinary creatures were ever to possess again," he said. "The electronics inside these robots, the workings that control their movements, the brains, if I may use that word, are so advanced, no mortal could possibly understand them, let alone change them in any significant way."

"No wonder," Hassad said.

"What does that mean?"

"It means I understand why you people have all but gone out of business. You quit before you start. We've got a saying, 'The difficult we do at once, the impossible just takes a little longer.'"

Oss Tiss stiffened into a military brace—thumbs of his eight-fingered hands where his seams would have been if he'd had seams, shoulders back, golden eyes with their vertical slits narrow straight ahead, forked tongue locked inside tight lips. His telepathic voice was a controlled monotone.

"We cannot convert these robots into military transports that will carry us to the Source. It is not possible. Sir!"

He said that with respect.

And the bassoe laughed at him. "Means we've only got till dark."

Dawn of the following day found them winging their way slowly through the low cloud cover that shrouded the plateau top of Mount Tassar. Ahmed Hassad and Soo Toy rode astride the neck of one mechanical pterosaur, with three of the Elite Guard clinging to the giant claws beneath them. The two other pterosaurs flew with them at a careful distance, one guided by Oss Tiss, the other by his next in command, bringing the rest of the guardsmen.

The jerry-rigged steering mechanism on the pterosaur Hassad and Soo Toy rode admittedly left much to be desired, but it functioned well enough so long as left turns were avoided. Circling to the right, Hassad brought his bird down through the mists, saw the ground, braked by dragging the giant claws, severely bruising the Elite Guard clinging there, crushed the breast of the bird into the ground, and finally stopped.

The other two pterosaurs crash-landed nearby.

Hassad jumped down and helped Soo Toy to the ground.

"Thanks for a pleasant flight," she said, ill-tempered.

"You expected lunch?" he asked.

Then he roared at Oss Tiss. "Over here! Join up!"

They joined up and moved out.

Only two of the Elite Guard had fallen to their deaths on the way here, and Ahmed Hassad led the remaining forces across the final few kilometers.

Finally, it was done!

They had penetrated the Shield, they had climbed the mountain, they were here. They were standing on the crest of a hill, and an easy road led the remaining distance down to the towering black obsidian cubes that had to be the Source. They were enjoying this moment of victory, of achievement, when another earthquake shook them down.

A veritable demon of a quake. It seemed the entire planet was going to be destroyed then and there. None of them believed, when the quake had finally ended, that they had in truth survived.

But they survived—if only just.

And when Oss Tiss staggered to the side of Ahmed Hassad, he found the big human staring at the great black cubes of the Source with narrowed eyes.

"Y' see that?" Hassad asked.

"What, sir?"

"The vertical lines are no longer vertical."

"They are not?"

"If they're not slanted to the right, I'm slanted to the left."

Oss Tiss looked hard. "You are not slanted, sir."

"Means this is it."

"Yes, sir."

"We're going under."

"That is correct, sir. The sinking has begun."

"Ahmed!" Soo Toy exclaimed. "What are you saying?"

"I'm saying the Atlantis bit was not camel droppings, after all." Hassad's tone was matter-of-fact. "This island is going down. In an hour, a half hour, a few minutes— who knows?"

They felt another shake, and the ground seemed to move several feet to the right.

"Like that," Hassad said.

"Any time," Oss Tiss agreed.

"What'll we *do*?" Soo Toy shrieked.

"Get the Lassa Crystal," Hassad said. "Get the Shield turned off. And get the hell out of here."

"My people will rescue us," Oss Tiss told her.

"But the button!" Soo Toy grabbed Hassad. "To turn off the Shield—that button! It's inside those buildings!"

"You're right."

"How do we get in?"

Hassad studied the featureless walls.

"Good question," he said.

CHAPTER 24

The mangrove swamp on the South Cliss was gone.

The island, like some gigantic creature settling down into a nest, had lowered itself comfortably into the ocean a depth of several hundred meters. The sea had accepted the change with no difficulty at all, sending combers hissing in, ten, twenty, thirty meters high to cover the great trees, to seethe and boil for a few moments, and then to become quiet again.

The jungle had been next.

Shrieking flying creatures had swarmed up as the seas had come in, and had flown to higher ground. Climbing and crawling creatures had drowned. Most of those had died silently without complaint, their eyes wide and staring as the water had closed over them. Some had clung to floating refuse in the hissing, booming turbulence, only to die later. Some had floated away, and these would be washed up on distant shores to go on living.

Each shuddering quake meant the island had settled again, that great reaches of coastal area had disappeared, and that the sea was racing up the long slopes in steady, inexorable pursuit of all living things. Soon the very peak of the island would disappear and the sea would resume its endless ways.

How much time was there left?

Perhaps an hour.

A few minutes more.

Or less.

Harry Borg pushed himself up from the ground, a fighter floored by a lucky punch in the tenth round of a fight he'd been winning. He was furious. Another shot like that last one could very well cost him the fight, and he wasn't half whipped yet.

He roared at the young lads with him. "Get up! Can't let a lousy earthquake beat yuh!"

The lads rolled to their feet. They looked at each other, pained.

"He's got to be kidding," their expressions said.

"He's gone bananas," their expressions said.

"Sir," Homer said, spitting on his big hands. "We can whip the biggest damn earthquake ever came along— bring on the next one!"

He had said it with a straight face.

The others broke up laughing.

Harry Borg looked at them as they got to their feet, his anger turning to pride. They were some kind of lads! Half naked, half starved, worn to the bone with almost constant uphill running, standing on an island that was due to go under any time now, drowning them, and they could laugh—weak laughter, thin laughter, and maybe a little giddy, but laughter nonetheless.

"Ten-hut!" Chad said.

"Shape up or ship out!" Eddie echoed.

They fell into a ragged line, shoulders braced.

Arnie giggled, his eyes glassy.

"At ease!" Harry growled.

A huge man, Harry Borg, powerful, with the muscled arms and thighs of a weight lifter, the flat belly and narrow waist of a boxer. His heavy jaw, covered with a reddish-brown beard, was mud-caked and rain-soaked now; his eyes burned with dark blue fire.

He was worn. He was ragged. He was as dirty as a hog in a wallow.

He was formidable!

Behind him the black obsidian cubes of the Source, each as big as a downtown building, were stacked in a random geometric heap like a giant child's blocks, forgotten, waiting. There were stairways, there were what seemed to be balconies, there were low walls and terraces.

He turned to glare at the cubes.

"Got to be a way in," he said.

Certainly no way in was apparent. All the sides were smooth, glistening with rain. No doors. No windows.

"Time's short," he said. "Hear?"

"Sir," they said.

"Split up. Go hard and fast. Keep in touch."

"On your count," they said.

"Go!"

They raced away. Each took a different route, up stairways, along terraces, vaulting low walls. A constant telepathic chirping passed between them.

"Nothing here."

"Going higher."

"Dead end this way."

Harry strode straight at the nearest building face. His shoulders were bunched, his arms swinging, his heavy chin was tucked down against his chest, his hands balled into hard-knuckled fists: He was a fighting man who was not going to let any goddamn black enigma defeat him at the last moment.

He was damned well going to search every inch of that wall as it had never been searched before, raking it, scouring it, staring at it until he found an entrance. Or else! And it was this look, this attitude of relentless determination that made the difference.

Old Mind saw it and was moved.

Gleaming and bright, a giant lens appeared, like a huge eye opening, in a wall high up. From it, a shaft of intense blue light streamed down, and Harry Borg was caught in the beam, a performer center stage in a dark theater. He was caught, then sucked up, tumbling. His arms and legs flailed helplessly. He yelled in startled rage. Then he vanished into the lens.

The young lads watched him go.

"Iron Balls found a door," Homer said.

"You know it!"

"Outa sight!"

"Think he's dead?"

"Not Iron Balls—not that easy."

And there were others who had seen Harry Borg go.

On the hill to the east, about to advance to the road, Hassad and the others had been close enough to the stacked obsidian cubes to have had their attention caught by the sudden ray of intense blue light, to have seen the tiny, tumbling figure of Harry Borg disappear.

Lori, Tippi, Sam, Illia, Guss, and Sissi had seen blue light flash on the far side of the cubes, but they had had no sure knowledge of what the blue light had meant. Sam thought an entrance might have opened and closed on that side, and they began to work their way around the buildings in that direction.

Chad now saw Hassad's group.

"Bogies coming in," he informed the others of the cadre telepathically. "Form on me, middle terrace."

"Right now!" Arnie said.

"What bogies?" Homer asked.

"Hassad, his bird, eight or nine Ussirs."

"They armed?"

Chad was watching them, counting, as Hassad led the others down the road toward the cubes at a run.

"No arms. Like us, they're bare-handed."

"Gotta knock their heads."

"Wait for me!" Sam Barnstable's telepathic voice was distant but urgent. "Where the hell are you?' he asked.

"Sam!" Chad exclaimed, startled. "You here?"

"Damn betcha!"

Now telepathic voices began cracking back and forth, a party line gone public. Some voices were distant, some were close. Some were angry, some were threatening, some were glad, some were alarmed.

"Where's Harry?" Lori wanted to know.

"Inside," Chad answered. "What're *you* doing here?"

"Oh, Chad." Illia sighed.

"Illia!"

Ahmed Hassad ordered them all to surrender.

"Lie face down!" he said. "You won't be hurt."
"Go to hell!" they said.

Inside, Harry Borg could hear none of this. Telepathy did not penetrate the obsidian walls.

He was skidding across a smooth, polished floor on his back, disoriented, confused, unable to get a purchase or right himself before he slammed into a wall. Then he lay for a moment, panting.

He was not hurt—but he was hugely angered.

"What the hell's goin' on?"

"Harry Borg," Old Mind said. "The human from Earth."

The voice was, of course, telepathic. It had no visible source, it was just there, inside Harry's head: it was information delivered to Harry's mind in a form he could understand—words of his language. But still Harry looked warily about, distrustingly, as he got to his feet.

"That's me. Who're you?"

"The god Uss!"

"Horse puckey!"

"You don't believe in gods?"

"No way!"

"All right, then. I am a device."

"Y' mean you're a computer?"

"Yes."

"I'll be damned! And you—you're in charge?"

"Yes."

"Tell me—is this island going to sink?"

"Yes."

"When?"

"Within the hour."

"An hour! You goin' with it?"

"Yes."

"The whole works? Everything? All this?"

He was looking around the room in which he'd found himself. It was long, narrow. Shining columns supported a high ceiling. There were carved figures of essans on pedestals; there were murals depicting distant star gatherings, spaceships, strange beings. There were floating forms, unattached, some transparent, some solid. Every small sound echoed hollowly as if the space were huge, the walls far off.

It was like a beautifully kept museum.

"All of this," Old Mind said. "Everything."

"I could get you out," Harry said. "Tell me where and how to turn off that Shield. There's ships waiting to come in."

"Not possible."

"To turn off the Shield?"

"To get me out."

Harry looked around. It was like talking to himself. It was crazy.

"C'mon!" he said angrily. "I gotta get that Lassa Crystal! I've gotta turn off that Shield! I've gotta get the hell outa here! If you can't go—okay! But I'm wasting time!"

"I understand."

"Let's move it!"

"Move, then—in the direction you are now facing."

"Straight ahead." Harry began moving at a running walk, hurrying.

"An hour's not much time," he said. "There's a lot to do."

The sound of his worn boots splatting on the smooth floor echoed. He was told to turn left, and he turned left. Passing through another rectangular opening, he found himself in a room where the walls were scored by vertical and horizontal lines.

"C'mon!" he said. "Where's the switch? The button?"

"First this," the voice of Old Mind said.

"What's this?"

"The Library of Tassar."

"I want the crystal!" Harry said. "The Lassa Crystal!"

"This is important," Old Mind said.

"There isn't time!"

"Take time."

One of the squares, scribed within vertical and horizontal lines on the wall before Harry, opened to reveal a lighted compartment, and within the compartment a shining case of black material, suitcase-size, handled. An inner mechanism brought the case forward and presented it to Harry.

"Take it."

Harry grabbed the handle of the case and jerked it out.

"What the hell?"

"Knowledge," Old Mind said. "Knowledge of the Ancients."

"All right, I've got it. Now the crystal, okay?"

"Turn to your left."

Harry turned, found a corridor before him, and began his hurried running walk again. This was way-out—following the orders of a telepathic voice, trusting it, going here, going there, with time running short. He looked at the case, feeling an impulse to throw it aside.

"No!" Old Mind said. Had he guessed Harry's impulse? "It is knowledge that will take you to the stars."

Harry tightened his grip on the case. "Thanks a bunch!" he said.

"You do not want it?"

"Be a lot of good if I'm on the bottom of the ocean!"

"Turn to your right," Old Mind said patiently.

The building was caught in another tremor. The floor heaved under Harry's feet, sending him crashing into a wall. The sound of the quake boomed in the corridor as if a cannon had been fired. Harry waited it out, cursing, then ran on again.

"Another shot like that, we're gone!"

"Then peace."

"Peace, your ass! I've got things to do!"

"Turn right."

Harry, panting, turned as directed and found himself moving through a stadium-size room toward a distant door in a distant wall. All about him enormous shapes hummed quietly. Dynamos, generators, transmitters—Harry had no way of knowing what they were or what their function was.

"Some kind of powerhouse."

"Exactly."

Through the door, he was guided onto a walkway and, peering over a rail, he could see that he was high up on only one level of many levels that gave off a shaft that extended downward, dwindling in the distance.

"Big sucker!"

He stayed away from the rail then and hurried on. At the far end of the walkway a heavy door opened as he approached. He went through the door into what he was sure had to be a central control room.

"Where's the switch?"

"Switch?"

"To turn off the Shield!"

"The Lassa Crystal first."

Harry swore impatiently. "All right! Where?"

"Before you."

Before Harry was an enormous altar made of some glistening material, draped with shining cloth. There were three wide steps to climb. Harry moved up the steps. As if to welcome him, panels in the front of the altar spread wide. Others fell away. And there was revealed to him now an eye-blinding brilliance.

The Lassa Crystal!

Glittering, many-faceted, many-colored, it was of such dimensions that Harry would need two hands to lift it. It was diamondlike and yet without that kind of substance. It was transparent and yet substantial. It seemed imbued with life. It was vigorous. It was fiery.

It commanded.

"Yes," Harry whispered. "Yes, *ma'am*."

Several moments passed before he saw it all, before he understood even a portion of what he saw. The Lassa Crystal was beneath a window that opened to the sky. Under the Lassa Crystal a shaft extended downward into mirrors. The power of the sun passed through here, the life of it condensed, transmitted, reflected, sent out to satellites, then back to ground.

"What now?"

Harry was told to grasp the Lassa Crystal and lift it. And that took courage, as much as he had ever needed to do anything before. The Lassa Crystal proved ice-cold in his hands, and he had expected fire. It was almost weightless, as if it were providing half the effort required to rescue it. Harry narrowed his eyes to slits to protect them from glare and did as he was told. There was a beautifully carved chest made of something like ivory into which the Lassa Crystal fitted perfectly. Harry placed it carefully, locked it in.

The lights dimmed.

"They going out on us?" he asked.

"Soon," Old Mind answered.

"Let's get outa here!"

Now Harry had the chest in one hand, the case in the other. He was directed away from the altar and out of the room. He went, running. A corridor led to yet another room, wide, high, echoing. Three walls were shining metal, behind which, seen through slits, violet lights glowed, red lights blinked, green lights raced.

The fourth wall was a giant glass face, and this wall, glowing, held a Presence. A three-dimensional figure was shaping and reshaping, never a recognizable image, never like anything Harry had ever seen, yet always *almost* something familiar, something he knew.

"I am the god Uss!" The telepathic voice seemed to originate behind the giant screen.

"Horsefeathers!" Harry said.

"Infidel!" the telepathic voice roared.

"You're nothing but a cotton-pickin' computer!"

There was a long moment of silence. When the voice returned, it was tentative. "Cotton pickin'?"

"It means," Harry said, willing to lie a little, "you're an excellent computer."

"I am excellent," Old Mind said. "I know all there is to know."

"Bully for you."

Harry was impressed. But he was not so impressed that he had lost sight of his most urgent need. His eyes had left the screen and were searching for something that might be a switch, a key, a button. He had to get that Shield turned off; he had to get the hell out of here before another ten minutes were gone.

The floor beneath his feet was trembling.

"Much of what I know is in your hands," Old Mind said.

Harry held up the case. "Y' mean in this?"

"Yes. Infinitely condensed."

"Great!" he said with great sarcasm.

"With instruments, it can be read."

"What instruments?"

"They are—"

The telepathic voice became static, scratching, unintelligible as another enormous shaking came, driving Harry to his knees. The glowing screen went dark. Harry rode with the quake, deafened by the thunder it made, a thunder that was mind-numbing as it echoed, booming. He thought surely he must see the walls burst in at any moment, see roaring, tumbling torrents of water racing at him.

None came.

The great shaking quieted to mere trembling.

"Old Mind!" Harry yelled. "You still there?"

The giant screen glowed again. Feebly.

"Yes, I am here," Old Mind said distantly.

Harry had shoved to his feet.

"The switch! The button! Whatever turns off the Shield—where the hell is it?" He was looking about in a fury. "C'mon! Tell me."

The Presence on the screen, a geometric, transparent, convoluting, ever changing pattern of golden lines, faded almost to darkness, came back to shine brightly for a brief moment, then faded until it was hardly discernible.

Circuits were burning out!

Finally the voice returned, distant but clear. "Only the fittest may survive."

"What's that mean?"

A man's voice, astonished, angry, suddenly roared: "Harry Borg!"

Harry turned to find Ahmed Hassad. Ahmed Hassad? Here? Yes! All but naked, as he was himself, as huge and as powerful as he was himself. Ahmed Hassad! That damned handsome face, those shining black eyes, those white teeth—it could be no one else!

"How'd *you* get here?"

"A ray hit me. Bang! I'm here!"

"Who shall have the Lassa Crystal?" Old Mind asked. "Who shall have the wisdom of the Ancients?"

Hassad's eyes were on the ivory chest. "That the Lassa Crystal?" he asked.

"It's mine!"

"The hell it is!"

"Let it be decided now," Old Mind said. "Who is the fittest? Who shall survive?"

"You're crazy!" Harry yelled. "We're goin' down!"

"I'll take that crystal!" Hassad's chest swelled.

"Survival of the fittest," Old Mind said. "That is the oldest law of living things. I am not living. I cannot decide. You must prove who is the fittest, who shall have the Lassa Crystal."

"Bloody hell!" Harry cursed.

Hassad was charging.

CHAPTER 25

Oss Tiss and Soo Toy had seen Ahmed Hassad go.

The lens had appeared again, high up, and the beam of intense blue light had streamed down as it had before, this time in search of Hassad. Finding Hassad, it had sucked him up, tumbling, to disappear into the lens, yelling fury.

Soo Toy had screamed.

Oss Tiss had cursed.

With the huge Earthman gone, he, Oss Tiss, was in command, and across the tops of the black obsidian cubes he could see Earthmen running, gathering around the one with the white head, looking toward himself and his Elite Guard.

What was he to do?

The way the land was shaking and tipping, he knew the sea must be racing up the slopes even at this moment. Soon it would smother everything. How soon? Time could be measured now only in minutes, he was sure. And they were locked beneath the Shield, out of reach of the Ussir flight-craft he knew were hovering above, ready to dive in and rescue him, his soldiers, and the Lassa Crystal.

But the Lassa Crystal was locked inside the cubes!

And there was no entrance save the beam of blue light. He saw the beam flash again, reaching out in another

direction, finding another human to take up. The distance
and the angle prevented his knowing which human had
been caught, if indeed it was a human that had been taken.

"Zat!"

And the female human Hassad had left behind went
on screaming telepathic curses at him! As if all this massive calamity were *his* fault! She wanted him to find a
way into the cubes. Osis, yes! He would love to! But
how? The full sun, risen now well into the sky, glistened
on walls as smooth as new-laid eggs.

"There *is* no entrance!" he told Soo Toy.

"*I'll* find one!" she said.

And she ran, small and swift, like a darting bird.

Oss Tiss saw her disappear behind a towering black
face. Good riddance! He had never cared for her. As a
tasty before-meal snack, served with a dry kliss, perhaps—

Riss! There was no time for that now!

But what to do? What to do?

The humans had gathered about the taller one with the
white head. A fighting force beyond any doubt. Well,
then, here was something he understood, something about
which he could do something. Making war was the way
he had always earned his way.

What useful purpose would war serve now?

What useful purpose did war *ever* serve?

"Attack!" he ordered his Elite Guard.

And, good soldiers that they were, they charged.

"Crazy buggers are comin' at us," Sam said.

The Elite Guard were racing in, eight of them in all,
climbing long stairways, jumping walls, running across
the flat tops of the obsidian cubes. Their war cries, telepathic shrieks, shrill and senseless, were intended to ter-
rify.

"Eddie, Arnie," Chad said. "Go wide, circle."

They went, a pair of wide ends going deep. They crossed
the tops of two cubes before turning to close on the rear

of the startled Elite Guard. Chad and Homer moved apart
and then advanced. Sam rolled right up the middle.

They made contact.

And the Ussirs began flying in every which direction.

Tippi and Illia, Guss and Sissi had been left staring
open-mouthed when the intense blue beam had found Lori,
choosing her apparently by chance out of their small group
and whisking her away. Had it been with greater care than
the others? It had seemed so. She had seemed to float up
and away, and though she had waved her arms about as
if worried she'd lose her balance, she had gone into the
lens in an upright position, in a more dignified way, in a
manner perhaps befitting a woman with child.

With respect?

"Name of Osis! What now?" Guss asked.

"We've got to go higher!" Sissi said.

She had been looking to the east. That way gave her
a longer view, and after regaining her feet after the powerful shaking, she had had no doubt that the land had
dropped a long, long way—which meant, of course...

And there it was!

Distant and below, but sea beyond any doubt, a line
of smoking combers crawled up the slopes. And the combers had to be on all the slopes around the mountains, all
that was left of the island, moving closer as the island
dropped. The island had paused in its settling for the
moment; those hissing rollers were waiting.

"Hurry!" Guss said. "Run!"

They found a way that led upward, first across broken
lava, then along a path, then up a stairway of timeworn
stone. The females, Tippi, Illia, and Sissi, went first. Guss
followed, herding them, urging them on.

Lori Borg had found herself in an electronic bedlam.

There were no walls here, no floor, no ceiling—at least
none clearly apparent. It was as if she had been brought
into the center of a busily operating computer and sus-

pended, upright, amidst all the zipping, streaking, flashing impulses.

Zeros and ones were gathering and scattering.

Whatever their mission, their purpose, they went about it, ignoring her.

Gray eyes wide and apprehensive, yet not frightened, just desperate, she ducked flying lights, batted at flickering digits with waving arms.

"What's goin' on?" she shrieked.

"You are in Master Control," Old Mind answered.

"What the heck? Who—*where*?"

She had no idea whose voice it was, or where it had come from. Suddenly it was in her head, a bit fragmented, not threatening, shaky, as if very old or falling apart. She turned, and turned again, and realized that her footing was secure.

"The Shield—you may turn it off."

"Shield? Oh, my God, yes! How? Where?"

"There, there—before you..." The telepathic voice of Old Mind faded away.

She ran, arms and hands extended straight forward.

There was no handle, no button she could see. Only transparent tubes, tall twists of golden wires, flashing light sources, like blinking eyes, off and on, red, violet, green, blue.

"Oh, Blessed Mary—help me!"

She began snatching at random anything that came to hand, breaking, tearing. Rhythms were broken, paths interrupted, streaks sputtered, crashing.

She spun, turned, ripped, tore.

"Go off," she panted. "Go off!"

Soo Toy thought she had fallen into a blue well.

But it was not.

It was an entrance, lower than she, lighted with a glow that was very blue, and it accepted her as she stumbled through it, falling to her knees. She looked about then, her black eyes wide with her fright.

"Where am I?"

"Where you wanted to be," Old Mind answered.

"Ahmed!" she shrieked. "Who's talking?"

She was given no answer. But pushing up, she saw she was on a balcony, and leading down, a long, gradual reach, a stairway seemed to beckon her. There was no way back; the way she had come was closed, and only this way, the stairway, remained open.

"Ahmed!" she cried. "Answer me!"

She ran down the stairway swiftly, like a small bird.

Harry Borg set the ivory chest containing the Lassa Crystal carefully to one side and the case that contained the infinitely condensed knowledge of the Ancients to the other side and met, almost joyfully, the charging Ahmed Hassad.

They crashed together like rams battling on a rocky slope.

Two enormously powerful rams.

Necks bowed, legs driving, they met with such force, head crashing against head, that they were both stunned and bloodied. Each had no thought but to destroy the other. They wanted the Lassa Crystal, yes, but they wanted this contest as well. They wanted it proved once and for all who was the strongest, the most able. They wanted to satisfy themselves that none existed who, without weapons, with muscles and courage and bare hands alone, was better than himself.

The charge had been the first test.

Neither had given way, neither had sought to avoid, to shear off, to take less than the best the other had to give. And the impact, full on, had very nearly done for both of them.

They fell, equally battered.

They recovered at the same moment, gaining their feet again, to lunge for each other, roaring their rage. Hooked iron-claw fingers reached out to tear at faces and were half deflected, raking instead red furrows on cheeks and jaws, arms and chests. The iron fingers became fists then, swinging hammers that struck with the force of sledges against hard heads already bloodied.

Harry staggered.

Hassad was driven to one knee.

Getting up, Hassad brought a fist ripping up that caught Harry just under the chest, lifted him, and threw him onto his back. Leaping, Hassad threw himself atop the gagging, gasping Harry Borg, thinking he had the man's life for the taking, only to be met by feet suddenly drawn back, cocked, feet that fired like twin catapults, hitting Hassad in the chest and sending him flying backward to crash against a distant wall.

Neither man had yet been broken.

Now an earthquake intervened.

There was no holding balance, no moving against the other; there was only a fight to survive the shaking, to endure the booming, the side-to-side shuddering. The obsidian building made cracking sounds like high-powered rifles firing close at hand.

Old Mind's telepathic voice was faint, full of static. "Survival of the fittest . . . survival . . . survival . . ."

"You set us up!" Harry Borg roared.

His dark blue eyes, gone nearly black with rage, were fixed on Hassad, who was crouched and gathering for a spring at a distance, and yet he was raging at Old Mind both with his own booming voice and with telepathic fury.

"A last pleasure," Old Mind admitted.

"The Shield?" Harry demanded.

"I gave your mate that task. She has broken the Shield."

"Lori? Lori *here*?" Harry was shocked, outraged.

Hassad had thrown himself again, and Harry drove to meet him, his concern for Lori set aside for this greater need. They grappled on meeting, huge arms thrusting out, great hands gripping. Holds taken, the two nearly naked men heaved, twisted, tugged. Plaited muscles on wide shoulders, down arching backs, and on board-flat bellies ridged with the bone-cracking strain.

Neither was aware that seawater had raced in across the floor, that it was rising, ankle-deep, then shin-deep. The water sloshed against the far wall, spumed up, then receded.

Harry broke free of Hassad's grip and brought an iron-mallet fist down, striking Hassad's temple, tearing an ear, breaking a collarbone. Hassad was hardly aware of it. A fist of his own, swung like a stone club, struck Harry's face below his left eye. Bone gave, splintering, beneath the skin, and teeth were knocked into the back of Harry's mouth. Spitting teeth and blood, he caught Hassad's throat in the grip of his two hands.

"Now! Damn you!"

Another man would have died in that grip.

But this was not another man; this was Hassad. Both his hands, fisted together, drove upward to spear between Harry's straining forearms, and those forearms were blown apart with an explosive force. Hassad's fisted hands went on, high up, to come down, hunting a killing stroke, missing by narrow inches.

They grappled again, seeking purchase.

And the sea came back, rushing in again in greater volume. The crashing force of it knocked both men from their feet, drove them across the obsidian floor, gone slippery now, and sent them crashing into the wall.

Submerged in the blinding salt foam, Harry felt Hassad's powerful body go limp. Fearing a trick, he held his grip, and when the seawater retreated once again, Harry hauled the limp, almost lifeless Hassad erect. It had not been a trick. Hassad had been dazed, but, held by Harry, the moment had given him his senses back.

"Fool!" Hassad drove a sudden fist hard and deep into Harry's gut just under the rib cage, a blow to paralyze the strongest. Harry's breath was gone; he could not take another. On his back now, sliding across the floor, he was flat when the next rush of seawater came.

Soo Toy, flitting down the winding stairway, found herself suddenly looking into a turbulent lake that filled a room where a giant glass screen held a wavering geometric figure—a figure that seemed excited to the point of ecstasy—where walls held flashing lights and where two giant men she knew very well had battled before a rush of water had covered them.

When they had risen, when Hassad, suddenly recovered, had driven Harry Borg back across the floor to be engulfed in the next wave, she screamed shrilly.

"Ahmed! We're sinking!"

Her thin shriek reached Hassad.

Not alone did it reach his ears, but it reached his awareness as well—there was no time left to go on fighting Harry Borg!

Was there even time left to escape alive?

He dived under the water, searching.

Harry Borg, who had recovered his feet and was bracing himself against the rush of water, had reached the same conclusion at the same instant. He had heard Old Mind say that the Shield was gone—that Lori had broken it! Flight-craft, then, would have come in and must be waiting.

And he dived under the water, searching.

When it seemed his lungs would burst for want of air, his hands found and gripped a handle. Rising up, he saw he had the case holding the knowledge of the Ancients, then he was knocked down and submerged again by another onslaught of the sea.

When he finally gained his feet again, he saw Ahmed Hassad on the far side of the room, about to go through a doorway. Hassad was looking back.

Now Hassad held up the ivory chest.

Hassad had the Lassa Crystal!

When Harry was finally able to reach the doorway, he saw Hassad racing up a long flight of stairs, little Soo Toy flitting at his side, the Lassa Crystal in his hand.

Another huge cascade of seawater poured over Harry before he could reach the stairs. As he tumbled and floated in the raging turbulence, he heard, or thought he heard, what had to be the last thoughts of Old Mind: "Survival of the fittest."

And a static crackle that might have been crackling laughter.

And then nothing.

Old Mind was gone.

When the surging water had stilled for a moment, Harry rose up out of it, screaming, cursing, furious. He got his feet on the stairway and began climbing. He still had the case, and it made the running awkward. But he would not leave it, for that would have meant he had accomplished nothing at all after his fighting.

That damned Hassad had beaten him!

Though Harry's fighting was by no means over.

In the last crumbling of the island, the great obsidian cubes were shifting and settling, sinking, becoming still, sinking again. The staircase where Harry struggled upward was breaking. He leaped over buckled slabs, was forced to wait out shiftings. The seawater pursued him with the relentlessness of a horde of demons, ever at his heels, sometimes to his waist, dragging at him with a million wet fingers.

His breath was a hoarse roaring in his lungs. His rage kept him going.

Finally he burst into the open—and into a shifting, ray-laced battle scene.

Flight-craft of both the Ussir and the Jassan nations were flashing close above the tilted obsidian cubes. The deadly purple rays of the fighting craft were streaking the sky, searching targets. Harry saw a hit almost at once, a green Ussir craft exploding in a sudden flash of blinding light, to be followed close after by another hit, this time from a Jassan craft. The hits filled the air with cracking, booming sounds, with light almost unendurable.

There were two ships on the ground. Both were large. One had certainly been shot down. The other—he couldn't tell. He thought the figures moving about it were in the uniforms of Jassans.

"Chad!" Harry yelled telepathically.

He heard, surprisingly close at hand, Chad's answer. "Ho!"

Harry looked around. There was little land left the sea had not taken. From his position now, very high up, Harry could see tall, smoking combers racing in on land all around. For the moment the island was still, the sea holding, though the trembling beneath his feet told Harry that the final moments were not far off.

"Chad! Homer!" Harry yelled again.

"Coming!"

Harry saw Guss at the door of the ship that was down, waving at him furiously, beckoning. Closing in, he saw

Tippi's face, then Sissi's, then Illia's. But he did not see Lori anywhere.

"Lori!" he shouted telepathically.

"Harry!" she answered, unseen. "I'm okay!"

In this madhouse, this bedlam, in these last desperate moments, those words were sweet relief. Harry saw he could reach the ship ahead of the closing sea. But he could not feel success. Hassad, not he, had taken the Lassa Crystal.

"Where the hell are you, Chad?"

"Coming."

Chad, Homer, Eddie, Arnie, and Sam streamed into sight, running. Eddie's left arm hung wrong, flopping. Arnie hopped on a crippled leg. Sam's chest was red with blood. Homer's face was scored, bleeding. And Chad's left eye was battered closed, his cheeks pulped.

But Chad had an ivory chest, gripped by the handle!

"You got it!" Harry yelled. "The Lassa Crystal!"

"That what it is?" Chad said.

"Hell, yes!"

They were running to the ship.

"Name of God, how'd you get it from Hassad?"

"We cut him off from the Ussir ship," Chad told him. "He threw it at us, a baby to the wolves. While we were after this box, he had time to get away."

"His life first!" Harry said.

"Not quite."

"Whaddayuh mean?"

"Had his girl over one shoulder, an Ussir over the other."

"And he gave you the box?"

"So he could get away."

"Be go to hell!"

They reached the ship.

Harry threw the case he had carried aboard, then turned to lift a slumping Arnie and shove him into Guss's reaching hands. Eddie and Homer followed. Then Sam. Chad wanted to be last, but Harry all but threw Chad and the ivory chest into the ship. Then Harry gripped the sides of the hatchway.

The sea was at his feet.

He pulled himself aboard.

The flight-craft lifted away.

Ten meters, fifty, a hundred, then a thousand. All on the ship went to windows to look down, to watch the combers roaring in from all sides.

On an Ussir ship, Ahmed Hassad, Soo Toy, and Oss Tiss looked down.

Oss Tiss was miserable. "You saved my life," he said to Hassad.

"Couldn't let an old buddy die," Hassad said. "We've been through too much together."

"I was going to kill you."

"Yeah, I know."

"Now I am in your debt, I cannot kill you."

Hassad grinned at him. "So—wound me a little."

"Ahmed Hassad," Soo Toy said. "You are insane."

In another ship, Lori Borg, tired, frazzled, but wearily content, leaned back in a soft seat and patted her tummy, Charlie's place.

"You okay?" she asked her unborn child.

The kick she felt might have been an affirmative.

On a televisionlike screen that had been activated for her, she was being given a view inside the ship where Harry, Tippi, Guss, Sissi, Illia, Sam, and all the lads were riding. They were battered, some bloody, but all were safe.

"We made it!" she sighed.

And below...

The center of the island, the last, highest point to go, was the roof of a black obsidian cube. The seas from all sides met there, spouted up to cover the cube, then subsided. All the island was gone then, save the one very last top of the very last cube.

The sea quieted.

Except for the last few meters of the last black cube

and the refuse that cluttered the surface of the ocean, there was no sign that an island had ever been here before. And as the people in the ships watched, awed, there was a last final sinking, and that last cube sank slowly.

And then was gone.

Plop!

CHAPTER 26

The day the lights came back on was a day of great celebration in the nation of Jassa. There had been gloom of night all over the world of Essa for a period of more than a half year after the Source had sunk beneath the sea, and while everyone there had experienced electrical outages at one time or another, some for as long as several days because of some malfunction or other, none had imagined the inconvenience that would come with a power loss that went on and on and on and on and on.

Machines stood idle.

The males loafed a lot.

Females complained.

Oh, there was electricity of sorts, provided intermittently by jerry-rigged generators, and so life was able to proceed after a fashion. But no one liked it. And a lot of food *did* spoil, just as Lori Borg had predicted it would.

Fresh meat in particular.

And yat milk.

But when the new power station had been completed and the Lassa Crystal put in place, and when President of Jassa, Ros Moss, with elaborate ceremony, pressed the button that brought light again and once more set the nation humming—and, not incidentally, put an end to all the pleasant foolishness that is the inevitable consequence of being alone in the dark with members of the opposite sex for extended periods of time—there was such rejoicing that many citizens of Jassa became ill.

Some even threw up.

But there was less merriment in the nation of Ussir.

They, the Ussirs, were given light and power, too—because, at heart, the Jassans were not that cruel—but at such a cost! The monthly light bill of the average Ussir household would at least double, which in the opinion of many was not going to contribute to a lasting peace between the two nations in any substantial way.

Ahmed Hassad, along with his consort, Soo Toy, were put under house arrest by the Ussirs. They were not abused in any way, even though Ahmed Hassad had failed in his mission. They were in fact treated as honored guests, since they were remarkable specimens of their kind, and in Ahmed Hassad's view, the confinement was only a pleasant interlude. Given enough time, he was still certain, he would own the country.

"A year," he sold Soo Toy. "Eighteen months at the most."

"Sounds about right," she agreed. And went on feeding him grapes.

Harry Borg, since he had won, was treated better.

Though not much better.

His mate, Lori, was given the best of medical attention, together with the most elaborate security measures, when her child was born. The child proved to be a boy of eight pounds, seven ounces, and he was named Charlie, as promised. A cute little sonovagun. And they were all—Harry, Lori, Charlie, Tippi, Chad, Illia, Homer, Eddie, Arnie, and Sam—allowed to live as guests of Guss and Sissi, who were, not incidentally, joined in matehood in a small private ceremony.

At which Sissi wore blue.

White being out of the question, she blushingly admitted.

Harry had asked for—no, demanded—rather a lot in return for the service he had rendered in defeating the Ussirs and Ahmed Hassad and rescuing the Lassa Crystal. He had demanded free trade between Earth and Essa, with himself to be installed as Commissioner of Commerce, for openers. Exclusive rights to manufacture an extensive array of high-tech products. Citizenship. Voting rights. Complimentary tickets to all sporting events for himself and his cadre. Chauffeured transportation. And free lunches.

He was given a medal.

Each member of his cadre was given a scroll.

And they were all told they would be able to go back to Earth. Soon.

As for the rest of Harry's demands—since Jassa was a democracy in which all matters of any importance had to be considered and voted upon by a congress of elected individuals, there was going to be a period of time, Harry was told, before any final decisions on the bulk of his demands could be reached.

A matter of ten years, some thought.

Others considered fifty years closer to the mark.

There was, however, the case Harry had rescued along with the Lassa Crystal, the case that, according to Old Mind, held the wisdom of the Ancients infinitely compressed. Harry, as almost an afterthought, had kicked the case under a seat in the flight-craft that had lifted him from the obsidian cubes in the final moments before the island of Tassar had sunk beneath the sea, and he had not thought it necessary to mention it to any official.

Then or later.

He did mention it to Guss and to Los Ross one night while drinking the euphoria-inducing drink, vassle, by candlelight in a bistro just outside Larissa, the city by the bay, while waiting for Lori to give birth. Los Ross, a scientist to the bone, took an immediate interest. He said that it was too bad Harry had not been given the kriss that would enable him to read the infinitely compressed information but that he, Los Ross, would see what he could do about devising one. That, too, of course, was going to take a while.

Didn't everything?

But he said he would get right at it.

So, while everything had not yet worked out quite as Harry had hoped it would, he was on the whole content.

He and Lori and Tippi and his new son—all his people, in fact—were safe and well, and he had reason to hope things would go on as they were through all the years to come.

"I think they will," he told Lori.

"Unless something else happens," she said.

ABOUT THE AUTHOR

Ward Hawkins, born and raised in the Northwest, began his adult life with a high school education and a wife, and his professional career with the hammer and spikes of a heavy-construction worker. He took to writing as an "easier way," sold to pulp science-fiction magazines, *Thrilling Wonder*, etc., went on to the *Saturday Evening Post*, *Colliers*, the *American*, etc. When they went bust, he moved to L.A., joined the Writers Guild of America, and began writing for the motion-picture and television market—*Rawhide*, *Bonanza*, *High Chapparal*, *Little House on the Prairie*, *Voyage to the Bottom of the Sea*, etc.

He lives now in the L.A. area with Adeline, the only wife he has ever had, near his children and grandchildren, plays golf to a five handicap, and writes only what he enjoys most.